D1528612

# LIVING WITH ANIMALS

## Hardy's Justice

### Nellis C. Boyer

iUniverse, Inc.

New York   Bloomington

# Living with Animals

## Hardy's Justice

This is a work of fiction. All of the characters, names, incidents, organizations, and dialogue in this novel are either the products of the author's imagination or are used fictitiously.

iUniverse books may be ordered through booksellers or by contacting:

iUniverse
1663 Liberty Drive
Bloomington, IN 47403
www.iuniverse.com
1-800-Authors (1-800-288-4677)

Because of the dynamic nature of the Internet, any Web addresses or links contained in this book may have changed since publication and may no longer be valid. The views expressed in this work are solely those of the author and do not necessarily reflect the views of the publisher, and the publisher hereby disclaims any responsibility for them.

ISBN: 978-0-595-52362-7 (pbk)
ISBN: 978-0-595-62420-1 (ebk)

Printed in the United States of America

# CHAPTER ONE

Hardy had a clear line of sight to the door of Lester Scroggin's shack. It was now just a matter of time. He waited, sprawled on his belly in the dirt, anxious to get it over with. The .22 rested comfortably in his arms, cocked and ready to fire. "Come on, Lester," he growled.

He knew the old man's routine. It would start with coffee and torture. And now, like clockwork, Lester kicked open the front door, a steaming mug in one hand and a bag of dog food in the other. He stood in the shadow of the porch, drinking from the mug, and then he began to shake the bag of dry food. Hearing the noise, the chained animal struggled to her feet, her head bowed with the weight of her restraint.

She was a Border collie, what was left of her, mostly just bones showing through a shaggy mat of tri-colored hair. It was all she could do to raise herself, but she did, ever willing to please. Ten feet of heavy chain tethered her to a steel pole in the ground. She could move in a circle, dragging her burden around the rut she'd worn in her space, but the bucket of dirty water was fifteen feet away next to the bowl of food. She knew they were there, but they did her no good.

Not programmed to comprehend the deliberate, sadistic nature of the human, her canine brain reacted instinctively, and once again she was hopeful that this time there would be food. The old man shook the bag and grinned, watching in perverse pleasure as his captive swayed with the effort of standing upright.

Lester stepped off the porch and approached the creature. He stopped just short of her reach and held the bag out so the animal could smell the food. And then he spit into the dry dirt, kicked it into the dog's face, and folded the top of the bag shut. Hardy squeezed the trigger, his bullet catching Lester between the eyes, spinning him like a top and dropping him flat. Chunks of dog food spilled into the circle of death, and the starving animal fell on them, devouring morsel after morsel. Hardy stepped in quickly. He lifted the chain from the dog's neck and pulled her away, for eating too much too quickly would do more harm. He carried the dog to his truck and laid her on the front seat, then he returned to Lester and dragged him into the shack. He found the can of gasoline the old man kept out back and splashed it around inside the house and over the body. When he dropped his burning book of matches, Lester Scroggins exploded in a pillar of flame.

Hardy climbed into his truck and drove slowly down the rutted dirt road back to his house, the Border collie's head resting in his lap. It would be awhile before anyone bothered to report the fire, if at all. The doctor's only concern was for his patient, as the deed was long overdue. He'd warned the man. He'd told him he wouldn't tolerate any more cruelty, but Lester kept on and on, paying no attention. And now Hardy felt good. He stroked the dog's head and talked to her as they pulled into his long gravel driveway and parked close to the house. He'd prepared a nice pad of blankets for her in the kitchen, and when she was settled there, silently watching him, he prepared a thick gruel of kibble and warm water. She eagerly gulped her first portion and he fed every few hours, allowing her weakened body to readjust.

The fire chief speculated it was Lester's own carelessness that did him in. The body had been reduced to a charcoal lump, and even if the medical examiner had thought to look for a bullet hole, he wouldn't have found one. As luck would have it, a beam fell when the roof collapsed, crushing the old man's toasted skull.

Hardy had watched his neighbor go crazier and crazier, shooting wildlife in the valley, taking a chunk out of Hardy's house with a .30-06 last year, dumping poisoned chicken guts along the road, and sadistically torturing and almost killing Bella.

Bella was back to a normal diet after a week of careful feeding, and her coat was beginning to thicken and regain its luster. Though she had the run of the house and outside in the back where the yard was fenced, she slept inside on his bed at night. She loved him, and she knew he had saved her. It was a good match, for he had wanted another dog, having lost Earl, his black Lab, two months earlier to old age.

As the small town's veterinarian, Hardy had seen it all when it came to people and animals—at least he thought he had until Lester. Hardy had had an epiphany when he'd turned sixty-three earlier that year; he realized the only changes he could effect in the world were things he tackled head on, and this realization at once relieved him from the depressing burden of fighting to preserve the world's threatened creatures and their environments and empowered him to take action in his own world. He could not save the whales or the tigers or the elephants, and in truth he feared no one could, for greedy influences worldwide always seemed to undermine the noble deeds of those who fought the good fight. The constant back and forth between catastrophe and triumph had worn him to a frazzle, and because the gesture now seemed hopeless, he'd stopped sending money to his favorite causes. But he could save one Border collie down the road. That much was within his reach. And so he crossed the first name off the top of his carefully compiled list.

The bulldozers came and cleaned up the old man's place, scraping the soiled ground with big shovels and hauling the debris to the county dump. When Hardy walked Bella down the road a month later, he saw that the iron bar which had held her prisoner was flattened into the dirt. Weeds had begun to take root where the shack once stood. When they stopped, she sniffed the air, but that was all; then she licked the back of his hand and pulled him forward, for the creek lay straight ahead, at road's end, and she was eager to play in the water. They slid down a little bank, and he freed her and sat while she pounced into the slow-running, shallow depths. He envied her ability to live in the moment.

It was August, and the water was lower than usual. If they had a normal winter, rains would swell the creek waist deep, and the water would rush in a torrent past his house. Bella couldn't swim then, for she'd be swept downstream by the current; hopefully, she would know not to try. Hardy thought she was two at the most, and he debated about spaying her, but he decided to let it go for now. She was a fine specimen of her breed, and pups would be nice, a family for him again. The malnutrition she'd suffered had not damaged her, at least not that he could discern, and she had recovered quickly. She came and buried her head between his knees, and then she looked up, one eye blue, one eye brown, and seemed to smile. Hardy felt a deep contentment.

That night, as they sat together in the living room, the dog's head resting on his slipper, Hardy tried to read, but eventually he closed his book and surrendered to his thoughts. It had always puzzled him how people got through life without the company of animals. In his practice he'd cared for dogs, cats, and farm animals, but he'd also treated birds, turtles, snakes, wild creatures, even a butterfly, though his attempt at supergluing its torn wing had failed. All were brought to him by folks who cared deeply and were terrified at the thought of losing these friends. He'd seen the death of companion animals render clients depressed for years, affecting them more deeply than the death of close relatives, a fact most were embarrassed to admit. Yet there were others who never sought these relationships, never allowed themselves to share the unconditional devotion a nonhuman friend could offer. He felt sorry for them and dismissed them. They were probably people he wouldn't care to know.

# CHAPTER TWO

Hardy John's house sat on the northern edge of his twenty acres. The cozy California-style structure had an accommodating front porch, which created a nice addition to the interior space in the summertime. Combsville Creek ran along his southern boundary, splitting his property from his neighbor's. Combsville, a northern California hamlet, lay in the middle of Little Flat Valley. Huge oaks, plentiful streams, and rich soil made it a pleasant place to live.

Hardy had fenced and cross-fenced his land, creating separate pastures. But he hadn't fenced in the front yard, where the long driveway made a circle around a huge oak and fed back onto the country road. His profession often included middle of the night sprints, and he didn't like to fuss with a gate in emergencies, especially when he was called to deliver a foal or a calf. Bella knew the county road was off limits and dangerous, so Hardy didn't worry about her while he worked on his gates. He had decided to buy a few goats, some lamas, and maybe an alpaca or two, something for her to tend, for she was a working dog who needed something to work.

Alice and Maybelle, two of his outside cats, draped themselves over the top railing of the wooden fence like lifeless, stuffed animals, paws dangling in midair, eyes closed. The inside cats, Cooney, Possum, and Wolf, watched the goings-on from the ledge of the front window. Although the cats could wander anywhere they wished, some simply preferred to be outside while others remained in, and he honored their wishes. Alice opened one eye, squinting at him as he pounded in the last nail and satisfied himself that the enclosure was sturdy.

"Good to go, Bella. Maybe we'll pick up our goats tomorrow." The dog pricked up her ears at the word *go,* for it usually meant a ride in the truck, one of her favorite activities, but today it meant *fence okay.* "Let's have some lunch," he added. She liked that, too, for Hardy usually gave her a slice of American cheese. They ate on the porch, content with a magnificent August afternoon.

When they were finished, he drove the truck into town to join his son at the veterinary clinic. Will, a recent veterinary school graduate, was learning the practice and, hopefully, would take over some day. Will's mother, Willa, had also been a vet and had worked side by side with her husband until cancer ended her life twelve years ago. She had urged Will to take up the science, join the family practice, and help his dad, and he had, finding the need to work with animals was in his blood.

Fortunately, Will had inherited his father's charisma, as becoming a successful veterinarian depended largely upon winning the trust of the human caretaker. Hardy had known this from the get-go, but it hadn't been a problem for him. He was a natural. His prematurely gray hair, ice-blue soul-probing eyes, wide smile, steady voice, and reassuring hand all combined to reinforce his image as the compassionate country vet, the human you could trust with the life of your animal friend. Hardy deserved their trust, for he was a skilled surgeon, a brilliant diagnostician, and an empathetic and humane doctor—the total package.

The clinic was two blocks from downtown. He parked in the lot behind the small building and entered through the back door with Bella. She accompanied him everywhere now, and she had come to know the clinic and her padded bed there almost as well as her place by the fireplace at home. He grabbed a white lab coat, and Bella found her mat, settling down as she had been taught to do.

The practice was designed to be a hands-on operation. Human companions participated in their pet's treatment if they wished, holding their animal while Hardy or Will did the exam. The owner's presence calmed the patient and reassured the caretakers, making them feel included. Most people liked to participate. A separate room in the back held individual kennels and a surgery area that was equipped with the latest medical devices. Four chairs were lined up under the front window, and an attractive young woman fidgeted in one of them, holding a small terrier in her lap. A huge malamute, its tongue hanging out the side of its mouth, sprawled on the stainless steel table in the middle of the room, and a nice-looking couple stood alongside, the man with a tight grip on the dog's collar, the woman dabbing her eyes with a Kleenex. Hardy joined his son and smiled, placing his hand on the dog's head. "How is Custer today, Doctor? Do we have a problem?"

"Just a foxtail between the toes, Dr. Johns, painful, but a long way from the heart." It was a tried but true cliché that always seemed to have its intended reassuring effect on the humans, and Will had readily adopted it into his veterinary speak. Hardy watched as his son extracted the bloody sticker. The two of them had thought it best to address each other formally at the clinic, although they were having a hard time with it. If either one slipped up, they were to add a quarter to the glass jar by the sink, a penalty they'd agreed upon. The jar was almost full. It wasn't easy for Hardy to address his twenty-four year old son as "Doctor," but it was coming.

As the big dog sambaed out the door, dragging his owners behind, Will rubbed disinfectant over the examination table and nodded to the young woman. She stepped forward, smiling coyly and placing Emily on the table. Both doctors knew Emily, for she had been mysteriously afflicted with a plethora of nebulous maladies ever since Will had begun working at the clinic. Hardy excused himself, finding something to do in the back room. But he listened, since he couldn't help overhearing anyway, and chuckled at the problems the poor little dog had suddenly developed. The young woman was good looking enough and obviously interested in Will. Hardy decided he would suggest a date and put an end to these unnecessary doctor bills. He heard the conversation drift toward the door and his son say, "Tomorrow at eight, then."

Before Hardy could begin interrogating his son, the bell over the door jangled furiously, accompanied by a banging of cages and angry curses. A stocky, middle-aged man juggling three pet carriers staggered toward the examination table. He dropped two carriers on the floor and pushed one onto the table. He was out of breath and wheezing.

"I need these cats put down. I ain't gonna take care of 'em. That damn bitch left me, and if she thinks she's comin' back to get these cats, she's got another think comin'." He wore a threadbare sleeveless undershirt, and tattoos covered his thick, hairy arms, wrist to shoulder. An uneven stubble of red whiskers shadowed the lower half of his sweaty face.

Hardy pushed Will aside and joined the foul-smelling man at the table. He carefully removed a big, healthy-looking female tabby from the carrier. As he stroked her soft body, his voice fell to a low whisper and he said, "Is this animal sick?"

The man glared at him, his eyes shrinking to narrow slits. "No, it ain't sick,"he spewed angrily, "I can't take care of 'em, like I tole you."

"Do these animals belong to you, sir?" purred Hardy, his blood pressure dropping with each caress of the cat's back, her innocent purr matching his own. His voice became a  controlled abstraction, as if he had glimpsed the bigger picture and knew precisely what had to be done.

The would-be client looked for somewhere to spit but swallowed instead and yelled, "Man, my old lady stuck me with 'em, and I don't want 'em. Now, you goin' to hep me or not?"

Hardy examined the other two cats, both fine-looking animals. The man stood by, snarling at him. "They're her cats, she got this comin'."

"I'll take the cats off your hands, sir," said Hardy, offering him one last chance, "but I don't kill healthy animals for someone's convenience."

The man became outraged, "If you won't do it, I know someone who will," he shouted, kicking at the cages on the floor. "I was trying not to have to drive to the next county."

The doctor struck like a cobra. "No!" he grabbed a hairy arm. "I'll do it, no need for that," he soothed. "Calm down. Have a seat while I prepare the solutions." Hardy cocked his head at Will. "Doctor, help this fellow. Sit him down. I'll just be a minute."

Will hesitated, silently questioning his father, then led the man to a chair as Hardy disappeared behind the wall at the back. Will returned to the examination table and stroked the tabby, who lay licking her paw, unaware of her impending demise. Hardy reappeared in no time, three big syringes in his hand, a grim look on his face.

"Doctor, close the blinds please," he said, nodding at Will. Then he addressed the man. "Sir, if you want to assist, this will go a lot quicker." The man grinned and stepped forward, and Hardy directed him to stand and hold the cat's legs. "Not too tight, we don't want to alert her that anything unusual is about to take place."

The man stood at the table as instructed, his big hands gripping the cat's front legs, and Hardy set two of the syringes on the table, the third remaining in his hand as he squirted a drop to push out any air. "Just like that, hold steady now, and it will all be over in a second." Will couldn't believe what he was watching, for his father would never agree to put down a healthy animal.

In one swift, smooth, downward swing, Hardy plunged the syringe into the man's exposed upper arm and depressed the plunger. "It will all be over in a second," he repeated. The man's legs wobbled, and he collapsed, banging his head on the table as he fell in a heap on the floor. The tabby jumped, frightened by the noise, and Hardy gathered her in his arms. "Not to worry, dear. It's painless."

Will stood frozen, his mouth hanging open, his arms dangling like wet spaghetti at his sides.

"This was *not* a healthy animal, Son. He needed to be put down."

Hardy threw the two empty syringes back in a drawer and said, "We'll wait until dark and then drive him home. He's an IV drug user, by the looks of his veins, so it's just an overdose. Fish out his wallet and tell me who he is and where he lives."

# CHAPTER THREE

Will locked the door and turned the open sign around, while Hardy dragged the dead man to the back room and covered him with a sheet. Then, since it was only three, Hardy turned the sign around again, opened the blinds, and unlocked the door. Will was operating in a state of robot-like shock, unable to come to grips with what had taken place. When Mrs. Oberson brought Ralph, her Doberman, in for his routine shots, Will blanched at the sight of the syringes, so Hardy sent him to the back while he took care of the dog. Will sat and stared at the lump under the sheet, listening as his father talked calmly to Mrs. Oberson in the next room, as if nothing out of the ordinary had taken place. When he heard them leave, he confronted his dad. "Do you think we can get away with this ... murder? That's what it is, you know, murder."

The fear and vulnerability on the young man's face tore at Hardy's heart. "Of course, I'll get away with it. This was a piece of human garbage, Son. And I did the deed, not you, so you're not to worry. Would you rather I'd killed three fine, helpless animals than that one useless man? You know he would have taken them to that monster, Skiles, and *he* wouldn't have given it a second thought. Or maybe he'd have bashed their heads in with a hammer himself. Believe me, Will, this is not even worth discussing. This is what right and wrong is about, and I've finally come to realize that I *can* make a difference. And this man sought me out, he wasn't even on my list, so it was meant to be. Someone was looking after those cats."

"You have a list?" asked Will, swallowing hard.

"I do," Hardy declared, "and never you mind about that. Now, I heard you made a date with Emily's person tomorrow. That's my boy. She looks like a fine young lady. Where are you going to take her?"

Will sat on a stool, his head in his hands. He looked up, his face a muddle of confusion. "I don't know if I can make the switch so fast, Dad. We have a body to dispose of, and you're asking me about a date. What's the plan? What are we going to do with Mr. Jacobsen?"

"According to his license, he lives out in the boonies. We'll drive him home, simple as that. He said his wife's gone, so I see no problem. Soon as it's dark, we'll leave. I'll drive his car; you and Bella follow in my truck. We'll come back here when it's done." They carried Jacobsen to his old Mazda and pushed him down in the front seat. Hardy donned a pair of thin latex surgical gloves, took his place behind the wheel and set out for the man's rural homestead. When they pulled into the driveway, the house was dark. Hardy pulled Jacobsen up, positioned him behind the steering wheel, and steadied the unruly head, which flopped around like he was drunk. Who knew how long it would take for anyone to find him. His mailbox was way down at the end of the road. Maybe his wife would come looking for her cats, but she wouldn't find them; maybe that was just a tall tale in the first place.

Will drove them back to the clinic. Hardy loaded the three cats in his truck, and Bella was overjoyed, thinking the whole game was a ton of fun.

"Put it out of your mind, Son," Hardy said. "If anything, we did the world some good today."

Strangely enough, Will was able to put it out of his mind. The man, Jacobsen, wouldn't stick with him; probably locked in some mental safe house that his brain had conjured up. And since Hardy had made the whole incident sound so noble, he couldn't even worry much about it. He turned his attention instead to Lois, Emily's owner, and their date. He would take her to dinner at Paul's Steak House over in Gridley—it was the best place around—and then maybe they would catch a movie, depending on what was playing. His father was right, the world was better off without the likes of that man. But shit, thought Will, he'd mentioned a list.

Bella was hungry by the time they were through with their chores, and so was Hardy for that matter, so he fried them up a couple of cheese sandwiches and threw a potato in the microwave. He sat in the kitchen at the little table Willa had bought from the antique shop in town, drinking a beer and waiting for the ding. Bella lay at his side, saliva running down her chin, the smell of the cooking food prompting her tail to swish back and forth in anticipation. He was sorry he'd had to involve Will today; that was the last thing he'd wanted, but there had been no way around it. The kid's moral compass was strong. He'd sort things out and realize it was for the best.

The microwave tinged, and he removed the potato, cutting it in half so that it would cool. He flipped the grilled cheese onto separate plates, cutting Bella's into strips and buttering her half of the spud. "Here you go, babe.

It's hot, so make it last." After she woofed down the sandwich, she settled on her belly and licked the butter off the potato, then she bit it into chunks and daintily chewed each one until her plate was clean. The new cats were stalking the house, smelling the sofa, and climbing over the furniture. He would keep them in for a few days and then let them decide if they wanted to be outside cats or inside cats. He'd have to give them shots and test them for diseases, but that could come later; they'd been through enough for the moment. Bella stretched out in the living room as Hardy picked up his book and tried to read. But he couldn't keep his eyes open and soon fell asleep on the sofa. When he woke at two thirty, having to pee, all three of the new cats lay on his body: one across his legs, one on his stomach, and the tabby on his shoulder, her chin snuggled against Hardy's. They slept and purred, and by God, if that wasn't gratitude, he didn't know what to call it. He hated to move, but he had to. They followed him to bed, finding comfortable spots beside him, and Bella let them stay, for she knew they needed him.

Will called from the clinic at nine the next morning, his voice strained and anxious. "Are you coming in today? Have you heard anything about anything?"

Hardy laughed. "I'll bring lunch, and no, I've heard nothing of interest. I want to clean the back room—you know, mop it good and disinfect it, to make sure we got rid of that garbage we spilled last night."

"Yeah, good idea. I'll see you later then." Will signed off, feeling like a man at sea without a life vest and knowing there was nothing he could do about it.

Hardy had a plan for this day and unfortunately it didn't include Bella, for he was worried she might get hurt if he brought her along. She was upset about not being included, and he tried to reason with her. "It's not safe, babe, not today. You know I wouldn't ask you to stay home unless I had a good reason." He left her in the fenced back yard, and she moped about, finally settling down inside her house. "See you soon," he called, as he drove down the driveway to the dirt road. He followed the road past Lester's old digs to where the creek took over; he parked there and waded across, coming out in a meadow of dry grass. Carrying a black plastic trash bag that held the things he was going to need, he trudged along to the edge of the meadow where the grass gave way to a thick forest of gnarled oaks and tall pines. He knew exactly where the Griggs set their snares for the black bears they illegally trapped, killed, and butchered, selling their parts to phony healers locally and overseas. A nasty business, "as nasty as it gets," he said aloud.

And then he saw the snare, baited and set, invisible to anyone who didn't know what he was looking for. A bear family was there already, a mother and two cubs, drawn by the smell of the meat that hung from a wire, dripping red blood on the ground beneath. The mother tried to warn her cub, but he was impetuous, and, like any kid, he didn't listen. The cub snatched at the bait, triggering the snare. The line zipped tight around his little leg and snapped, flinging his small body into the air. He howled in fright and pain, and the mother bellowed and went crazy. As the cub dangled twenty feet off the ground, swinging from the branch, the mother flailed overhead with her hairy paws, but he was too high. The sound she made was enough to break a decent person's heart, but Hardy knew it would bring the indecent, and he waited. "For every action there is an equal and opposite reaction—Newton. Ready when you are, Griggs—Hardy."

He withdrew his own snare from his bag and quickly camouflaged it in the middle of the trail. He then attached his line to a thick, pliable willow and ratcheted it down to the breaking point. He'd get at least one, and, with luck, he might get two. He completed his task without fear, for the sow was distracted by her cub's quandary. Hardy was barely forty feet away, hidden in the woods, when he heard them running, probably Griggs and his boy. They would have their weapons, but if it happened the way it should, they wouldn't get a chance to use them.

The mother continued to bellow and cry, slapping the air beneath her dangling baby while her second cub cowered in the brush close by. The footfalls got louder and closer, and then he saw them, Griggs and Griggs. They ran directly into his hidden circle, and he cut the wire, releasing the willow. The loop snapped tight around their legs, yanking them off the ground feet first. Their shotguns flew into the brush and their bodies swung wildly upside down five feet in the air, a bouquet of screaming, smelly humans presented precisely at bear height. The sow heard them and turned, her anger boiling into a terrifying rage. She charged the helpless predators, tearing into them, ripping chunks of flesh from their bodies as they dangled. They screamed in terror, but not for long.

Hardy took advantage of the sow's preoccupation to slip behind the tree that held the cub and cut the snare with a whack of his knife. The tiny body fell to the ground and rolled into the underbrush, bruised, scared, but not badly hurt. The mother could do the rest. When she heard his cries, she stopped mauling the Griggs and galloped back to her babies. Hardy had hurried to the safety of his truck, for a mother bear wronged was not something he wanted to engage. It had not been a pleasant way to die, but it had been fairly quick and was certainly deserved. And he knew the bears wouldn't have fared as well had it gone the other way. Their paws would have been cut off for souvenirs, their gall bladders sent to China, their heads mounted on plaques, and their coats dried and made into bedspreads. All in all, Griggs and Griggs got a pretty fair deal, considering the number of bears they'd slaughtered over the years. He felt good about it, and he crossed them off his list.

# CHAPTER FOUR

It was lunch time when Hardy returned home and freed Bella. He made cheese sandwiches, a thermos of ice tea, bagged it all up, and drove to the clinic. He and Will took turns bringing the midday meal so they didn't have to close the clinic. Their clients seemed to appreciate the effort, for many came in on their lunch hours. Hardy sat at the examination table, feeding Bella pieces of sandwich, while Will attended a surgery patient in the back room. The dog waited politely and patiently. A real lady, thought Hardy, as he tore the last piece of sandwich and fed it to her in several bites. "Good Bella."

"I'd like you to take a look at the Lab in the back, Dad, er, Doctor," said Will, thumbing through a chart on his clipboard. "He's been in a fight, and I did the best I could, but I'm not sure it's good enough. He's a new client, name of Henry; his owner, a Mr. Garcia, brought him in early this morning." Will looked tired, dark circles sagged beneath his eyes, and he hadn't shaved; a brown stubble covered his chin and cheeks.

"Have a sandwich, Doctor, you look terrible. This isn't because of what happened yesterday, I hope. Did you sleep last night?"

"For a little while. It's not about that. I had to make a call in the middle of the night. Missy Abraham's cow had her calf. Three thirty in the morning. I was afraid I was going to have to call you. It was breach and all legs, but I managed." He sat at the table and grabbed a sandwich. "It's a great feeling, bringing new life into this world, isn't it, Dad?"

"That it is, Doctor. You owe the jar a quarter."

"Oh, come on," pleaded Will. "Let's not make that the rule when it's just us. Sometimes I need to call you Dad." He grinned, "Bringing new life into the world is awesome, *Dad*."

"Okay, not when it's just the two of us." He walked to the back and opened the cage door. The Lab had been mauled on its head and neck. With its torn flesh now brought together by stitches, it lay on its side, still under the influence of the anesthetic. Hardy didn't like what he saw. "What did this Garcia say happened to Henry? These injuries look like someone used him for bait. Labs aren't known for being fighters. My Earl would have walked a city block to avoid a confrontation."

"He said Henry got out of his yard and another dog attacked him. He didn't know what kind of dog, just a big one. Sounded like he knew more than he was telling me."

"Looks like you did a good stitch job; have to see how he is when he wakes up. Poor Henry. Reminds me of Earl. You going on your date tonight?" he asked, changing the subject.

"Yeah, hope I can stay awake. We're going for a steak and maybe a movie. Can you close up here so I can catch a few winks?"

"Go on home. Bella and I will take over today."

Will rented a small place in town. Martha, their part-time helper in the clinic, cleaned house for him once a week. She was scheduled to clean that afternoon, but he gave her the day off so he could sleep. She futzed around at the clinic instead, finding things to do that didn't really need doing, but Hardy didn't care. She was a good worker, and he paid her a decent wage. When Henry started to stir, Martha noticed the dog was acting strangely and called him to come look. He lifted Henry onto a gurney and rolled him under the surgery light. The dog's eyes didn't focus, rolling off in different directions, and a deep puncture wound in the back of his neck oozed dark blood through Will's stitches. Hardy checked Will's notes and gave the dog a shot of clotting factor to curtail the bleeding, which should have already stopped. He found Garcia's phone number and called him, wanting more information on what had happened.

The man was vague. He said he didn't know how Henry had gotten out of his yard and was unable to describe the dog that had attacked, even though he said he had broken up the fight. Not satisfied, Hardy decided to drive by Garcia's house on his way home. If he felt it was warranted, Hardy sometimes took a patient home to monitor during the night. He was worried about Henry, but after he considered the pros and cons of moving the dog, he decided to leave him at the clinic. Garcia's statements bothered the doctor more than anything. It could have been a random dogfight, but the more the man talked, the less likely that sounded, and his broken English didn't make things any clearer.

Hardy locked the clinic's doors and set off to find Garcia's house. He located the two-lane dirt road and followed it past ramshackle shacks, broken-down trailers, and abandoned stacks of junk, shameful insults to the landscape. Land abuse was second only to animal abuse in sending Hardy's blood pressure soaring to dangerous levels. It was the general lack of caring that got to him. Seeing junk piled all over the countryside made him heartsick, and this particular road was one of the worst he'd come across. Gritting his teeth, he continued bumping along until he found the number on a post in the front yard.

Surprisingly, Garcia's house was tidy and neat, a refreshing jewel in the surrounding wasteland. It had a small front porch and chicken wire fencing around the front yard with a metal gate that swung open. The driveway down the side of the property led to a large metal building. Hardy left Bella in the truck and began walking toward it. Suddenly a man appeared on the porch of the little house. He waved his arms and yelled, "Buenas tardes," as he hurried to intercept the doctor. The anxious stranger introduced himself as Hector Garcia, Henry's owner. Hardy told him he'd come to give him a report on the dog's condition, but he continued to walk toward the metal building. Garcia stepped in front of him, blocking the way, waving his arms and yelling, "No, no, por favor, Señor."

Hardy was a big man, and now he was an angry big man. He pushed Garcia aside, strode to the door of the building, and flung it open. It was as he'd suspected. Bales of hay piled to form a square fighting arena, metal pens, bloody dirt, cattle prods, and bleachers on one side for the watchers and participants in the deadly sport of dogfighting.

"Is this how Henry got mauled? Was he used for bait? Where are the rest of the dogs?" bellowed Hardy, grabbing Garcia and shaking the terrified man until his gold teeth rattled in his head.

"No, no, not here," yelled Garcia. "No dogs here." Hardy threw him loose and strode around the property, which was nothing more than a weedy patch of land. He saw no animals, but there were piles of dirt that might have been graves, for bodies were buried somewhere. The whole place reeked of death.

"Fighting dogs is against the law," boomed the doctor. And the cowed man, who followed behind, whimpering, could do nothing but shake his head and repeat, "No, no, no. Otros hombres."

Hardy had quickly sized up Garcia, realizing he was only a caretaker. The building was being used by other, more unscrupulous men. Garcia now spoke openly and slowly, and the doctor understood enough Spanish to ascertain that Henry had been mauled by accident during a dogfight. That did answer the question why he was brought in for treatment, since bait dogs were usually disposed of rather than treated; that way there were no questions to answer, no vet bills. Hardy learned the next fight was scheduled for the coming Saturday, and he warned Garcia to be gone that night if he wanted to stay out of jail. Rather than mow them all down with a shotgun, he'd turn this bust over to the local law enforcement, for he knew the sheriff would score big points closing down a dog fighting operation. They were hot topics at the moment.

"Henry might not make it. He's hurt real bad," Hardy warned. "Muy malo." Apparently an out-of-work laborer, Garcia had been coerced into the job in exchange for a place to live. The man had five kids, a pregnant wife, and no green card, and still he'd brought his dog in for treatment. Hardy had to give him something for that.

"Just don't be here Saturday, and say a prayer for Henry."

The shaken man thanked the doctor. "Gracias, Señor Doctor."

Hardy walked back to his truck and Bella. "What a mess, babe. You don't wanna know." She wagged her tail in wide sweeps, dusting the dashboard, and licked his cheek with her warm, wet tongue. He rested his arm around her neck as they drove away.

It was almost dark, and as they neared the clinic, a premonition overwhelmed him. He had had them many times in the past, and they sickened him, because they were usually true. And, sure enough, when he stopped to check on Henry, he found that the dog had died. He pulled a blanket over the still body and called Mitch Downey, the sheriff. Then he found Garcia's chart and called him. In the background he could hear children crying, and Garcia thanked him and asked if he could pick up the body the next day. The family wanted to have a burial ceremony. Hardy said that would be a nice thing to do.

He drove home wondering how Will's date was going. He wished for pleasant things and good news, but when he pushed the button on his answering machine, he got neither. Craig Bowerman's mare was foaling and having trouble. "Where the hell are you, man? Get over here as soon as you get this message."

The call had come fifteen minutes earlier, so he rushed back to his truck, Bella at his heels, and they took off, fishtailing down his drive. Bowerman's place was just down the road. He screeched to a stop next to their barn, where the lights blazed and the doors stood open, waiting for him. "Thank God," yelled Craig, when he saw Hardy and Bella.

The barn was a modern wonder, a clean, knotty pine structure, with stainless steel doors, a tall ceiling, and a wide cement aisle running down the middle separating two rows of box stalls. Craig and his wife Celia knelt beside Queenie, their three-year-old champion quarter horse mare, who lay on her side snorting and straining, trying to push the foal from her body. She lifted her head, lunging forward as if that would help, but it didn't. Hardy fell to his knees, rolled up his sleeves, and slid his hand inside the horse, trying to feel the foal and determine its position. It was turned wrong, so he massaged the mare's uterus and the foal, when he could feel it. Eventually he knew he had it right and in position, and Queenie knew too, because she heaved and the wet baby slid out of her, a quivering mass of jelly-covered horse. Queenie squealed, and Craig and Celia clapped their hands and cheered.

Hardy wiped his arms and hands on a towel and cleaned the foals eyes and nose of debris, and then he stepped aside and let Queenie take over. The mare hefted herself up and nuzzled the baby, nudging it with her muzzle, waking it to the world, and then the foal gathered herself, pushing her awkward body upright, wobbling on four spindly legs.

"She's a beauty," said Hardy, stroking Queenie's rump. "You did good, girl."

Craig and Celia were crying, and Craig grabbed Hardy and hugged him. "Thanks, man, I knew you'd come in time."

The foal found her mother's milk and began to nurse.

"Sometimes things work out," said the doctor. "I'll check in with you tomorrow." Bella had stood respectfully in the entrance to the stall, having enough sense not to interfere, and now Hardy praised her and patted her head, "You're a good girl too, babe. Let's go home."

# CHAPTER FIVE

Hardy settled on the sofa and closed his eyes. Bella lay on the floor beside him, and the cats were scattered around the room, sleeping in various poses. Woofie lay sprawled over the vent in the floor, where he sopped up cool air in the summer and heat in the winter. Hardy usually pushed him off, but this night he didn't bother. The house was comfortable enough, and he was tired. The last thing he remembered was wondering about Will's date.

The morning came too early. He showered, dressed, and made a pot of coffee, letting it brew while he fed the animals and cleaned out the cats' litter boxes. It was his routine, and it was about to get a whole lot busier if he got the lamas, goats, and whatever else he'd promised Bella. While he was tucking his shirt into his jeans, the phone rang. It was Craig, thanking him again for last night and letting him know that Queenie and the foal were just fine. "We owe you a dinner out," he said. Hardy thanked them, saying that wasn't necessary, and said he'd come check on everybody in a few days. He was on his way out the door when Will arrived with the local newspaper. "Thought I'd stop by and have a cup of coffee with you. I don't suppose you've seen this," he said, dropping the paper on the kitchen table.

"Help yourself. How was the date?" Hardy picked up the paper.

Will didn't answer. He just watched his father's face as he read the headline aloud. "Local Men Mauled by Bears." A smile spread over Hardy's face. "Huh, those Griggs guys finally got their due. Paper says they got caught in their own snare. Imagine that. Illegal snare, by the way. They been trapping illegally for years, and everybody around here knows it. Who found 'em?"

"Read on."

He continued reading aloud. "Boy Scout Troup number 34, on their annual nature hike, discovered the grizzly remains late yesterday. Many of the boys were traumatized and had to be placed under a doctor's care.'" Hardy peered over the paper at Will. "Tsk, tsk, tsk, now *that's* a shame." He laid the paper on the table. "Who'd a thought Boy Scouts would be out in that neck of the woods. Why, there's bears out there! That's just irresponsible. Somebody ought to have a talk with that troop leader. Now, tell me, how was the date? I've been itchin' to hear. And I delivered Bowerman's foal last night, so we're even, that and Missy's calf. And Henry passed away. Garcia's coming to pick up the body. He's living in a house that's sponsoring dogfights. There's going to be a bust this Saturday. I called the sheriff. The date?"

"Are you finished?" Will set his mug on the table and spoke calmly. "You first. You answer my question, and I'll answer yours. And what I want to know is, were the Griggs on that list of yours?"

"Of course they were," spewed Hardy, indignantly. "The Griggs were terrible people, but you can see right here in black and white, the paper says they got caught in their own snare. Now, are you going to tell me about that date or not?"

Will studied his father's blank expression and drank from his mug. Realizing the futility of further interrogation, he said, "We had a nice dinner. I was rested up and felt good, thanks to you letting me go home early. And we didn't do a movie. We're saving that for next time."

"So, there's going to be a next time! That's great, that's what I wanted to hear. Now, we better get to the clinic, because I think Garcia's coming early. He's a good man, just got mixed up in the wrong thing at the wrong place, and he's in way over his head. They're going to have a funeral for Henry. That's a nice thing to do. Can't fault people like that. Don't charge them anything. I'll cover it."

They opened the clinic at nine, and the Garcia family was waiting in the parking lot. All seven of them—five kids, two adults—piled out of an old Ford Taurus, and Will ceremoniously handed over the stiff, towel-wrapped body of their dog, Henry. The kids were sniffling, and Mrs. Garcia wept openly, tears running down her chubby cheeks. Hector accepted the body solemnly and held out a fistful of bills, but Hardy shoved them back, saying, "De nada."

"Gracias, gracias, Señor Doctor," said Hector, bowing and sliding his feet backward toward the door, holding Henry in his outstretched arms. The family followed in a little line. And Hardy warned, "Sabado, vamanos ustedes."

"Vamanos," said Hector, nodding his head.

"Quite a little ceremony right there," said Will, when they had gone. "It's going down on Saturday?"

"That's what Garcia told me. The sheriff said he'd be there. I can't take on a whole group. Got to save myself for my list," he chuckled.

"Well, there's nothing yet about tattoo man. Somebody's going to smell him pretty soon."

"The windows in his car were rolled up, right?"

"I think so. Yeah, I'm sure they were. Geez, this is a hell of a discussion to be having with your father—with anyone, for that matter."

"I'm sorry, it wasn't my intention to involve you in any of this, but that man wasn't planned. He just happened."

"Yeah, I know. Let's not talk about it anymore. What's done is done. And he deserved it. That's what's getting me through. It was like you gave the shot to the right one instead of the wrong one."

"Ones, plural. Remember, we traded one life for three: three good ones for one bad, a hell of a deal."

Sheriff Mitch Downey was excited about Hardy's tip. Dog fighting had made big headlines recently because of the ultra-rich football star who'd been jailed for bankrolling fights and killing dogs. Mitch could be a hero to the locals, and maybe the nation, if he handled this bust and the publicity correctly. He briefed his men, alerted the surrounding jurisdictions should he need back up, and told the press to stand by for a big story. Now all he had to do was hope nobody tipped the bad guys and the fight took place as scheduled. He had three days to wait. Hardy relaxed, knowing the sheriff was on it, for he had other activities planned.

Later that day, Lois came in without her dog. Hardy was glad she had dropped that pretense, for it meant she could concentrate on Will. She was a pretty girl with wide-set brown eyes, a high forehead, a mane of auburn hair that fell on her shoulders, and a little bow of a mouth that she painted bright red. She was a bit taller than Will, and he was five foot nine. She smiled a lot, which Hardy found pleasing, and her laugh sounded like a tinkling bell. He could probably get used to it. But what he admired most about Lois was her conversation. She talked intelligently and didn't blather. He listened in when he had the chance. She was concerned with animal welfare, and he believed she was serious, not just playing to Will's background. She was involved with several groups that handled lawsuits on behalf of animals, and from what he could gather, she was working toward a law degree. Lois was no dummy.

When Will asked Hardy to close again so he and Lois could go to dinner, the old man wholeheartedly agreed, urging the youngsters to go have fun.

Willa would have liked Lois, he thought. As he sat with the animals for company, the clinic cat, Sophie, in his lap and Bella at his feet, he felt a tinge of loneliness. He knew he shouldn't feel lonely, for he had the animals, but he couldn't help it. It was his damn humanness. He missed Willa. She had understood the depth of his love for the animals and respected it, for she had felt it too. Will was the only close human tie he had left, and now Will had his own life. But that was the way things were, and it was too difficult to find a human who didn't let you down sooner or later, so he'd stick to Bella and the rest. The loneliness would pass. It always did.

# CHAPTER SIX

Hardy fed Sophie, leaving one of the cage doors open should she wish to spend the night inside, and he fed Bella too, since they were going on a little trip and might not get home until late. He had all the tools he needed in his toolbox, and the only thing he didn't like about this mission was the long drive. Something terrible was going on in the hills above the town. He had found out about it by accident, overhearing a conversation in the local coffee shop. It had turned his stomach, so of course he'd added it to his list. This was something so evil he was sure people would react if they knew, but there was the bureaucracy, and things got tied up in court and took forever. And by then it might be too late. He drove slowly, his arm around Bella's neck, taking it easy on the curves that carried them up into the hills. It wasn't quite dark yet, and darkness would be necessary.

He'd given up trying to understand why people did what they did, but this was a no-brainer. It was a scheme driven by greed, pure and simple. The participants, who lived in several states, stole horses and sold them for slaughter. Most of the meat was shipped overseas, to France mainly—damn French horse-eaters. The stolen horses were brought in over a period of months and were kept in a secret location until the thieves had enough of them to make the effort worthwhile. Then they were shipped to a slaughterhouse in Texas, where the "good ole boys" took over. The missing animals were on watch lists that the police distributed to places where the horses might turn up, like slaughterhouses, but the Texas boys paid no attention to watch lists. A lot of fine horseflesh ended up on somebody's plate. This knowledge turned his stomach and enraged him. To Hardy's way of thinking, horses were special. He saw them as magnificent creatures which enriched human experience;

symbols of freedom of spirit that was America at her finest. That human beings could eat them was beyond impossible for his mind to process.

As he drove, his thoughts wandered to the slaughterhouses and their horrendous deeds, and he remembered what one traumatized defector had said to him. "Ever look a beautiful Holstein in her big brown eyes, let her lick your hand with her rough, pink tongue, hit her in the head with your stun gun, slit her throat, and watch the blood run down a trough around your boots as she died? And we call evil people 'animals.' We got that all wrong." The depressed man had committed suicide the next day.

It was dark now. A thin moon illuminated the jagged outcroppings, and Hardy knew he'd found the place, for it was just as the man had described: a little sunken valley hidden between two rocky peaks. He parked the truck on the wide shoulder, called Bella, and climbed to where he could look down. Wearing his night vision goggles, he could see at least a hundred head of horses milling in a herd far below. There appeared to be only one way in or out of the canyon: a narrow pass between the cliffs. He and Bella would have to climb the rocks. It was a perfect hideout, very inaccessible.

"Come on, girl, I'm going to put you to work tonight." Hardy and Bella made their way down, she much faster and with more agility than he. He slipped, groped, rolled, and fell most of the way, all the while thinking about getting back up. But he had a coil of rope over his shoulder and an idea in his head. They stalked as quietly as nature allowed, pushing through a field of tall grass and fallen branches that opened onto a dusty, narrow trail. Hardy had hoped the hostages were not guarded, but when the gate that blocked the entrance to the canyon came into view, he saw a lone man leaning on the rocks beside it. As he watched, the man sat down, pulled his cowboy hat over his eyes, and wrapped his arms around his knees.

Hardy motioned for Bella to be still and quiet, and she knew instinctively what he was telling her. He waited, wanting more signals from the man sitting on the ground. After twenty minutes, his arms slipped down and his head fell backward against the rock, and Hardy was sure the guard had fallen asleep. He waved to Bella, and the two of them moved forward, invisible in the darkness, padding silently down the trail toward the gate. What if it was locked? He hadn't thought of that. He could shoot it open, for he wore his pistol in a holster, but he didn't want to shoot the man, and that's what would happen: the guard would wake, try to stop him, and Hardy would have to shoot.

They reached the target, a twelve-foot metal range gate. He could hear the man snoring. The enclosure was directly in front of him, and there was no lock. He raised his arm and lifted the bar. The gate was mounted a little higher than the ground, so it swung open silently and easily. Hardy propped it open with a rock and signaled Bella. He stepped aside quickly as she charged into the herd, which milled about alertly, aware that something was happening. All they needed was a leader, just one to start the run. Suddenly a big black horse bolted forward, Bella at his heels, and in a matter of seconds the herd thundered through the open gate and down the trail. Bella had peeled away after the leader. She and Hardy took off running back in the direction they had come, through the field to the rock cliffs. Hardy fastened a loop of his rope around Bella's chest, tying it to his waist, and up they climbed, the big dog dragging him when he faltered.

They reached the truck in good time, the thunder of hooves ringing in their ears, and Hardy watched through his goggles as horses scattered throughout the countryside. He swung his sights back to the gate and saw the man clinging to his rock perch as the last horse flew by on his way to freedom. "Good job, Bella! That's what you're born to do! Good girl!" The climb back up had been much faster than the climb down, and it was all Bella's doing. He grabbed her snout and kissed her.

When they got home, he called Sheriff Downey's house and told him about the horses running loose, advising him they were stolen and probably very much missed by their owners. Hardy wasn't sure of the ringleaders, but he gave the names he'd overheard and the name of the slaughterhouse in Texas. "You should be able to put them out of business, Sheriff. This kind of thing doesn't make for very good publicity. Keep my name out of it, you understand? I'm a secret informant, nothing more."

Downey was overwhelmed. "You're making me one busy man, Hardy. You're a one-man vendetta, but you watch it now. We don't want you getting yourself killed. Just be careful, and keep me in the loop. Okay?"

Hardy understood. He was making the sheriff's career. By the time he had finished with his list, Sheriff Downey would be famous.

Two days later, the headline in the local paper read, "Horse Thief Ring Broken Up by Local Sheriff." Will dropped the paper on Hardy's kitchen table and poured himself a mug of coffee. "Sheriff Downey's on a roll. Hell, he'll be running for president if we don't watch out."

And the next night, Saturday, Downey and his men ambushed the dogfighters out at Garcia's place, pulling off another coup. The headline on Monday read, "Downey Drops Dogfighters," and the article went on to tell how the sheriff and his men had stopped the fight before any dogs had been hurt, confiscating the animals and a pile of money. It was another feather in Downey's feathery new cap.

"What about Hector and his family?" asked Hardy, when the sheriff called later that night to thank him again for the tip.

"He's staying there. The man who owns the house didn't know any of this was taking place, and he's real shook up about it, believe me. He's a dog lover, and when I told him what was going on, he about had a stroke. Those dogfighters had Garcia thinking he had to play along or else. Apparently they threatened his family, but poor Henry was the only one they got around to."

"Yeah, Henry—he reminded me of my Earl. 'Night, Mitchell, and good work."

# CHAPTER SEVEN

Hardy mused about his age and his antics of the past week. It wasn't as if he was out playing golf. Scrambling up and down cliffs and tromping through woods was rough. He supposed he'd keep going as long as his body would let him, but he was sore, and he had a bad bruise on his rear end where he'd hit the rocks the other night. Bella was fine, but she was a lot younger than he was.

It was Sunday. He'd given Will the day off. The clinic was open seven days a week, but the kid needed a break. Hardy's life, however, *was* the clinic, and he had no place else to go anyway, other than his little side trips. Sundays were usually slow, but there was the occasional emergency, so he was always ready. While Bella snoozed in her bed by the window and Sophie napped on top of a stool, her legs hanging over the sides, Hardy fiddled with his computer, trying to make it print billing statements. This was a task usually undertaken by Martha, but she had been ill for the past week with flu or hoof and mouth disease, so she said. Hardy didn't like the computer. He was too old to care about learning how to master it, yet he knew it was important in the modern world, so he didn't put his foot through the monitor. He chuckled at the thought of adding it to his list. Instead, he walked away and went to fold towels. Folding towels was something he had mastered all by himself a long time ago, after Willa passed away. They washed lots of bloody sheets, towels, and rags at the clinic, and he folded them and stacked them neatly on the shelf. Doing laundry was soothing he had found, mind numbing but soothing, and his body needed a rest.

As he closed the linen closet, the little bell over the front door dinged. Bella awoke and sat up, her ears pricking forward as a woman carrying a cat in her arms entered. Hardy advanced, offering to take the animal, but she clutched it to her breast and stared at him, her big sad eyes pleading for a miracle. He knew the look, but he didn't know the woman. She hadn't been in before. She was a tiny person, probably his age, with short graying hair and the big blue eyes.

"Something's wrong with my Fluffy," she said, almost apologetically, as if the cat's predicament were her fault. "She has this awful, runny diarrhea all the time, and I don't know what to do." Realizing she hadn't introduced herself, she did a little curtsey and said, "I'm sorry. My name is Estelle Greenwood, and I'm just so worried about my cat." Tears collected in the corners of her sad eyes.

Hardy reached for the animal, but she clutched it closer to her body. Invoking his most empathetic voice, he coaxed, "Ms. Greenwood, would you like to put Fluffy on the examination table there so I can have a look? Please, we have to start somewhere. Can you tell me her age?"

Estelle Greenwood nodded and gently placed the docile animal on the table, propping a protective hand at each end of its body. "She's ten now. I've had her since she was a kitten, and she's been spayed and had all her shots. Lately it's just this awful diarrhea."

"Is she eating and drinking water?" the doctor inquired, smiling at the little woman.

"Yes, but it comes right back out the other end."

Estelle relinquished her protective position at the table as Hardy stepped forward. He stroked the small calico cat crouched on the cold steel, looked in her mouth, and palpated her abdomen. He felt ropey growths in the intestines, probably cancerous tumors, and undoubtedly the cause of Fluffy's bowel problems. Never one to hold back the truth, he said, "It feels like tumors in the intestines. They could be cancerous." The little cat was brave and didn't utter a sound while Hardy squeezed and poked, though he knew it must have been painful for her.

Estelle Greenwood didn't fare so well. She broke into tears and began to wail. Hardy offered her his box of Kleenex and rested a hand on her shoulder. He remained silent, for he knew people needed time to process a statement such as the one he had just uttered. Regaining her composure, she asked, "Is there something we can do? An operation?"

He shook his head slowly. "I'm afraid an operation wouldn't help. The growths feel too advanced. It wouldn't be a solution, and Fluffy might not survive. My advice would be to make her as comfortable as you can for the time she has left."

"Is she in pain?"

Hardy hated this question, but he answered as honestly as he could. He thought Fluffy probably was having some pain, especially when she moved her bowels.

"Probably," he said.

"I can't put her to sleep, not yet," cried Estelle, clutching the little cat again.

"I can give Fluffy some pills," Hardy offered. "They might help with the diarrhea."

"Thank you, Doctor, please." He filled a bottle with the medication, took her billing information, and told her to call him at any time, day or night.

Estelle and Fluffy left. He figured the cat had two weeks tops, if she continued to eat and drink. A sad case, but one he saw repeated often; if not cancer, it was some other terrible disease. Putting an animal down was always difficult for him. He wished he had more towels to fold, more simple towel-folding dilemmas to deal with instead of life and death.

How did you know when it was time? Short of obvious pain, which animals hid very well, how did anyone know when it was time to end the life of another creature? Some people had no problems ending life, human or animal, yet others agonized over the prospect. He had not given a second thought to Lester. Once he'd made up his mind, that was it: garbage to the dumps. But he'd warned him, so that counted for something. And Lester had paid him no mind, and Lester was evil, pure evil. So were the Griggs. No problems with putting any of them down. He'd have more trouble over Fluffy than the rest of the human flotsam combined. And tattoo man? More walking human waste. But no longer. What about him? Perhaps he should take a drive out to the boonies and have a look-see. No, too risky. Hardy talked himself out of it, and good thing, for the next morning's newspaper had it covered.

Will dropped the morning paper on his father's kitchen table and poured a mug of coffee. "Here we go," he yelled. "Finally! What a relief. 'Overdose Victim Found in Car,' it's on the second front page. 'Habitual drug user overdoses on barbiturates.' Man, I'd hate to be the one to have to deal with that body."

"Yeah," said Hardy reading the article, "not good. Says here he just got out of jail for abusing a six-year-old child! You're welcome, world." Hardy stood and took a deep bow.

"I don't think you should be so cavalier about taking human life, Dad—child abuser, animal abuser, any human life."

"You're young, Son. Wait until you've walked a mile in my boots before you make comments like that. Come on, let's go. We're going to be late again."

"It's you I worry about, not them. You don't want to spend the rest of your life in some jail, do you?"

Hardy dismissed that statement as utter nonsense. "They ought to be pinning medals on me, but Sheriff Downey's getting the glory, and that's how I want it." Hardy was out the door walking to his truck, Bella at his heels.

They drove their separate vehicles. When they arrived at the clinic, Will was anxious to continue his dialogue with his father, but a message on the answering machine took precedence.

"Oh, hell, it's that Estelle Greenwood, the woman I told you about with the calico cat, Fluffy. Fluffy's disappeared and she's hysterical." He grabbed Fluffy's chart and found Estelle's address. "She's out where we live. I'll be back soon. Call her and tell her I'm on my way."

Estelle stood in her front yard, waving her arms as Hardy pulled into the driveway. "She's gone, and I can't find her, and she was out all night," she screamed. "What can I do?" Hardy got out of his truck and hurried to her side. He wondered if he should touch her or take her hand. Towels would help. He wished he had towels for her to fold.

"Okay, tell me what happened," he said. "When did you last see Fluffy?" He tried to sound both gentle and professional.

Estelle gasped and launched into a chaotic, running dialogue. "She went out like she always does, just around five, and then she didn't come back in, and I walked up and down the street calling for her, and she always comes when I call, but she didn't come, and I can't find her! She was outside *all* night, and she never stays out at night. I'm afraid of predators, so I keep her in the house. Why is she doing this, Doctor? Why is she tormenting me?"

"Tormenting you?" Hardy stared at the tiny woman, puzzled by her statement. "You think Fluffy is purposely staying gone to torment you?"

Estelle buried her face in her hands and began to cry. "No, no, of course not, but she is ... tormenting me. I feel so guilty. I know she doesn't mean to, but not knowing where she's gone is torturing me. It's my fault. I never should have let her go outside yesterday. She was getting too thin and too weak. I'm afraid she's gone off and died somewhere, and I'll never get to see her again. I'll never get to say good-bye."

"Can we sit down here on the porch?" asked Hardy. He felt the weight of the world settle on his shoulders, and it was heavy. As they sat side by side, she cried, and he listened to her sobs. After a while he said, "You're probably correct in what you said, Ms. Greenwood ... Estelle, if I may?" She nodded and continued softly sobbing.

"Sometimes, when an animal knows it's dying, it simply goes off to be alone. That's probably what happened to your Fluffy. They're following their instinct, and you or I might very well want to do the same when our time comes. It's Nature's way. You have to accept it. Can you do that, Estelle? After all, you and Fluffy had many good years, I'm sure. She didn't do this to hurt you; she did it to spare you. Can you see it in that light?"

"I know you're right, but it just hurts so much to lose her, to know I'll never see her or hold her in my arms again. She was my best friend."

Hardy patted Estelle's shoulder. She sniffed, but the tears finally stopped.

"Time will soften this wound, Estelle. It always does. And I get kittens in the clinic, and they need homes and someone to love them. Give it a while and think about saving another life."

She was quiet for a long time, and then she said, "Thank you for coming to my house, Doctor Johns. You certainly went above and beyond the call of duty for me today. I appreciate your compassion. I just need time, like you said." She dabbed at her eyes and stood. He stood up, too. And then she grabbed his arm, leaned forward, and kissed his cheek.

It was just a little thank you kiss, but it caught him off guard. A woman hadn't kissed him for years. He interacted with them daily, but a kiss was not professional, and he didn't know how to handle it. He blushed, stammered good-bye, and got into his truck. She turned and went into her house. As he backed out of her driveway, Bella sniffed him, curious at the scent of a strange female on her man.

# CHAPTER EIGHT

Hardy thought about the kiss as he drove back to the clinic. It was just a peck, a thank you for your time and effort. Was the woman married? He knew absolutely nothing about her other than what he'd written in her chart, and that was more about Fluffy. He'd call her in a few weeks and see if she'd take a kitten. That was a good opening. Good for a kitten too, a win-win. Not that he wanted to get involved with a woman, he told himself. He was just curious what it would be like to have one again.

"Well, what happened?" asked Will.

Hardy told him about the missing animal, but then he hesitated. "And she kissed me good-bye," he added.

Will did a double take. "A kiss? Really? Hey, how about that?! I haven't gotten a kiss from Lois yet, so you're one up on me."

"Lois and you haven't kissed? How many dates have you had?

"Two dinners."

"Well, what's the matter with you? Are you trying to be a friend? Is that what you want, a friend? Hell, I can be your friend. You need a woman, you know, for sex."

"Hey! Watch it, old man. I know what I need and what to call it. Hearing it come from you makes me feel like a little kid. Lois is a class act. I can't rush into things with her."

"I wouldn't call a good-night kiss rushing into things. Promise me, next time you go to dinner, you kiss her good night. She's probably thinking something's wrong with you. Maybe you need some practice. You can use Bella. Bella likes to be kissed, just don't hurt her nose, it's very sensitive."

"Get a grip, Dad. I don't need kissing practice on a dog."

"I kiss my dog all the time. Nothing wrong with kissing your dog, huh, Bella?" He broke into a soliloquy of baby talk, cooing and blathering. "Come here, honey, show Uncle Will how to kiss." Hardy leaned over and stuck his face in front of Bella, and she gave him a big sloppy swipe with her tongue, wagging her tail like crazy.

"Atta girl! See, that's how to do it. Stick your face down there and give it a try, Will. She may not like you enough, though."

"That's okay, Dad, I get it. Bella and I can remain good friends. We don't need hugs and kisses, huh, girl?" He threw her ball across the room, and she bounded after it.

"That's a shallow gesture," said Hardy, wrinkling his nose.

"Okay, next date I kiss Lois good night, and, who knows, maybe it'll lead to something more."

"There you go. That's the right attitude. Now, anything going on around here, business-wise? Any patients?"

"The Pattersons are bringing in a shelter dog for a checkup. They just adopted him. Golden retriever. Man, they get some nice dogs at that place. Makes you wonder how folks can give them up."

"You'll break your mind trying to figure that one out," said Hardy. "I got a special errand to do today, so it's my turn for some time off. I'll check with you later."

Will raised his eyebrows. "Stay out of trouble, okay?"

"Always."

When Hardy and Bella returned to the house, he carefully backed his truck into the garage and slid the inflated raft off the overhead storage area into the bed. It was navy surplus, gray rubber, and it just fit. Then he placed one of his larger collapsible metal cages inside the raft, threw a tarp over the whole shebang, and set off for a drive into the countryside, Raccoon Flats, to be more precise. The Flats were in the middle of nowhere and they were another dismal place, not because God had planned it that way, but because man persisted in altering the landscape. Piles of litter grew like strange new life forms along the gravel road. A ways down, the gravel gave way to dirt. Every trailer and every shack sat buried in old cars, broken down appliances, and evidence of human inhabitance that smothered the weeds fighting to gain purchase in the parched, red soil.

Bella's body twitched nervously as Hardy steered the truck along the ruts and over the bumps. His destination was a falling-down mud-brick house at the end of the road. It sat conveniently alone at the edge of a very dark lake. In front of the house, propped on end in the dirt, was an assortment of steel traps, ugly in size and shape. Each trap had a rope attached to one end. A flea-bitten hound dog stood and growled at them from the side of the house.

Hardy commanded Bella to stay in the safety of the vehicle, then he set his .22 on the seat and got out. The hound eyed him, leaning into her chain, and then laid back down, burying her muzzle in the dirt. Hardy moved toward the house, and as he did, a slight man stepped forward and stood in the open doorway, grinning at him. He was not as old as Hardy, but he looked withered and ancient. His face was covered with whiskers, and the few teeth in his mouth were the color of coffee. He wore overalls with suspenders, no shirt, just his bare dirty body, and work boots with the laces hanging loose. "Whatta you doin' out here?" He yelled at the doctor. "I ain't called ya'."

Hardy didn't want to engage the man in conversation. He wanted to let him know what was on the agenda, nothing more. "I brought you a present," he said, "a boat to float in your lake." He gestured at the raft in the back of his truck. "Come take a look."

Gordy Rumsey seemed pleased, and he shuffled to the truck and watched as Hardy threw off the tarp, exposing the raft and the collapsed steel cage. "That's real nice. You brung me another cage too?"

"Yeah, for bigger animals. I'll take the raft down to the lake for you. It'll be easier to unload it right into the water." Hardy backed the truck to the edge of the lake as Gordy walked alongside, smacking his gums and spitting into the dirt. Bella bounced from one foot to the other in the passenger seat, terrified by the man's scent. Hardy had never seen her so upset. "Easy girl," he whispered, "everything's going to be just fine."

He stopped short of the water's edge, slid the raft and its contents to the ground, and set about assembling the cage. "I can do that," protested Gordy, but Hardy insisted, as it was his gift. When he was finished, Hardy set the steel cage in the middle of the raft. Gordy looked puzzled. "Whatcha do that fer?" he asked.

Hardy shook his head and picked up his .22 from the seat of the truck. The men stood at the shoreline, the raft between them, and Hardy raised the gun.

"Get in the cage," he said. "Try it out."

The dirty man scratched himself. "I ain't getting in no cage," he spat, growling through a crooked grin.

"In!" commanded Hardy, pointing his rifle at the man's head.

Gordy crouched, looking stupider than usual, a twisted smirk on his face. "This is some joke, huh? You playin' with me, huh, Doc?" Then, like a cowed animal, he did as he was told. He hunched over and crawled into the cage. It was plenty big enough.

Hardy slammed the door shut and threw the lock. Gordy Rumsey squatted in the cage, grinning through the bars, waiting for Hardy's next move as if it was some fun game they were playing. Hardy took great satisfaction in the moment, savoring the look of the man in the cage, but something, he knew, was missing.

He pulled the plugs that held the air in the raft and shoved it into the lake. The raft floated quietly out toward the deep middle, and Gordy kept grinning at Hardy while air streamed from the exposed holes, hissing like a dozen punctured balloons. Then the raft began to list with the weight of the man and the steel, and finally Gordy understood. He began to scream, presenting Hardy with the missing element. He needed to hear Gordy scream like he imagined the innocent victims had, the hundreds of animals he'd sunk into the lake and drowned in his filthy cages. Perhaps their spirits would tear him apart when they met in the depths. Gordy's last scream was more of a gurgle, as the cage slipped off the deflated raft and sank slowly to the bottom of Bottomless Lake.

He climbed back into the truck and wrapped his arms around Bella, who trembled with fright. "It's okay, girl. He's gone." Hardy parked in front of the house and unclipped the hound, who took off bellowing. Then he did a quick search of the inside for any other hapless creatures. He found a yellow cat cowering in a trap with a rope attached, no doubt one of Gordy's intended victims. He set it in the back of the truck and started home. How many Gordys were there in the world, he wondered? The thought set him shivering.

He let the yellow cat loose in the house when they got back, and it immediately ran for cover under the sofa. He'd find the litter box and the food and water on his own, and by tomorrow he'd know every nook and cranny in the place. That's how it always went down. A neighbor would probably look after the hound, for those dogs were appreciated by the hunter folks in Raccoon Flats.

It was four o'clock. He called the clinic, hoping Will didn't need him, for he wanted to take a nap. Will told him to stay home and said he'd stop by later. Not much going on.

"Easy for him to say, huh, Bella?" She had regained her composure, and Hardy knew he had witnessed proof of an animal's ability to sense the presence of evil. He lay dozing, his arm resting on her back, and they snored in unison. Will woke them at six when he let the screen door slam shut.

Hardy sat up and rubbed his eyes. "No date tonight?"

"No. She's out of town at some convention, some animal advocates group. How come you don't go to those kinds of things? You're the biggest animal advocate I know."

"Humph. I prefer to work alone. Get more done that way, avoid the bureaucracy. Paperwork slows everything down."

"Yeah, I've seen you in action."

"Yup."

Will sat beside his father on the sofa. "Listen, Dad, about this list of yours. Do you really have one?"

Hardy saw the easy way around it, saying, "No, of course not. I was just pullin' your leg. You want to go out for some Mexican food?"

Will apparently believed him, for a look of relief spread across his face. "Yeah, let's go eat."

They took Hardy's truck and drove downtown to Los Arboles, where they found a quiet table at the back and ordered their usual. Just as the food arrived, so did Estelle Greenwood with a little girl in tow. Estelle noticed Hardy and waved at him. She and the girl sat at the only remaining table, by the front window. Every now and then, Hardy glanced at Estelle and found her glancing back. "That's Estelle, the calico cat lady," Hardy confided to Will. "Should I go say hello?"

"The one who kissed you?" Will turned to look and Hardy kicked him. "Don't look just 'cause I said it was her. Look later, when she's not looking."

On the way out, Hardy and Will stopped at Estelle's table and exchanged cordial hellos. She introduced the young girl, her granddaughter, May, and Hardy presented Will. There was no mention of Fluffy, so Hardy guessed the cat hadn't returned, and he didn't bring it up, not wanting to spoil her evening.

"Well," Hardy asked as they climbed into his truck, "what do you think of her?"

Will shrugged. "Seems nice enough, pretty little face. What do *you* think of her is the thing. Is she single? She has a granddaughter."

I didn't see any sign of a man in her chart or at her house. I want to give her a kitten. She needs to replace Fluffy."

"Maybe you could find out if she's single and ask her to dinner. You've already got your kiss."

"Maybe I will."

Will had been playing along, but now he said, "Seriously, Dad, before you flirt anymore, find out if she's married. Save yourself from hurt feelings and an angry husband."

# CHAPTER NINE

Two days later, Estelle Greenwood banged the door to the clinic open, a shallow box in her arms and a terrified look on her face. Hardy and Will were standing at the examination table, clipping mats of hair off a fat cat who had tangled with a sticker bush. She hurried toward them with her bundle. "Look, he crawled under a cabinet in my garage and I pulled him out. His leg is chewed up, and it smells awful." An orange and white cat, its right rear leg mangled and putrid, lay in the box, able only to raise its head. Hardy carried the box to the surgery table. A cursory examination told him the animal was dying; infection from the rotting leg was flowing through his system.

"If he's going to live, we have to amputate that leg immediately. This mess has been festering for at least two weeks. He's probably a stray that got hit by a car and couldn't go any further. Have you seen him around before?"

"He might have been eating the dry food I've been leaving out in case Fluffy comes home."

Hardy knew Fluffy was not coming home. "You'll attract wild animals if you do that, you know." He said it as gently as he could.

Ignoring his words, she said, "Please help this cat, Dr. Johns. Don't let him die. I can care for him."

Hardy set to work preparing the cat for surgery. The leg would have to come off at the hip joint so the cat would have balance. Hardy explained the procedure and the likely aftermath as he worked. "He'll use his tail like a rudder. I've seen three-legged cats walk, and that's what they do. He ought to get along just fine. You might have to scratch under his chin for him. He won't be able to do that on the one side."

Will assisted his dad, and Estelle waited in the outer room, pacing the floor nervously. The answering machine picked up their calls, and no other patients came in. The operation took an hour, and their chief concern was the amount of anesthetic the animal could tolerate. Will carefully monitored his breathing, standing by with a tiny oxygen mask. When it was over, Estelle was called in and allowed a visit with her new cat, who was still out cold. He was one leg lighter, but at least he would live. They placed him on a soft towel in a warm cage to recover.

"He can go home tomorrow," said Hardy. "Would you like me to drop him off, seeing as our houses are so near each other? I practically go right by yours every day. He's going to need neutering, but let's get him over one amputation before we do the other; looks to be about a year old, maybe a little less." Now he felt himself beginning to blather. He wanted to ask her if she was married, and the only way he could think to do that was just come out with it, so he did. "Are you married, Estelle?"

The question caught her off guard, but she answered, "No, I'm not married, I'm a widow."

Relieved, Hardy said, "So am I," and they laughed. "You know what I mean," he said. "I'd like to ask you to have dinner with me sometime, and of course I didn't want to do that if you were married." They laughed again.

"Of course not," she said. "I mean, yes, I'd like to have dinner with you, and I can because I'm *not* married." More laughter.

"How about tomorrow when I bring the cat? Maybe we could catch a bite then." "Oh, I don't think I'd want to leave him alone his first night." She twittered nervously, twisting her fingers into knots. "I know, why don't I fix dinner for us, that way we don't have to leave Hardy alone."

"Hardy?" asked Hardy, perplexed.

"I'm naming him after you, Hardy Johns, because you saved his life."

"Well, I'm honored, Estelle. I don't think I've had an animal named after me before."

"Good. Then I'll see you both tomorrow  night about six. You'll call me if any complications arise?"

"Of course, but they won't. I don't mean to inconvenience you, but I'm a  vegetarian."

"So was my husband!" she exclaimed, "What a coincidence! In that case, I have a special dish for you. It's very tasty."

Will had been listening from the back, and as Estelle left, he joined his father.

"Good for you, you've got a namesake and a dinner date. Not too shabby, a good-luck tabby."

"Good-luck Hardy pulled himself into the right garage, I'd say."

The following morning, Hardy the lucky tabby was awake but woozy. His temperature was back to cat normal, now that the killer leg with its terrible infection had been severed from his body. By the end of the day, he had eaten and drunk water, so Hardy loaded him into a carrier and set him in the cab of his truck along with a bag of antibiotics. Bella sniffed the carrier. It was occupying her space, after all, but she was used to sharing the truck. He dropped the dog at his house, not wanting to leave her in the truck while he and Estelle ate. "I'll be home early, girl," he said as he fixed her dinner. She didn't like it when he said those words, for it meant he was going out again, leaving her with the cats. And all they wanted to do was lie around.

Hardy arrived at Estelle's house a few minutes later with Hardy. She saw him coming and opened the door. "Put him down and we'll let him out," she said. "I've made a bed in the kitchen, and I've got the litter box and food in there beside it. Of course, he can go anywhere he wants in the house, but I'm not going to let him outside for a while."

"That's a good idea. Let him get to know the house first." Hardy opened the cage door, and the cat dragged itself out. It wobbled on three legs and immediately made a beeline for the darkness under the sofa. "That's were my new ones all go first too," said the doctor.

"We'll leave him alone and let him get acclimated," said Estelle. "Would you like a glass of wine? I have white or red."

"Red, please."

The crisp, cheery blue-and-white checkered décor of her living room was a stark contrast to the worn-out browns and reds of Hardy's faded place. Estelle sat next to him on the sofa, keenly aware that the cat was beneath her, watching her feet. "I hope Hardy likes it here," she said. "It's all I've got to offer."

"It's certainly nicer than my run-down digs, Estelle. Hardy's a damn lucky feline, if you ask me. How long have you been a widow?"

"Bernie died in 1994. It was an accident. He fell off a platform three stories high. He was in construction, you see. It was quick but nasty way to go." She sipped her wine and shook her head. "And you met May, my daughter's child. My daughter is single and travels quite a bit for her job, so sometimes she leaves May with me. The girl's good company, and I do get lonely. That's why I wanted to keep Hardy, because you were right, I don't think Fluffy's ever coming home." She refilled their glasses and suggested they move to the kitchen while she assembled her famous vegetarian tacos. "I've told you about me, now tell me about you, Hardy."

He told her of his wife, his love of animals, and how sometimes he, too, became lonely for human company. She was a good listener.

"I'd be happy to go to dinner with you anytime you get lonely for people," she said, "if that dog of yours will tolerate another female. I notice how she watches me when I come into the clinic. She's very jealous. What did you do that she loves you so much?"

"Same thing you did when you brought Hardy into the clinic, I saved her life."

They finished dinner and talked for another hour, then Hardy thanked Estelle and said good night. He returned home before nine. Bella greeted him with her usual enthusiasm, but his time she stopped and sniffed a bit longer, for it was that same scent again, the scent of that woman.

Hardy the cat didn't come out from under the sofa that night, and he wouldn't come out the next morning. Estelle lay on her side, coaxing him with a chunk of tuna, but he growled and hissed at her. She had to give him his antibiotics, however, so she grabbed the loose skin on his neck and slid him out slowly, talking to him all the while, until finally she held him in her arms. He laid back his ears, squinted his eyes, and cringed at the dreaded human touch, waiting for the worst, but when she scratched him under his chin, he stretched out his neck and rubbed against her fingers, purring loudly.. Estelle knew then and there that Hardy was hers for the scratching.

# CHAPTER TEN

Estelle brought Hardy in for a check up a few days later, not that he really needed to be seen by the doctor but because she wanted to. She wanted to show him off and visit with the other Hardy. Will deferred to his father, disappearing into the back while Hardy examined the cat. "My, you're doing a fine job with him, Estelle. He's so docile. How did you tame him so quickly?" The doctor was truly astonished, for he could tell the animal had been feral until Estelle rescued him.

"Watch, I'll show you." She began scratching under the cat's chin, and he melted in her arms, purring and gyrating, happy as a clam. "It seems to hypnotize him. He's totally tame now. He even sleeps on my bed."

"You must have a way with creatures, like my friend, Marion. I was hoping you'd take one of her kittens, but you found Hardy. Marion does animal rescue work and has a lot of critters, not just cats."

Estelle perked up. "I could take a kitten, Hardy. My goodness, I can have more than one cat, and Hardy might like having someone to play with when he's able. Can I meet this woman? A kitten would be such fun."

Hardy nodded, agreeing with her. "Well, sure, Estelle, I can introduce you. Let me give her a call, and I'll let you know."

As Estelle left the clinic with Hardy the cat in her arms, a huge Rottweiler dragged a young couple into the room. The dog didn't see the cat, but the cat saw the dog, and it was all Estelle could do to contain him. She covered his eyes and scratched his chin and hurried to her car, promising herself that for everyone's safety, Hardy's future trips to the clinic would be in the cat carrier.

When the doctor got a break, he called Marion Myles and asked if he could bring a friend by to look at her kittens. He explained the recent events in Estelle's animal household. Marion said she only had three kittens at the moment, but of course he could bring the woman by anytime. Marion always had five or six dogs in residence; she picked them up in the middle of the road or at Wal-Mart, wherever they'd been dumped, and she wasn't sure how many cats roamed her twenty acres. Most of them circulated around her house, going in and out as they pleased, but some were wild and came only to eat the food she put out in the mornings. She kept a large pond where ducks and geese swam, unafraid of the raccoons and skunks who hunted at night, and she was proud of her chicken house which sheltered its little clutch of mixed breed hens and their rooster. Her property was fenced against larger predators; she patrolled the perimeter often, looking for ruts dug under the wire by Wiley coyote or his friends. This time of year she usually had kittens left from spring litters or new late arrivals. Her large laundry room had a fold-down table that accommodated several roomy cages for sick animals or those that needed to be contained for one reason or another.

Marion was of Estelle's vintage, but she was a free spirit and a loner, never married, and always an outdoors person. She was stocky, built more like a man than a woman, and she wore her thick gray hair in a short bob. The creases in the corners of her soft blue eyes crinkled when she smiled, and her skin was tanned and weather-beaten. She drove a tractor, rototilled her fields, and did anything a man could do except lift bales of hay. For that and other heavy stuff she had to hire her neighbor's boy, Billy. People who knew of her love of the animals and concern for their welfare sometimes took advantage, asking her to take pets they no longer wanted, which she usually did. Sometimes she found homes for the creatures, but often as not she ended up keeping them. She knew people abused her compassionate nature, but she overlooked it in favor of lives saved.

Over the years, Marion and Hardy had developed a symbiotic relationship. He could place animals, having access to the public, and she fostered them until he found the right people. Occasionally it worked the opposite: he received an animal that was not adoptable and she accepted it with open arms. This was usually a cat testing positive for feline AIDS, a deaf cat, or a cat with some odd deformity. As a rule, people who spent their hard-earned money at his clinic were compassionate and caring. Marion was just more so.

He called Estelle and asked if she would like to meet Marion that evening and possibly pick out a kitten. Estelle was ecstatic. Hardy filled her in about his friend on the way, taking note that she had brought her cat carrier. Bella rode in the back of the truck's extended cab, her head resting on the seat between the two in the front. Estelle's scent was disturbing, and Bella didn't like it. When they arrived at the ranch, Hardy let Bella out, telling her to stay on the grassy area in front of the house. She settled on a nice shady spot beneath a large oak and rested her head on her paw, waiting for them to come outside again and retrieve her.

Marion invited them in and offered a glass of ice tea, which they gladly accepted, as the evening was still quite warm. They sat out back on a wide deck that overlooked their valley. It was a spectacular setting. You could hear the geese honking and the ducks quacking and the chickens clucking about. Estelle was smitten. "What a wonderful location you have here, Marion, and Hardy tells me you run this place all by yourself."

Marion blushed and chuckled. "Once in a while I have to hire Billy, the boy across the way, to help. Other than that, yes, I do most of the work, and it's constant; it never stops. There's always something to trim or mow or feed or water at the hacienda, and then there are the animals. It's a damn fortunate thing my daddy left me some money. Hardy tells me you just saved the life of a cat and now you want a kitten. I've got a couple beauties for you to look at." They finished their drinks, and Marion said, "Glad I don't have to choose one. Shall we go have a look-see?"

Hardy and Estelle followed her back into the house and into the laundry room. The big cages had platforms and climbing posts, and one held three kittens: a brightly defined calico, an orange tabby, and a fluffy black-and-white baby.

"Oh, my, you're right. How will I ever choose?" exhaled Estelle.

"You could take them all," said Marion, half jokingly.

"I could, couldn't I?" she said, realizing there was no reason she couldn't. There was no one to say, "No, you can't have all of them."

Marion opened the cage and handed her the black-and-white female. "I'll close the laundry room door, and you can bring them out and play with them for a while. Maybe you'll get a special feel toward one or another. I'll be out on the deck."

"I'll come and sit with you, Marion. We'll let Estelle bond," said Hardy. They left her alone in the room with the kittens. Hardy had a pretty good inkling of what was going to happen, and so did Marion. They sat on the deck watching the sun sink lower and lower, and Marion said, "She's as bad as me. She's going to take all three."

"I think you're right. Won't surprise me a bit, but she's very good with animals. They like her. Except Bella, and I think she's jealous. She's jealous of anyone who comes around me for any length of time. Of course, I realize I *am* a handsome devil."

"And you don't think too much of yourself, Hardy Johns. That's what I always liked about you." They laughed. Marion heard the laundry room door bang open as it hit the wall. "Come on. She's made her decision."

The noise Marion heard was Estelle's carrier banging the door open, for the three kittens made it lopsided and hard to control as they rolled about inside. Estelle grinned and shrugged her shoulders. "Okay, I'll take all three. I certainly can't choose one over the others, and they get along so well."

"Good girl!" Hardy carried the kittens to his truck, Bella at his heels. Estelle thanked Marion and asked for her phone number, telling her she thought she would like to know more about animal rescue work. Marion gladly gave it to her, saying, "There's so much to be done, always."

"What a wonderful woman she is," said Estelle, gripping her carrier in her lap.

"I suppose it's something you're born with, this love of animals. Don't you think so, Hardy?"

"Yes, and what Marion does, the rescue work, requires empathy. You must be able to feel the way the animal feels, put yourself in his skin, so to speak, to be truly good at it. Some people have it, others don't. I come into contact with both kinds, and I don't much care for the ones who don't, but I do what I can to even the score."

"Like working with Marion?"

He smiled. "That's part of it."

# CHAPTER ELEVEN

Estelle had taken home two female kittens and one male, and Hardy needed neutering now. So, all in all, she was looking at a sizeable vet bill. But the doctor let her slide, for she had graciously taken on more than was called for, and he appreciated her kindness. She did have the necessary empathy. She just had to learn how to control it, to channel it in the right direction rather than let it turn her into an emotional wreck and render her incapable of helping when the need arose. She could be trained, however, and Hardy gave that serious thought.

Although he worked alone when it involved his list, certain high-profile assignments required a group effort. And that's when Marion became involved, for she kept close tabs on animal welfare issues in the county. An urgent mission was on the agenda, and Hardy, needing a helper, decided Estelle just might be an excellent choice. She was ready and eager, and he rather believed she had fallen for him. He liked her, too, for that matter. She would certainly see the justice in the act, for it was hard to overlook. Will and he had argued about various solutions. The younger man took a conservative stance, a mistake Hardy attributed to his son's youth and inexperience.

"You can't wait for the bureaucracy to do the right thing, Son, because they just don't seem to get around to it. We're dealing with lives here, you understand, not inanimate objects."

Estelle would agree with him, of that he was sure. His only dilemma was knowing whether she could keep a secret. He decided to take the chance and ask for her help. That night after work, Hardy and Bella ate dinner with Estelle and the cats. Estelle had stocked Bella's favorite dry dog food so that she could be included in their dinners. The big dog was slowly coming around to the strange-smelling woman who seemed to care so much for her person. These cats were more fun than Hardy's, because they liked to play and his didn't. The kittens scrambled over the crouching Bella, playing king of the hill, and she rolled on her back and let them pounce on her. It was becoming obvious that Bella would make an excellent mother. When three-legged Hardy hopped up, wanting to join in, Bella stopped him with a paw; then, realizing he was one leg light, she began licking him, knocking him off balance with each wet swipe. It was heart warming to watch.. Estelle and the doctor felt as if they had suddenly become parents again.

After dinner they sat in the living room drinking coffee, and Hardy told her what was in the wind. She listened raptly, eager to be a part of the plan as he explained it. "Out on Danbury Road, there's a farm where a group of men raise geese. They force-feed the birds, shoving grain down their throats to fatten their livers for pâté. This is a cruel, inhumane practice, and there's a petition before the county court right now to outlaw it, but sources tell us certain officials have been bribed to look the other way and are arranging for the petition to fail. You and I and a few others are going to make the court's decision moot. Are you with us, Estelle? Are you ready to become a member of the humane underground?"

She was entranced by his words, her eyes big as saucers. She nodded her head in agreement and said, "How?"

"Wednesday night there's a meeting at the courthouse to decide the issue. The concerned parties will all be there, and the geese will be unattended. We'll arrive at Danbury Road after dark, free them from their pens, herd them into our van, and take them to Marion's place. She's arranged for rescue groups to filter them out all over the country. Bella's job will be rounding them up; that's what she was born to do." Hearing her name, Bella rolled over and stood, throwing kittens helter-skelter. Her ears pitched forward and her tail thrashed back and forth, knowing something was up.

Estelle was electrified. "So we're working with Marion and the rescue group? Oh, this is so exciting! I'll do my best to be a good helper to you, Hardy." She threw her arms around his neck and kissed him hard on the lips. Before he knew it, they were rushing to her bedroom. They fell on the bed, pulling at each other's clothing, recovering quickly from their prolonged absence from the game. Bella barked and jumped on the bed too, wanting to be part of whatever was going on, but Hardy pushed her off and warned her to stay down or go outside. Testosterone levels were heightened by the thrill of impending danger and the reawakening of sexual desire, and their lovemaking was passionate and tender, reminding them both that they were still viable sexual beings.

When it was over, they lay in each other's arms, panting and dripping wet. Viable, perhaps, but unaccustomed. Engaging in physical lovemaking was much more strenuous than climbing up and down cliffs, Hardy realized. Estelle turned on her side and wiped his forehead with the end of the sheet. "You're a wonderful lover," she said. "It's been such a long time for me. I hope I was okay."

He stroked her arm, "Long for me too, honey, and you were perfect.

We make a good team, and if we're this good now, think how great we'd be with a little practice."

She giggled. "We could work on that, you know; practice once in a while."

"Definitely." He rolled over and looked at Bella. She sulked by the door, her head resting on her paw. "Come here, babe. It's okay. You're my girl too." She slunk to the bedside and raised her head up under his hand. "My girl." He stroked her, and she lay by the bed, finding reassurance in his words, for she had heard them often, and she knew they were good.

Hardy dressed, and Estelle put on her bathrobe. They sat once again in the living room, where he finished telling her the details. "I'll pick you up here after dark, and wear black clothes, if you have them." He took her hands in his. "Most important, don't say anything about this to anyone. We could go to jail if we get caught, so you must keep quiet. The safety of the group depends on absolute secrecy. Got it?"

"Got it," she declared earnestly, and then she said, "Hardy, does Will know about the plan?"

"Ha! No, he's too conservative to participate in such a hands-on operation. For God's sake, don't say anything to him. He'd make my life hell. Bella and I gotta go now, honey, and tonight was special for me. I want you to know that."

She kissed his cheek. "Me too."

Estelle watched Hardy's truck ramble down the road, feeling her life enriched by the man who was willing to share his secrets and his body with her. She felt herself growing stronger, and she loved him for it. And she vowed to do her very best to help him succeed, no matter what it was he asked her to do.

# CHAPTER TWELVE

Estelle was wired. She'd cleaned her house, raked her front yard, groomed the cats, and was running out of chores when Marion phoned. It was Wednesday, G-Day, and she asked Estelle to meet at her ranch at three that afternoon for a briefing. Hardy wouldn't be there, but Marion would introduce her to the group. Estelle tingled with excitement as she hung up.

She had found a pair of black jeans, a black shirt, and a black windbreaker in her closet. She bought a black scarf downtown, and she had black boots. At two forty-five she climbed into her a red Honda Accord and drove out to Marion's ranch. When she saw the dozen or so trucks and cars assembled in front of Marion's place, Estelle finally realized she was part of something. It was really happening, and it was big. After Hardy brought her into the fold the other night, she'd watched the newspapers for articles about geese and had found several. The farmers tried to defend their practice against cruelty charges, but really how could they? Force-feeding geese until their livers exploded? Any sane person would think it was a no-brainer on the side of the geese. And Marion's coconspirators, aware of the political chicanery, had already decided the case.

Realizing the initial introduction to the group might be intimidating, Marion met Estelle at the door and greeted her warmly. Then, wrapping her arm inside the newcomer's, she led her into the living room, where everyone had congregated. Marion introduced Estelle as Hardy's friend. Estelle immediately felt comfortable with the sincere, earnest people who seemed to be normal, rational thinking folk. Many were her age, which was a relief, for she'd been worried they might be college kids out for a thrill. She had nearly misjudged "the Movement," as it was called by those present.

When Marion got a chance, she pulled Estelle aside and explained that the group was indeed much more than a pastime for people who had nothing better to do with their lives. "The Movement is a belief system founded on the idea that actions speak louder than words. These are concerned citizens who don't accept the things they're told they can't change. They find the courage and change them. Wisdom is knowing the difference." Tears filled Marion's eyes as she related their mission statement. Estelle could sense that the woman was deeply invested in her words as she reiterated the oft-stated proposition that the human race needed to reevaluate its relationship with all living things if it wished to survive. All forms of life were sacred and interrelated, Marion said, and the destruction of any one might well spell the destruction of all. The Movement fought their battles as priorities dictated, and their membership was growing, expanding whenever outrageous crimes against nature and the innocent occurred. The people were rebelling, and Estelle, if she wished, could be part of the force now. When Marion was finished talking, Estelle felt charged and empowered, capable of achieving great accomplishments and meaningful deeds for the first time in her life.

Marion outlined the timeline for delivery of the truck with the geese to her ranch and the departure times of the people in the group. It seemed like a simple operation. They all agreed to meet back at Marion's at eleven that night for disbursement of the cargo. Since Estelle was working with Hardy and Bella in the actual liberating of the flock, she was on special duty. Hardy would tell her what to do when the time came.

They adjourned, and Estelle drove home to wait, feeling so energized she could hardly stand herself. But she was also a bit scared. Hardy would calm her, and she'd feel strong again in his presence. She dressed in her black outfit, admiring herself in the hallway mirror. It was a good thing she'd bought the scarf, she thought, for her silver hair shone as bright as a light atop a lamppost. Thinking she looked like a ninja all dressed in black, she bent her knees and chopped the air with her hands, then she did a few side kicks and felt a sharp pain in her hip. Fearful of throwing something out of joint, she stopped performing and contented herself with the image in the mirror.

Darkness at last enveloped the yard, and shortly afterward, Hardy and Bella arrived. He wore black clothes, and Bella had a black scarf tied around her neck. Estelle watched from her front window as he got out of his truck and started up the walk. She let him ring the bell, waited a moment, fussed with her hair, and then hurried to greet him. She knew now was not the time to play coy, but she couldn't help herself. When she opened the door, he smiled, stepped forward, took her face in his hands, and kissed her. That was all she needed. Her courage soared. "How do I look?" she whispered.

"Perfect. Like a dark ninja lady. So let's go, missy. It's time."

She climbed into the cab and petted Bella's head, which hung over the seat back between them as usual. "I like your scarf," she told the dog. "Where'd you get it, Hardy?"

"That? It's one of Willa's aprons, actually. It just fits. Kinda cuts down on the sheen of her coat. Her coat shines just like your hair in the moonlight. Two pretty girls."

Estelle fidgeted in her seat as they drove toward the destination. "Are you nervous?" she asked.

"Me? No I don't get nervous, just anxious to get the job over with."

"You?"

"Yes, I've never done anything like this before."

He laughed. "Don't be nervous, Estelle. This is an easy job. Everyone's gone to the meeting. All we have to do is steal the geese, and that's mainly Bella's job."

They rode the rest of the way in silence. Fifteen minutes later they were well into the countryside. Hardy slowed the truck, killed the lights, and turned left down a gravel road. A light shone at the end of the drive "That's where the geese are kept," Hardy said. "Now we wait for the van. It should be here any minute." He pulled the truck off the road and parked under a stand of oaks.

"How do you know no one's watching the geese?" asked Estelle.

"We don't, absolutely. One of our informants, a fellow who used to work here, says the geese are unguarded during the night. Now that there's been all the fuss in the newspapers, we're not sure. We'll find out, though, won't we?" He grinned.

"What will we do if someone *is* there?"

"I don't know, Estelle," he said, becoming annoyed by her questions. "Knock him out, I guess. I sure as hell don't want to shoot anybody tonight."

"You have a gun?" she asked, breathlessly.

Hardy couldn't tell if she was afraid or aroused. Her tone rather aroused *him*.

"I carry a pistol, yes. Of course, I have my .22 and a couple of other long guns."

"Oh," she exhaled, her breathing heavier now.

Just then they heard tires on the gravel. A large, dark, moving van pulled alongside Hardy's truck. Hardy handed Estelle a flashlight. "Blink this twice at him through the window."

She did, and as the van proceeded down the drive, Hardy moved out behind it and trailed it to the end of the road where the barn stood. A single floodlight was mounted high on a corner of the barn's roof. They parked side by side. The man in the van slid down from the cab; a black ski mask covered his head and face, and he wore the black uniform. He nodded and motioned toward the barn door, and the three of them crept forward. The man quietly lifted the iron bar that locked the door, and Hardy grabbed the door handle and pulled the slider open. Estelle stood behind him, peering under Hardy's arm. She saw no humans, only hundreds of geese crammed together in wire pens that spanned the length of the building, separated by a wide cement aisle. The man ran back to the van, turned it around, and backed it through the entrance, the top of the vehicle wedging neatly under the doorframe. Hardy pulled the slider closed tight against the metal sides, leaving no space for the geese to escape except into the van. After flipping on the barn lights, they pulled out the telescoping loading ramp and proceeded to unlock the geese pens, shooing the large animals out into the aisle toward the ramp.

"Bella, lead!" commanded Hardy. The beautiful Border collie was in her element as she dodged and prodded, nipped and head-butted the flock of confused geese up the ramp into their transport. The first few were the most difficult, but once one or two waddled up, the others followed. Within ten minutes, all the geese were loaded, the slider was closed, and the little convoy was rumbling back down the drive. When they hit the country road, the van accelerated, beating a retreat to Marion's ranch, where anxious rescue personnel awaited their cargo.

The van parked inside a fenced area at Marion's, and the process began in reverse, unloading and reloading separate groups into smaller vehicles. Bella was indispensable, herding twenty here, twenty there. All in all, they had liberated three hundred geese. Never again would humans shove grain into their stomachs with long prods. And even though the geese probably didn't realize they were safe, that fact was a source of great joy to their rescuers.

Marion kept ten. She clipped the metal tags from their wings so they couldn't be identified and then let Bella herd them to her large pond. The caper was deemed a huge success, and the team scattered quickly, agreeing to meet again in a week for a celebration at Marion's hacienda. By the time Hardy took Estelle home, it was one in the morning. They toasted themselves with a glass of wine, tossed the cats off her bed, and made adrenaline-fueled love.

The hero of the night, Bella, settled down on the living room rug, distracted by a big soup bone Estelle had bought for that very purpose.

# CHAPTER THIRTEEN

Will dropped the newspaper on Hardy's kitchen table two mornings later. The break-in and theft hadn't been discovered until morning, too late to make the next edition, so by now the goose caper was old news, for gossip traveled fast among the townsfolk.

"So, the geese got liberated? Good thing,'cause the court turned the petitioners down."

"We knew they would. The supervisors were paid off, Will. I told you not to trust the bureaucracy. You got to take a stand, make things turn out right."

Will shook his head and poured a mug of coffee. "I guess I don't want to know if you had anything to do with it. Just don't tell me, okay?"

"Don't you worry about that." Hardy read the headline aloud because it tickled him: "Rustlers Hustle Geese Away—Pâté Passé." Well, thank the Lord and the geese rustlers," he said. "Now, how's your love life going?"

"Lois and I are becoming quite an item," Will said, smugly. How about you and Cat Woman?"

"You had sex with her yet?" asked Hardy, ignoring his question.

Will blushed and stood, leaving his mug on the table. "I've got to go open up that clinic of ours. Sometimes people actually expect us to be there at nine."

"I'll take that as a no," said Hardy. "Son, you've got to take the initiative. Is she frigid?"

The remark stopped Will at the door, and he turned to his father.

"Why all the interest in my sex life, Dad? You never cared a hoot what I was doing before. And no, Lois isn't frigid."

Hardy looked his son in the eye. "Because I've been reacquainted myself with the joys of lovemaking, and I now remember how good it can be. And it's healthy for you. I just want you to be healthy, like me."

"You old son of a gun," said Will, slapping his hand on the wall. "You got to third base before I did! Well, good for you, Dad. So I guess you don't forget how no matter how old you get."

"You better go open up the business," he cackled, trying to sound decrepit. "People might be waiting, and it takes us old guys a while to pull our breeches on."

By the time Hardy arrived, several cars were already parked in the lot. He entered the clinic through the rear door, grabbed a white coat, and joined his son and a young couple at the side of a large German shepherd who lay on the steel examination table.

"What have we here?" he asked.

Will introduced his father to the McElroys and said he thought the dog, Larry, had an infection and that he was drawing blood for the necessary tests. Larry's temp was 104, and Will recommended they leave the dog until he got the test results back from the lab. It was a twenty-four-hour turnaround, and as the dog was dehydrated, he could begin IV fluids immediately. The McElroys agreed to leave their Larry. They wanted to do the right thing, whatever was best for him, they said. So Will prepared a double cage on the lower level, padding it with soft blankets, and led the weakened animal to it. Larry climbed in without a fuss and lay still, wanting only to sleep.

An hour later, another dog came in, a cocker spaniel, and his owner, a worried young woman, said the dog had been throwing up all night. Long strings of drool hung from his mouth. Hardy wiped them away, but they kept coming. The cocker's temp was elevated also, so Hardy drew blood, recommending the same panel of tests Will had just ordered for Larry. The woman left her dog, but she wasn't happy about it, and she insisted they call immediately when the results came back, which of course they always did anyway.

They knew something was terribly wrong when a few minutes later, another dog arrived, same symptoms, and then another, and then several cats, all vomiting and in circulatory distress. By the end of the day, the cages in the clinic were full, and Hardy was on the phone with the local authorities. It was becoming evident that the animals had been poisoned, most likely by a commercial food they had eaten rather than by some lone nut on a mission, for the victims came from all over the county. By morning, the blood tests confirmed his suspicions, and the news media had hold of the story. A pesticide, outlawed in the United States, had been found in certain brands of dry and wet food that had been processed in China for companies in America. It had gotten through government checkpoints and was killing pets all over the United States. And now they begin to die in Hardy's clinic, their kidneys and livers failing.

Will was shattered. His voice cracked with the stress of tending to the dying animals, his body was wracked with sleeplessness, and he railed against everyone involved.

"How could our country let this kind of thing happen? Why do we allow China to make food for America's pets? To save a few bucks? Wouldn't Americans pay a little more for dog food made here, where we know it's safe? It just doesn't make sense. For God's sake, China of all places—the whole country's polluted. It's polluting its own environment and everyone else's, and nobody gives a damn. Everything they make is contaminated with lead. Good God, why do we put up with it? What's the matter with America? We can spend billions on war, but we can't protect our pets and our children from goods made in China? The whole world's crazy, Dad."

"Now you're getting it, Son," sighed an equally weary Hardy. "And China's responsible for the decimation of hundreds of animal species. Endangered? Hell, they don't give a damn. That just makes the poor creature more desirable. Poachers make big bucks smuggling endangered animals into China, and the scarcer that animal becomes, the higher the price on his head. They raise dogs and cats and tigers to eat. They keep bears in cages, draining their gall bladders and they demand illegal elephant tusks. And they call themselves this great old civilized country. Bullshit! They may be old, but they're far from civilized. Nothing makes me crazier than talking about China!" he concluded, banging his fist on the examination table.

The McElroys arrived and sadly carried Larry's limp body to their car. Wanting to keep him close, they would bury him in their yard. When Hardy confirmed their beloved companion was a victim of the tainted food epidemic, they hastily hired an attorney. "He was our child," said Mr. McElroy, tears filling his eyes, "and we aren't letting him go without a fight."

Warnings were now updated regularly on every radio and television news station. Names of the affected brands were posted on the Internet, and the list grew daily. Hardy and Will tried to keep current. As more animals died, sick ones filled their cages.

"Needless suffering," said Will. "It's enough to make you want to kill somebody."

"Kill who, the Chinese? How about the inspectors who passed the stuff through customs? Nobody on our side caught the problem. We're to blame as well. This kind of thing …," Hardy shook his head. "Something terrible has to happen before anything gets done about it, and it's always over money. That's why you got to take the bull by the horns. Sometimes you win, and sometimes you get gored, but if you don't grab the horns, you're not even in the game."

# CHAPTER FOURTEEN

Some of their clients pulled through, but many of them died painful, lingering deaths. Hardy thanked God that the brand of food he fed Bella wasn't contaminated. Losing her would have finished him. And Estelle's cats were safe, as well as his own, so they'd been lucky. He shook his head at the blame game being played by those who had dropped the ball and let the poisoned food pass through customs. If they didn't have enough inspectors, as they claimed, then they should either hire more people or stop bringing in things that needed inspecting. It seemed simple enough to him. Food for America's dogs and cats ought to be made in America anyway. People would pay a little more if that's what it took to keep their beloved companions safe.

Estelle, Hardy, and Bella were going to a celebration at Marion's that evening. It had been several weeks since the goose caper, but the pet food scare had delayed their party, for nobody felt like partying when dogs and cats all over the country were dying.

Hardy had tied a big pink bow around Bella's neck, and when the Border collie pranced into Marion's living room, everyone clapped and called her name, for she had been the star that night, and now she knew she was being honored. She carried on with her favorite activities, sniffing pant legs, munching dog cookies, and frolicking with the cats, while the relaxed group gathered on the deck, drinking wine and watching the sunset. The sky was awash in a hazy orange. It was late September. The days were growing noticeably shorter, and a strange electricity filled the air. Everyone felt good about the accomplishment. Marion called upon the geese transporters to share the outcomes of their journeys, and they did, reporting successful missions, one and all.

Three hundred geese had been relocated to rural locales where they could live out their ornery lives in safety. It was a great victory. When everyone had had plenty of time to settle into a mellow mood, Marion said she had an announcement. It was important, and she made sure all the guests were paying attention by clanging a large cowbell that hung off the end of her deck.

"We have a formidable task confronting us, dear group. I will understand if, after hearing what I am about to say, you decide not to participate. Do not be afraid to say no thank you. We will understand." Seeing that her ominous introduction had captured the attention of the mellowest among them, she continued. "Our covert agents have discovered that something very disturbing is about to rear its ugly head in our midst. We had hoped this abomination wouldn't find us, but, as we all know, man's ingenuity in his quest for blood knows no bounds."

"What is it?" yelled one of the men, fired by her oratory.

Sparks flew from her eyes as she spat the evil words. "A game park featuring canned hunts! Pay your money and shoot the exotic animal of your choice, no questions asked."

A collective gasp escaped the crowd, and angry shouts arose as the members cursed and swore to obliterate any such operation. Marion stood stoically, hands on her hips, watching the reaction and gauging the temperature of their rage. The man who had spoken earlier cried out," Hell, Marion, those shooting galleries are in Texas, not out here."

"Not any more, Roy."

"Where is this place?" he yelled.

"We're not even sure yet. We think it's in Cowell County, near Rowland. It's being kept ultra secret, and we know they don't have permits for the types of animal they're bringing in. They're planning on the big cats—tigers, lions, cheetahs, you name it—and, of course, all the antelopes and buffaloes. There's mention of a few elephants and zebras, zoo animals bought on the sly. It's sick. I don't mean to ruin our celebration, but disrupting this coming abhorrence is going to be the next big objective for those of you who wish to participate. We don't know how we're going to tackle it yet. We'll need to form committees, like always, but it *will* go down, I promise you that. Okay, now that I've said my speech, go on back to having a good time."

Hardy turned to Estelle, clinking his glass on hers. "Here's to bigger, badder targets, and lots of dart guns, 'cause that's what it's going to take to pull this one off." Estelle smiled and drank her wine, not sure what he meant but certain she'd learn when the time came.

People broke into groups, eagerly discussing what they'd just been told. Hardy noticed Marion waving at him from across the deck. He excused himself, telling Estelle he'd be right back, and joined the hostess, who took his arm and led him through the kitchen into the empty living room. She sat him down on the sofa. She talked softly, urgently, and her words were like flint hitting flint. "This thing I just talked about is going to require your help exclusively in one area: sedatives. We're going to need large quantities to get the cats out. We won't be sure about the others animals until we see them in action, but I thought I'd better tell you now so you can stock up slowly and not make it too obvious when you order the stuff. If it looks like you're sedating a zoo, someone might get nosey."

"That's good thinking. I can start ordering little by little tomorrow. How soon is this going down, any idea?"

"Not yet. As I said, we're not even sure of the location. We should know a lot more by next week. I'll keep you informed." She fidgeted in her seat and clasped her hands in her lap. "One other thing, Hardy, and I hope you'll understand why I'm bringing it up. Are you absolutely confident in your friend Estelle's devotion to the group? Any misstatement to the wrong people could ruin everything for all of us. We must be sure of our loyalties."

Hardy rested his hand on Marion's and smiled. "I'm as sure of her as I am of Bella. My two girls are loyal, but I'll remind her again what's at stake, for I'm heavily invested here, too, especially with the latest item on our agenda."

"Good, then, I feel better. Just talk to her one more time, for me." She stood and pulled him up. "Come on. We'd better join the guests before they think we're up to something covert, for that's the nature of *this* beast."

Estelle had integrated herself into the gathering and was talking animatedly with several women. Hardy marveled at how the shy woman had emerged from her shell and become a contributing force. She had strong opinions and wasn't afraid to voice them. Rather than procrastinate, she got right to the heart of things, a trait he admired. She had only needed a catalyst to jolt her out of suspended animation, and that had been Hardy the cat. He thought it fitting that a cat should be a catalyst. They said good-bye to everyone at midnight; they weren't the first to leave, but not the last either. Estelle snuggled beside him as they drove home, Bella's muzzle resting against her head, blowing soft warm air into her ear. Hardy decided to forgo any serious talk, for it was late and they were both tired. When they arrived at her house, he walked her to the door and kissed her good night.

"Come to the clinic at noon tomorrow, and we can eat lunch together. I'll make you a sandwich," he said.

"That would be nice. I will."

He could talk to her then about Marion's security issues. He didn't want to say the wrong thing and hurt her feelings. She was sensitive, which played well with her empathy, but her empathy was an emotion under cultivation, and he didn't want to upset any balances.

Hardy was a little tipsy when he climbed into bed. When he awoke in the morning, cats surrounded his head like a furry hat. Bella lay across his feet, one cat blanketed his stomach, and another was nestled under his arm. He opened his eyes and lay still, wondering whether he should move. He stared at the ceiling, for it seemed a good time to ponder. He was comfortable, though considerably warm under all the cats and Bella, but he was a lucky man, he thought, to have so many fine creatures that cared for him. He shouldn't move; it wouldn't be fair to those who surrounded him, who literally leaned on him. He closed his eyes and decided to go back to sleep so as not to disturb them, but all at once he had to pee. Damn it, he would have to get up to do that. He pushed himself to his elbows, and Esther, stretched across his stomach, opened one eye, yawned, and squinted at him, as if to say, "Oh no, you're not doing *that* again." He must have gotten up during the night and disturbed her. Bella was awake, and she rolled over, freeing his legs.

"Sorry, you guys, but I've got to go. You can stay here as long as you want. I won't make the bed, okay?" He shuffled into the bathroom and heard the kitchen door slam. "Will's here," he yelled to the animals. "Make coffee, Will," he shouted down the hall. "I'll be right out."

The cats did aerobics. Gripping the blankets with their claws, they pushed their rumps in the air, stretching their elongated bodies like weenies, and then they reversed, shoving their heads high, dragging their stomachs along the blankets, front legs rigid. After the workout, they followed Hardy to the kitchen for breakfast and a poo, and then they returned to his bed, where they would spend the rest of their day napping. Will's coffee was brewing, and he'd dropped the newspaper on the table. If anything, their morning routine was predictable.

Hardy's gray hair stuck up in spikes, and a stubble of whiskers shadowed his chin. He scratched his stomach through an opening in his pajama top where he was missing a button, and Will shook his head at the sight of the man. "How was your party last night? Did you have a good time?"

"Very, very good. Yes, lots of nice people. Someday maybe I can introduce you to the group, you know, the one I told you about." Hardy had mentioned the group to his son without disclosing their true purpose, but Will hadn't been interested, so he'd let it drop. "Animal welfare people. You have an open invitation, whenever you're ready."

"Thanks, Dad, I'll consider it."

"Lois might be interested. She's into that kind of thing."

"Yeah, I'll mention it to her," he said, distracted by an article in the paper.

Hardy suddenly remembered that he'd invited Estelle to lunch at the clinic. "I'm making sandwiches for Estelle and me. She's coming to the clinic at noon for lunch. Shall I make **one** for you? Bologna and cheese?"

"I'll grab a bite downtown, if you guys want to be alone," he said, absently, still reading his article.

"Okay, yes, that might be good, because I do have some rather touchy things to talk to her about, come to think of it."

"Touchy?" Will dropped the paper and raised his eyebrows. "You're not asking her to marry you, are you?"

"What?" The idea of remarrying hadn't occurred to Hardy, so Will's question startled him. "Of course not. Why would I do that?"

"Well, people get remarried all the time, Dad, so they don't have to live alone. Is that something I have to explain to you?" Will looked skeptical, like his father was putting him on.

"Well, I'm not lonely at the moment. I've got plenty of company. I got so many bed partners I could hardly move this morning. Bet you can't say that."

"The hairy kind, you mean. No, I can't compete with you on that." Will finished his coffee and left to open up shop, while Hardy made sandwiches, a plain cheese for him and two bologna and cheese, one for Bella and the other for Estelle.

She was punctual, arriving at noon sharp, which was another quality of hers that he admired. After Will left to grab a bite downtown, they sat at the exam table, a paper towel covering its surface. And as he laid out her sandwich, he attempted a delicate presentation of the touchy subject. "Estelle, dear, there's something Marion asked me talk to you about, and it is simply to remind you how very cautious we must be as members of the Movement. I assured her that you were loyal and intelligent enough to keep your mouth shut, and she pretty much took my word for it. Just tell me once more that you realize how important this secrecy is, and I'll never bring it up again, I promise."

Estelle listened politely to his speech, and when he finished talking she said, "I'm not stupid, Hardy. I know how important secrecy is to the Movement, and because I think I love you, I certainly wouldn't do anything that would take you away from me and put you in jail. Is that clear?" She bit into her sandwich and waited for his answer.

"Couldn't be clearer," he said. She might as well have hit him over the head with a sledgehammer.

# Chapter Fifteen

Hardy didn't remember anything Estelle had said that afternoon after "I love you," and when she left and Will returned, he must have looked shocked, because Will said, "What's wrong with you, Dad, you look white as a ghost."

Hardy sat on a stool at the examination table, his hands on the cold steel, his fingers spread wide. "She said she loves me, Will. What am I going to do?" The words rattled in his throat as if he'd received the death penalty and was waiting for a lethal injection.

"She said that?" Will pulled up a stool and sat beside his father, staring into his dad's terrified eyes. "Holy cow, she's a fast worker. But why do you look like you're about to have a coronary? Let me listen to your heart." He plugged his stethoscope into his ears and held it to his father's chest. "Are you breathing, Dad? I can't hear a sound. Cough or something."

Hardy looked down at the apparatus Will held over his heart and grabbed it away, tossing it on the counter. "That thing's been broken for a year. I hope you haven't been diagnosing patients with it," he snarled. He jumped up and began to pace the width of the room, hands clasped behind his back, head down, counting the steps under his breath. Suddenly he stopped and wheeled around, facing his son.

"How could a nice woman like that love an old fart like me?" He stood in the middle of the room, waiting for an answer. "I knew she liked me, at least I suspected, what with the sex and all. But love? At our age?"

"How do you feel about her? Honestly, Dad, couldn't you love someone again? You like sex, at least that's what you said, and they kind of go together, and women don't like one without the other usually, unless they get paid for it. You know what I mean."

"I just never thought it would happen again. Willa, your mother, is the one I love, and she died. I didn't stop loving her because of that, Will. I still love your mother, so how can I love another woman?"

Will was clearly exasperated by his father's comments. "But Mom's physically gone, Dad. You can't hold her and kiss her and make love to her. Of course you still carry the love for her in your heart, but all animals need others of their kind to comfort, sleep beside, keep warm—you know how it works. You're no different, and Mom would want you to have a companion, someone who can care for you like she did. I know there's plenty of love in your heart. You certainly share it with your four-legged friends."

Hardy responded without blinking an eye. "That's different," he snapped. "The bond I share with my animals is pure and unconditional, unpolluted. Humans are corrupt, even Estelle. Sooner or later she's bound to ruin the relationship we have. She can't help it; it's in her human genes. I don't need some new person sharing my life, anyway. I've got you, and I'm not lonely very often, you know. Bottom line, I can't tell the woman I love her back, so if she still wants to hang around and have sex once in a while, it's her call. Thanks for the talk. I feel a lot better." He grabbed his son and wrapped him in a hug.

Will hugged him back and said, "Well, I'm glad we got your love life straightened out, now maybe you can help me with mine. Lois has invited me to go to a convention in Las Vegas at the end of October. I'd be gone a week, and it sounds like fun. Do you think you could get along without me? I'm supposed to let her know so she can make the reservation."

"That's wonderful!" said Hardy, slapping Will on the back. "Of course I can get along, and you'll have a great time in Vegas. That's quite a town, you know. Your mother and I went there a few times. I imagine it's changed a lot since then, though. That was back in the seventies."

That evening, Hardy ate dinner at Estelle's house. He felt odd. It was as if they shared a lopsided secret, her end heavier than his, but he was confident in his position, having diagnosed the dilemma that afternoon.

She had prepared a vegetarian salad and baked her own bread. They sat on the back patio in the shade of the overhang, sipping ice tea and watching the sunset. Bella lay sleeping on the grass at the edge of Estelle's marvelous flower garden. Estelle had promised Hardy a surprise as soon as it got dark. "I have to make sure all the cats are in the house," she said, as she caught up with the last kitten and slipped it into the kitchen. When it was completely dark, she handed him a big flashlight. "Point it into the flower garden. It's magic."

He did, and a dozen fluorescent eyes caught the beam and danced in the light. "Come on, follow me," she whispered. She crept down a path among tall spikes of delphinium, the blue and white flowers that towered throughout the garden.

"Look, there's one, it's a moth! Look, Hardy, it's as big as a humming bird. There's another! Aren't they beautiful?" She shone her light, illuminating the wondrous creatures. The huge, multicolored moths hovered here and there, inserting their long proboscises into each blossom before darting on to the next. "The cats go crazy over them. That's why I have to put them inside when it gets dark. Hardy caught one and mauled it, and I tried to save it, but once the wing is torn, there's nothing you can do. I cried and cried over that poor thing. I set it in a flowerpot, and it just withered away. I even tried to feed it honey water, but it wouldn't eat. It was a tragedy."

The doctor had once tried to superglue the big wing of a butterfly back together, and it hadn't worked either. "Yes, I know, I've had a similar experience."

They returned to the porch. The flash of their lights seemed to create glowing phosphorous trails as the moths fed from the flowers and then flitted off to the mimosas bordering the creek at the back of Estelle's property.

"It's easy to follow them. I can do it for hours," she said.

"You're a good woman, Estelle." He put his arm around her shoulder, "Anyone who cries over torn moth wings has a good heart."

# CHAPTER SIXTEEN

Hardy was preparing an order for a large quantity of sedative and several boxes of darts that delivered the drug. In a few weeks, he would order the same quantities again, and if necessary, again. He had the dart guns but rarely needed to use them. While he sat at the surgery table preparing his list, he heard the client bell tinkle, and shortly afterward Will stuck his head around the corner and said, "Dad, come out here. I think you'd like to see this."

The scene before him took his breath away. Bella stood nose to nose with a male Border collie equal to her in beauty and size. The two of them wagged their tails and sniffed appropriately, seemingly enchanted with each other.

Will introduced his father to the dog's person. "Dad, this is Mr. Hollis, and that's Buster." Buster turned and sat at the mention of his name.

"What a beauty," said Hardy.

"Yours too," said Hollis, admiring Bella, "And she's not been spayed?"

"No, I was kind of hoping I might breed her and keep a pup. Haven't found a suitable mate yet, although I really haven't been looking. Just stalling on the spaying, I guess. She's such a great dog, it seems a shame not to let her have a litter, although as a veterinarian I must wholeheartedly approve and recommend spaying and neutering. There are way too many unwanted strays in this world." He cleared his throat, hoping his ambivalence didn't sound completely foolish.

Hardy and Hollis eyed each other and each other's dogs. They walked a slow circle around the animals, who were sitting together in the middle of the room, looking like images in a mirror.

"Is Buster still all together?" asked the doctor, stroking an imaginary beard.

"Got all the necessary parts," answered Hollis, hands clasped behind his back.

"Well, then, Mr. Hollis, what would you think of letting Buster mate with my Bella here? You could have the pick of the litter and as many of the pups as you wanted. I just want one to keep Bella company."

"Dr. Johns, I was thinking that would be a wonderful idea, for won't we get some lovely pups, and you being a vet and all, you can keep right on top of things, medically speaking."

"It's a deal, then," said Hardy, grabbing Hollis's hand and shaking it. "I'll get your number and call you when Bella comes into heat. It should be soon. And you can bring Buster to my ranch, if you like. I think the female feels more relaxed if she's on her own turf, and most males, once they get a whiff, couldn't care less where they do it."

Hollis laughed, "Ain't that the truth." He nodded his head knowingly, attached Buster's leash, and led him to the door. "Goodbye, Bella. Be a good girl."

She followed Buster to the door, and Hardy called her back. "Not yet, honey, you'll see him again soon enough."

"Well," said Will, "that was a fortunate encounter. The Hollises just moved here from Oregon, and he brought Buster in for his yearly shots. That's why we haven't seen the dog before."

"He looks like a perfect sire. Sometimes good things just drop into your lap. Baby Bellas, can you picture it?" Bella had returned to her mat, and when she heard her name, she rolled onto her back, her feet in the air and her tongue hanging out the side of her mouth.

"What a vision you are, my dear. Yes, Buster's a lucky dog."

Hardy had put his personal list aside, what with the geese caper and recent activities of the Movement, but that evening as the clinic prepared to close, he took a phone call that forced him into action.

Estelle was near hysteria as she related how the drunken man, his clothes stained with blood, had just staggered across the creek behind her house. He had a large bow over one shoulder and a quiver of steel tipped arrows over the other and was dragging a squealing goat that had an arrow sticking through its neck.

"Go inside and stay there," commanded the doctor. "I'll handle this." He left the closing duties to Will and peeled out of the parking lot, roaring toward Estelle's place. This was the last time Noble Mathers would wound and kill with his murderous arrows. He should have taken care of him sooner, but there had been the distractions. Now he feared it was too late to save a life. Bella bounced across the back seat of Hardy's truck as he screeched to a stop. He ordered her to stay down, grabbed his .22, and ran into the pasture behind Estelle's house.

The ugliness unfolding before him turned his stomach. The injured animal shrieked in terror as a drunken Mathers dragged it through the dirt. Hardy called out to him, for he wanted Mathers to see his own death. They were fifty feet from each other. Noble Mathers dropped the squealing goat, pulled an arrow from his quiver, and fumbled, trying to load it in the bow. When he had it set, he pulled the bow string taught, aiming at Hardy. Hardy waited a moment, allowing for the man's drunkenness, and then fired, slamming Noble in the shoulder. The force of the bullet knocked him backwards, causing him to release the arrow, which shot straight up overhead as he sprawled on his back beside his helpless, bleeding victim. The terrible weapon of death reached its apex, hung for a moment, and then turned, beginning its downward spiral trajectory, gaining speed as it spun and returned from whence it had come, piercing Noble's chest and heart and pinning him to the bloody soil.

Hardy ran to the goat, gathered it in his arms, and carried it to Estelle's porch. She had been watching, and she threw the door open and motioned to the table where she had spread a clean blanket. "Put him here," she yelled, and then, urgently, "save his life, Hardy, you can do it."

"My truck, Estelle, bring my bag of tricks." She ran to the truck, grabbed his satchel, and ran back to the kitchen, Bella beside her. Hardy found a syringe of sedative and administered it to the goat, calming his terrifying screams, then he snapped the arrow's shaft and pulled it out quickly, plugging the hole with a wad of gauze soaked in antiseptic. "Hold it in place," he instructed, "while I thread my needle."

He stitched both holes in the goat's neck, and the bleeding stopped. "The arrow missed the jugular and just went through flesh. This is one lucky goat, Estelle." The sedated creature lay still, his breathing regular and calm. Hardy carried him to the truck and laid him on a blanket in the bed. "I'll take him directly to the clinic. He should be up on his feet tomorrow. Afraid we can't say the same for old Noble. I feel like I ought to apologize for soiling your dirt with the likes of him. You'd better call the sheriff. Tell him there's been a hunting accident, which I guess is true. That arrow accidentally killed the right animal. I can help Downey figure it out if I have to. You didn't see any of this, is that right?"

Estelle smiled, grinning ear to ear, and embraced him, giving him a big kiss on the cheek. "Just that trespasser in my field, coming after me with a bow and arrow."

The sheriff arrived quickly, however, and Hardy decided to tell him what had happened, omitting the goat, for there was no other way to explain the bullet hole in Nobel's shoulder.

"Yeah, he came running at Estelle, ready to shoot her with that arrow, all drunker than usual. And I had to stop him, so I aimed high and hit his shoulder. That arrow coming down like it did was pure coincidence, really weird, like someone was up there guiding it."

Sheriff Downey didn't know what to say, other than he'd never seen anything like it during his whole career in law enforcement. And it was obvious that Noble had been done in by his own arrow. The forensics team would lift any prints, just to be sure.

"He was a bad man, Hardy. We all know that. I can't and won't say I'm sorry he's gone, and fittingly too, just like he killed everything that moved. That damn bow and arrow crap, about it being so pure, just cause Indians used to hunt like that. Hell, Indians knew what they were doing. These yahoos nowadays don't have a clue. If you don't kill with the first shot, you got an animal runnin' around with an arrow stickin' outta him. Imagine how that smarts. It's cruel, and this guy abused it worse than anybody. And what's he doing over on your land, Estelle? He must have been drunk outta his mind this time." Mitch yelled to his deputy, "Randy, bag this pile of shit and get it to the morgue. You two will have to come in and help us with the details for our report, anytime in the next few days."

"Will do, Sheriff."

Hardy waited for the sheriff and his deputy to leave, and then he told Estelle, "When they talk to you, don't mention the goat. It would just confuse things for them. Let the sheriff think it was you he was aiming at, like we said. It'll be easier for him to understand that way. He's a good man, but he's the law, and not everybody sees things like we do, honey. Mathers moved himself to the top of my list today."

Funny how things work out, how fate intercedes one way or the other, thought Hardy, as he drove the injured goat back to the clinic. Mathers had had some time left, but he chose to forfeit it over a goat. Hardy liked goats. He found them intelligent and capable of forming strong bonds with humans. It bothered him greatly the way they were routinely sacrificed in third-world countries. He'd seen it on television-- some history channel-- the friendly little animals eagerly following their human companions, clomping along, then somebody rips a knife across their throat, and bingo, gone.

That domestic animals exhibited trust toward their human caretakers filled him with despair. Cows and pigs, after all, were not raised because humans desired their companionship. But at least their betrayal was usually swift and unexpected. Shivers ran up his spine. Mathers, on the other hand, killed for "sport," which was murder in Hardy's book and spoke to the fact that humans were the ultimate bloodthirsty predators. Animals didn't kill for no reason. Ending the life of another creature was fun to the human predator, and several of the worst offenders were on his list. He would collect his "fun" too. But now he shook off the dark thoughts and attended to his helpless charge.

He made a thick layer of blankets in his largest cage and laid the goat on his side. He pulled his tongue out so he wouldn't choke, for he was still asleep with Hardy's drug. The animal, not yet fully grown, was the size of a big dog. His sleek, blood-stained hair was a steely gray, and he had a white blaze on his forehead. The skin around his mouth was pinking up, and Hardy was confident the goat would be fine. Knowing he'd saved the little life filled him with warmth and omnipotence. Nothing compared with the high he felt during these moments, for he was addicted to saving the lives of the innocent and taking the lives of the guilty.

# CHAPTER SEVENTEEN

The next morning Will dropped the newspaper on his father's kitchen table and brewed a pot of coffee. They had talked on the phone the previous evening when Hardy returned home after bedding down the goat, for Will had been worried about his hasty exit from the clinic. Hardy had related his story about the arrow seeking its mark and the goat in the cage, and now he gulped his coffee and hurriedly pulled on his pants, wanting to check on the animal. The paper had a brief article on the accident, mainly just bits their reporter had pulled from the sheriff last night in time for inclusion in the morning's edition. It recounted more or less exactly what Hardy had told Mitch. "Local Man Killed in Freak Accident" was the headline.

"See you at work," yelled Hardy, as he ran out the door. When he turned his key in the latch at the clinic, he could hear the bleating of the frightened animal, so he hurried around the corner to the row of cages. The goat sat up on it haunches, its head hanging low. Hardy released the latch and gently lifted the creature, placing him on a pad in the middle of the surgery room. Bella sat a respectful distance as instructed.

"You look good this morning, little one. How do you feel?" The goat tilted his head at the doctor's words and bleated. Hardy stroked the blaze and inspected the wounds. "Just need some time to heal, and you'll be good as new. Now, I wonder who you are. I think I'll make some calls."

He set up a pen around the goat, giving it a bucket of water and a pan of alfalfa pellets. The goat sunk his muzzle in the bucket, pulled a few long, deep swallows, and then tackled the alfalfa. His healthy appetite was a good sign. Hardy knew most of his neighbors, who were also Estelle's neighbors, and he called them, but no one was missing a goat. Then he called the sheriff and reported finding a goat, but none had been reported lost. Returning to the goat, he said, "We'll have to give you a name, Mr. Goat, because I can't keep calling you goat, so what's it to be?"

Just then the animal flicked his head, tossing a mouthful of pellets in the air. Bella, who had moved to the edge of the enclosure, reacted playfully, catching the flying morsels in her mouth. "All right, we'll call you Flicker. How's that?"

"Baaa."

"Good, I'm glad you think so, because Bella and I like it. Don't we, girl?"

Bella crouched, rump in the air, wanting to play. "Woof," she said, but Hardy called her off. "Flicker's not up to playing yet, honey."

Will had come in, tinkling the bell, and now he joined them, anxious to get a look at the new patient. "He's a nice-looking goat, Dad. Nobody claims him?"

"Nope, not yet. We just picked a name. He's Flicker."

Flicker inched forward, trying to lift his head over the top of the enclosure, but his bandages were restricting, and he gave up, drinking more water instead.

"Good name. Looks like he's a bit sore."

"I guess so, what with an arrow through his neck."

"He's one lucky goat."

"I reckon I'll keep him if nobody calls. I was going to get some stock for Bella anyway. I'll take him home in a few days. No need to keep him here."

Hardy let Will handle most of the morning's business, and he stayed in the back, keeping Bella and the goat company. At noon, Estelle arrived with a lunch she'd packed. It was a surprise, and she'd made enough for everyone, the goat included. Hardy was delighted. He fed celery sticks and carrots to Flicker, and Bella chewed on a big biscuit. Will took a break and had an egg salad sandwich with a side of cole slaw. It was like an indoor picnic.

"What a nice idea, Estelle, and you thought of everyone."

"I'm so relieved the goat's going to be okay. I hope nobody claims him so you can keep him, Hardy. I have to go give my report to the sheriff this afternoon, so I thought I'd make a day of it."

"I could go along and give mine too," said Hardy. "Maybe we ought to go together. Is that okay with you?"

"I was going to suggest it, because we want to keep our stories straight."

"Stories straight?" said Will.

"Yeah, in case one of us forgets the details," said Hardy.

Estelle and Hardy left in his truck, and Bella willingly stayed behind, her attachment to the goat already blossoming. They dozed together, their bodies touching through the wire pen.

Just before Hardy and Estelle returned, Will answered a call from a man claiming to be the goat's owner. He took the man's number and said he'd have the doctor call. Hardy was crestfallen upon learning the news, but he returned the call, politely asking that the man identify the goat. And when he did, Hardy inquired what the man was planning to do with the animal. The gruff voice was quick to answer. "I just bought him for slaughter. It has to be done now, before he gets any older and the meat gets tough. I was going to do it last week, but he got away from me."

Hardy's stomach churned, and his mind kicked into overdrive. "Listen, this goat's not going to be fit for eating, what with all the antibiotics I've pumped into him. He'd probably make you sick, and he's run up a sizeable veterinary bill. I'll cancel the bill and throw in a hundred dollars if you let me take him off your hands. How's that sound? I need a companion for my herding dog."

The man was quiet for a moment. "That's more than I paid for him, if you cancel your fee. Sure, why not? I can always get me another one."

"I'll send you a check. What's your address?"

"Flicker, you are one super lucky goat," said Estelle, who listened in the background." Thank God, Hardy," she said, as he hung up.

"Yeah, but he's just going to buy another one to butcher." He shook his head. "On second thought," he purred, "maybe I'll deliver his check in person."

"Dad, what are you scheming?" asked Will.

"I don't know yet," he pondered. "I'm hoping to come up with something."

Estelle caught the nuance in Hardy's voice and knew his brain was churning. Suddenly, she had an idea. "Does this guy sound like a country boy?"

"He did. Why? What's your idea, Estelle? No time to waste here."

"I was thinking, maybe if he isn't too terribly bright, we could put something over on him."

"Whatta you got?"

"I could print up a letter on my computer, make it sound real official, and print it in big fancy letters about how goat meat has been found to carry bugs, or poison, or something he'd understand. That way, maybe he'd be afraid to buy another goat to kill. We could scare him away, if he'd fall for it."

"That's a great idea, honey, but why stop at goats? Let's put the fear of God into him and include all animals. You go home and start working on the letter. Make it real scary stuff. And I'll pick it up after work and deliver it with his money. It's worth a try. Good girl." He grabbed her cheeks and kissed her, and Bella, responding to "good girl," wagged her tail and stood waiting for her pat on the head and kiss, which she got as Estelle hurried out the door.

"That Estelle's got a good head on her, Dad," Will said, as they worked side by side by side castrating an Old English bulldog.

"Yes, she does, and she's a genuinely good person. And she cries over torn moth wings."

"Well, there you go. She's the whole package."

Hardy left a little early, anxious to see what Estelle had created. She presented him with an official-looking document, printed on stiff, grainy paper that scared the hell out of him when he read it.

Attention: All Medical Personnel, USA

To Whom It May Concern:

Recent studies performed by the Federal Bureau of Food Investigation and the Department of Agriculture have found conclusive amounts of poisonous bacteria of the Lepidoptera strain in the meat of goats, cows, pigs, sheep, and chickens. Also found in our research were parasites, including ringworms, hookworms, roundworms, tapeworms, spider mites, scabies mites, and a number of mites too vicious to mention for fear of spreading panic among the general public.

We recommend that no sane person buy and eat goat meat or any of the above-mentioned meats but instead stick to crops such as corn, peas, beans, and anything that does not have a face and can look you in the eye when you kill it.

Yours, with the hope of a long, meat-free life,

Alfred B. Molina, Esq., MMD, ASC

U.S FBFI and the U.S. Dept. of Agriculture

"Well, if that doesn't turn the guy into a vegetarian, by God, I don't know what will," said Hardy, as he burst out laughing. "Good work, Estelle. FBFI? Lepidoptera?"

"Our beautiful, big moths. Good luck, Hardy. I hope it works."

Hardy took a copy of the letter, folded it neatly, and inserted in what looked like an official envelope. Then he drove to Mr. Babb's farm, a short distance from Estelle's place. He knocked on the door of the shack, and a thin, middle-aged man with a long hooked nose opened it immediately, as if he'd been standing there waiting. Hardy introduced himself, trying to sound dour and concerned, and handed the man a crisp one hundred dollar bill and the envelope.

"I think you should read the letter I received today before you do any more goat shopping, sir," Hardy said, watching as Babb withdrew the letter, unfolded it, and began to read.

The expression on his skinny face changed from greedy satisfaction to pure terror.

"My Lord God, this means we can't eat meat at all! What will I eat?" he cried, looking to the doctor to explain how the man should stay alive.

"I don't eat meat, sir. Haven't for years, and I get along fine. There's any number of things on the grocery shelves: beans, corn, peas. You take a good look. You'll learn quickly. Bread is good. Eat bread, man. One hundred dollars will buy a lot of loaves." Hardy left the shaken Mr. Babb clutching a one hundred dollar bill but too scared to spend it.

# CHAPTER EIGHTEEN

The hunting death of Noble Mathers seemed to be absorbed without much ado by the local community. Noble had been trespassing, hunting out of season, and pointing an arrow at Estelle Greenwood, well there was no defense for any of it. Plus everyone knew he was always drunk. A drunken hunter with a bow and steel-tipped arrows was a recipe for disaster. The inquiry was wrapped up in a matter of hours, and the incident forgotten. But a few days later, Hardy was patrolling the perimeters of his property along the creek and found a number of the horrendous arrows scattered over the ground. Mathers had apparently been stalking game on his land as well. He gathered the arrows. He ran his finger along the razor edge of one tip and realized it wouldn't have required much speed for the falling shaft to accomplish what it had. Bella shied away from the deadly instruments, her instinct infallibly warning her of danger.

It was October, the first rains had already come, and the creek ran fast. But it was still shallow, perhaps only six inches deep, and Hardy could walk across its thirty-foot width if he wore his rubber boots. Bella waded, licking the curls of water as they bumped over the rocky bottom. Occasionally a brown trout flitted out of the shadows and ran upstream. The seasons were changing, and Hardy liked it. He found the coolness in the air invigorating. Bella was a different dog. The sharp mornings put a snap in her gait, and she was energized, as if awakened from the hazy drag of the hot summer.

He had turned Flicker out in the first pasture by the house. The outside cats claimed the pasture's fence and had hardly let him adjust the gate. They had their noses up against the wood and metal, inspecting his progress as he tried to work. Cats were indeed the curious creatures they were said to be.

Now they were spread over the top rail on their stomachs, paws hanging, watching Flicker and Bella jump and run together.

The little goat had almost completely healed in one week, his young flesh eager to mend. Bella finished the romp and then sat looking at Hardy, her tongue hanging out and her eyes bright. She seemed to say, "See, look how much fun we have. Thank you for my friend." He knew she was happy, and for that he was glad. That evening when he spooned Bella's dinner into her bowl, he noticed a small stain of blood on her rear; she was in heat, and soon it would be time to invite Buster for a visit. He hurried to the kitchen, found the phone number, and gave Mr. Hollis the news.

"In twelve days, she should be ready to receive him. She's just begun the process."

"I can bring him anytime. You tell me when's best for you, Doctor."

They agreed on a date. When he finished with Hollis, he called Estelle, for he was excited beyond words at he thought of becoming a grandfather, which was how he had it figured. They'd leave them alone in the garage, he said. The pasture would allow too much room to run around, and Buster would be worn out before he had to perform. If Bella reacted typically, she'd lead him on a while before allowing the actual deed. Next, he called Will, who was just getting home, and told him the big news. "So, the rendezvous is October 20. You want to come over? Estelle's going to bring some wine, and I'm making a pot of chili."

"Do you think that's appropriate? Maybe the dogs will want to be alone."

"They will be. We're just celebrating the pre-conception in another room. Hollis is invited too, of course, since he's bringing a main ingredient, the father. Come on, it'll be fun. Ask Lois."

"What do I tell her, it's a pre-coitus party?"

"I prefer pre-conception, because coitus is a given."

"I'll tell her about the dinner invite, but maybe I won't say anything about mating dogs."

"Lois likes animals. She works for their welfare, doesn't she?"

"Yeah, okay, you're right. She'd probably think it very 'progressive.' That's her favorite word lately."

"See you in the morning."

The days passed quickly. While he waited, Hardy constructed a lean-to for the goat on the house side of the pasture and attached a trough for feed and a heavy tarp for shelter from the weather. Tomorrow night was the party for Bella and Buster. It was getting dark, and his work was finished, but he lingered, worried about leaving the animal outside at night. He'd heard coyotes calling, and he knew cougars were nearby as well. Since he didn't want Bella out either, the only solution was to bring the goat in. He picked him up gently and carried him to the kitchen, setting him down on the linoleum. Having her friend join her in the house made Bella ecstatic. As Hardy ate a bowl of leftover stew, she showed Flicker around, leading a procession of curious cats and the goat down the halls to the bedrooms and back to the living room. The goat's cloven hooves click-clacked on the wood and linoleum floors as the little procession clomped back into the kitchen. Hardy had finished his dinner and now stood with the broom, preparing to sweep up the pile of droppings Flicker had deposited upon entering the house. But as he began to sweep, the goat loosed a fountain of urine, and when Hardy bent to wipe it up, the remarkable moving plastic tablecloth caught his eye. Flicker had one end in his mouth and was sucking it down like a vacuum cleaner.

"No, no," he yelled, grabbing the plastic and pulling it back out of the animal's throat. "That's not good for you. You'll gum up your works."

The little goat looked at him, wagged his flag of a tail, and clip-clopped to the curtain hanging over the window, taking a mouthful.

"No, no!" yelled Hardy, pushing him away. "Okay, I see what I have to do, and that is make this kitchen goat proof." He studied the small room, removing anything that the goat could reach and might try to eat. He set the coffeepot on top of the refrigerator, shoved everything on the counters back against the splashboards, and laid out a nice mat for Bella and Flicker to share. He filled Willa's big turkey roaster to the brim with water, and as an afterthought, he spread a few newspapers on the floor. Finally he set the cats' litter boxes in the living room so all he had to do was close the kitchen door and the companions should be fine overnight. Any messes the goat made would be easy to clean off the linoleum.

"But you don't have to go to bed yet," he told them, "so settle down and behave, and we'll read for a while." They followed him to the sofa. When Flicker tried to take a bite out of the cushion, he thumped the goat's nose and addressed Bella. "Bella, watch this guy. Take him for a walk down the hall. And be good, Flicker, or you're going to have to go to bed early."

The goat and the dog wandered a bit, but they couldn't explore much beyond the hall, for Hardy had closed the doors to the bathroom and bedrooms, realizing that limiting access was the easiest way to mitigate damage. Eventually the two friends settled down together on a throw rug in the living room, where Hardy sat reading. At eleven, he called the animals into the kitchen, the goat trotting along behind the dog. "Good night, you two." Bella looked quizzically at the man, for she had never slept anywhere at night except with him on his bed. But when he closed the kitchen door, she was quiet, so Hardy assumed all was well and went to bed. He missed having the dog at his feet, but he knew he had to share her.

The next morning, Will's scream woke him from a deep sleep. He hurriedly stumbled to the kitchen and opened the door that had kept the animals contained. Will stood flattened against the stove, the goat nibbling at his pants. Before Hardy could explain, he yelled, "Why the hell is the goat in the kitchen, Dad? Look at the mess he's made." It was true, there *was* a mess. Apparently the goat had tipped over the water pan, and that had sent large amounts of poop floating around the floor. And the newspapers had disappeared; Flicker fodder he surmised. The water turned the reconstituted alfalfa pellets into a soft mush that the goat had tracked all over the kitchen table and the countertops. Hardy had forgotten that goats can jump. The curtain that he had tucked up high on top of the rod hung in tatters, a good part of it was missing but would no doubt reappear in another form soon enough. And the smell was not pleasant: like asparagus and spinach combined, and very strong.

"Where's the coffeepot, Dad?" demanded Will. "Did he eat it?"

Hardy became defensive. "Certainly not, I put it on top of the refrigerator. See, it's still there." He pointed to the pot, which seemed to be the only thing left undisturbed.

"Well, here's your paper." Will dropped the newspaper on the table. "Better grab it quick before the goat gets it. I'm going to stop downtown for breakfast. It's too tropical in here. By the way, Lois said she'd love to come over tonight, for the consumption."

"Conception, Will, we're not having a barbecue, for God's sake."

"Maybe you're making a mistake there," he smirked, casting an evil eye at Flicker. "See you at the clinic," he said as he slammed the door. Hardy reached for the goat but slid on the wet linoleum and fell backward into the mush. The goat and Bella licked his face as he lay there laughing, his hair taking on a greenish tinge. When he was up on his feet, on solid ground in the living room, he opened the front door to air out the house and led the goat to his pasture. Flicker made a beeline to the shelter and his alfalfa pellets, but Bella remained behind with Hardy, as if she knew that things had gone badly on her watch.

"What a gigantic mess," he said. "But it's my fault," he reassured Bella, patting her head, for he knew she felt guilty. He brought his bucket and mop from the garage and began the cleanup, first sopping up the green water and then wiping down the counters. He wore his rubber boots and his wet pajamas, for there was no sense dirtying another set of clothes. When all the green was gone, the smell remained, so he poured undiluted pine cleaner over everything, making himself slightly sick to his stomach. After two hours of work, the kitchen was back to normal except for the smell and the tattered curtains which he took down completely and threw away. Bella lay in the doorway watching his progress. He was sure she knew this would not happen again.

"From now on, Flicker will sleep in the pasture, and you and I will sleep in the house." Hardy had decided, and now he made a phone call. "Yes, I want the twenty by twenty-six, pitched roof, and I need it as fast as possible. Tomorrow? That's wonderful."

He hung up the phone and addressed the dog. "We're buying Flicker a barn with a door that closes, and at night we'll lock him in there so he's safe. How's that sound?"

"Woof!"

"I think so, too."

# CHAPTER NINETEEN

Hardy made it into the clinic by noon. When he noticed that Bella had gotten splashed with the green poop water, he set her in their big tub and gave her a nice bath as he wanted her to look ravishing for Buster later that evening. He fluffed her beautiful long hair with the blow-dryer, clipped her nails, and cleaned out her ears with Q-tips. She was a Border collie vision, and if Buster didn't realize what a babe she was, it was his loss.

"She looks great, but you still smell like asparagus," said Will. "Did you shower?"

"I fell in the mess. Of course, I showered," he said, annoyed that his son would have to ask such a question. "I'll go home and shower again, if that's what it takes. All I've done so far today is clean things. What time are you coming?"

"Lois and I will be there around seven. You're making chili?"

"Yes, and French bread. I'm not *making* the French bread, just serving it."

"I suspected as much. Why don't you go on home now, Dad. You've got a lot to do, and we're not busy here."

"I was hoping you'd say that. Come on, Bella. Let's go get ready for your big night."

Hardy seemed very nervous, so Estelle urged him to have a drink of wine or liquor, whatever it took to calm himself. He poured a tall scotch, neat, and as the liquor worked its magic, he loosened up and told her about the goat-in-the-kitchen affair and a few other assorted stories. She tidied up, dusting, replacing nibbled-on towels with fresh ones, and removing a few green hoof prints here and there that Hardy had missed. Hoof prints on the counter weren't good, and the alfalfa green had stained the Formica and was difficult to remove. Hardy stirred his chili with a flourish, poured himself a second scotch, and told Estelle about the big barn that he'd bought. "They bring it in panels and erect it in a day. Of course, you can do a cement floor or whatever, so there's still work, but it will make a safe refuge for Flicker during the nights."

"Isn't that an awfully big structure for one goat?"

"Oh, well, I've always wanted a barn," he said, jauntily, "needed one, really, and I'm planning on acquiring more animals. Flicker's just an unexpected early arrival."

Now the first and most important guests arrived, Hollis and Buster. Hardy welcomed them and ushered them into the living room. Hollis released Buster from his leash, and the two dogs sniffed each other. Buster's ears pricked forward, Bella's lay back, and they began a dance of jolting stops and starts, dodging around the furniture and knocking Willa's bric-a-brac to the floor with their tails. Because of the kitchen disaster and because he was weary of cleaning messes, Hardy suggested they put the dogs in the garage and leave them to their own devices, checking in every now and then. Estelle handed Hollis a glass of wine, which he accepted gratefully. "But how will we know if they've coupled," he asked, "if we don't see it happen?"

"We'll peek," tittered Hardy, a hint of the effects of the scotch apparent in his manner. "It takes a while once they're engaged, you know, so we've a good chance of catching them in the act."

"Whatever you say, Hardy, you're the doctor. And a hardy har, har," toasted Hollis.

Hardy led Bella down the hall to the garage, Buster literally on her tail, and Hollis followed close behind, and Estelle behind Hollis.

"Now, we'll leave them alone. That's the best way," Hardy said, raising an index finger to his lips and shushing the followers. "They're apt to mate several times, so I'm very hopeful something fruitful will come of this evening."

When Will and Lois arrived, the group drank and celebrated the occasion, toasting the yet-to-be-conceived Border collie pups. They took turns peeking into the garage, but all anyone saw was a lot of dog hair milling around in a circle.

"That's the courtship going on," Hardy explained. "Bella is not just some quick bump in the night," he huffed. "Shall we eat?"

He and Estelle had decided it best to eat in the dining room, for the smell of pine cleaner was still too strong in the kitchen. Hardy set his pot of chili in the middle of the table, adding two loaves of hot French bread and a green salad Estelle had made. They ate and drank their wine, talking, laughing, and wondering how things were progressing in the garage. "Go check," Estelle urged, and Hardy slipped from his seat and tiptoed down the hall. Why he was tiptoeing escaped him, but it seemed appropriate. When he nudged the door open, he gasped. Bella and Buster were stuck together, tail to tail. He felt he shouldn't be watching, but he couldn't pull himself away and close the door. When he didn't return to the table, Estelle joined him, leaning over his shoulder. And then Hollis arrived, and then Will and Lois. If the hall had been a boat, it would have capsized. There was complete silence. Everyone held their breath, as if breathing was suddenly taboo and something sacred was happening; and indeed it was, for Bella and Buster had successfully mated. And in sixty-three days, Bella would give birth to seven beautiful babies, but the humans didn't know that yet. Hardy backed up as he pulled the door closed, bumping into Estelle, who in turn shoved Hollis, who fell into Lois, who grabbed onto Will. They then stumbled back to the dining table, humbled by their collective experience.

"Wasn't that beautiful?" said Lois, tears in her eyes.

"It certainly was," said Estelle, nodding in agreement.

Mr. Hollis raised his glass. "I propose a toast to Bella and Buster and their progeny. May they live long, happy lives and love us as much as we love them."

"Here, here," said Hardy, releasing a large burp.

Will let the dogs back into the house as the mating had ended, and they were hungry. He fed them bowls of Hardy's finest dog food, wet and dry mixed together to form a thick gravy. When they finished feasting, the sated animals curled up together on the rug by the fireplace.

The humans continued their celebration until all the wine was drunk and at least five of the pups-to-be were spoken for, one each going to Hardy, Estelle, Hollis, Will, and Lois. Given the way their relationships were developing, Hardy had the feeling that none of the puppies would be living far from their mother.

It was a satisfying evening in more ways than one. Bella hardly raised her head when Hollis called Buster to go home. He had served her purpose, and she didn't need any more from him. "Please keep me informed on the possible pregnancy, and we'll see you real soon," said Hollis. They did not know what Bella knew, and she laid her head back down and closed her eyes, her instinct to mate fulfilled.

Will and Lois snuggled together on the sofa, looking for all the world like a couple in love. Hardy found himself wondering if the events of the evening, being so sexual in nature, had had an influence on them. He knew he was up for a bout if Estelle was game, and he wished the youngsters would leave so they could get at it.

At nine, he yawned and stretched and asked Will what time he was going to open in the morning. Seeing that they always opened at nine, Will found the question peculiar, until he realized that his father wanted him to go home. "See you in the morning, Dad," he called, as he led Lois to their car.

"It was a great fun evening," she yelled. "I'm sure we'll have pups."

He slammed the front door and turned to embrace Estelle, who stood behind him. "Doesn't all this dog sex make you horny, honey?"

She smiled and led him down the hall to his bedroom. "I intend to stay overnight, Doctor. I don't drive well in the dark."

# CHAPTER TWENTY

Will didn't stop by the next morning, which Hardy took to be a good sign. He hoped Lois had the young man tied to a bed frame but guessed that probably wasn't the case. She was too uptight for games. He slipped out of bed, tucked the blanket around Estelle's shoulders, and looked lovingly at Bella, who snored softly where his feet had been. Seeing his two girls sleeping in his bed left him feeling warm and fuzzy. As he shuffled down the hall, he felt content in knowing they were there.

Hardy was standing by his sink measuring coffee when the rumble of tires on his gravel drive startled him. He watched out the window as a long truck pulled into the yard and stopped at the entrance to his pasture. The barn! Of course. The barn was coming today, but with all the sexual activities, he'd forgotten about it. He hurried out to meet the man who stood poised to knock on his front door.

"I'm Bill, sir, here to erect your Built-Rite barn," said the burly man, a big smile on his face. "Where is it going to stand? I'll need electricity and a good, wide entrance."

Hardy hustled down the porch steps and motioned for Bill to follow. "It's for the goat, out there," he said, pointing to where Flicker stood, munching alfalfa pellets in his shelter. "I want it near that shelter, facing the house. You can plug in at the outlet under the window. I'll open both gates so you can drive right in there and unload. I'll move the goat."

"You buying this big barn just for one goat?"

"No, no, I'll be getting other animals. He's just the first. Hope you don't need me here, because I have to go to my clinic."

The man smiled again, "No, sir. My helper will be stopping by in a few hours, when I've got things laid out. But that's all I need, just a little muscle."

Hardy shooed Flicker into the adjoining field and swung open the double gates for the big truck. The grass and dirt was still packed hard enough to support the load, which allowed the truck to park close to the construction site. Hardy wished Bill luck and went back into the house, where Estelle and Bella watched the activity from the window.

Estelle had dressed. She gulped down her coffee and kissed his cheek. "Gotta run. I have a hair appointment."

"I'll call you later," he said, "and thanks for the lovely evening."

He dressed, shaved, and downed a mug of coffee. He liked it when things were happening. Activity made him come alive. Bella caught the vibe too, for she bounded into the pasture, looking for her friend, woofing at the burly man who busied himself laying out sections of walls like a giant puzzle. "Flicker's fine," called Hardy. "Come along now, Bella. It'll be a surprise when we get home." They took off down the drive, gravel flying under their tires, excitement in the air.

Will was talking with a middle-aged couple when Hardy and Bella blew into the clinic. An old cat lay on the examination table, and from the looks on everyone's faces, they were discussing euthanasia. And that was sure to bring down his mood. The old gray cat lay drooling, ribs and hip bones protruding from the almost hairless skin and eyes sunken in the dehydrated body. It was probably kidney failure. The cat had no doubt lived a good life, but his time had run out.

"Can you come take a look here, Doctor," called Will. Hardy threw on a white coat and joined them at the table. The woman had been crying, and the man was holding on, but just barely, according to Hardy's practiced assessment.

As he studied the cat, Hardy realized it was not old, as he had thought. It just appeared that way, because of neglect and or abuse. He looked to his son for an explanation.

"These folks, the Masons, found this cat lying in the gutter in front of a house across the street from theirs. They think the residents of that house have many more such animals, and they want to report abuse, but they've come here first to verify their suspicions and ask for our help."

Hardy laid his hand on the still form. The chest rose and fell almost imperceptibly, so he was careful to touch very lightly. "I want IV fluids administered to this animal immediately, Will, and he needs to be on a heating pad until his body temperature comes up. He's too cold."

"You think you can *save* him?" the man gasped, incredulous, as the woman smothered a shriek, covering her mouth with her hands.

"He's not dead yet," declared the doctor. "Yes, I think we can bring him back, if we act quickly, with a light hand. You folks have been instruments of salvation today."

Hardy prepared a heating pad and carried the cat to a cage. Inserting a feeding line was difficult, for the animal's veins had shriveled and shrunk, just like the rest of him, but Hardy finally got a line in and began the flow of life-giving fluids. The Masons paced the room while he worked. When he finished tending the animal, they told him what they knew about the people across the street. "We see them bring lots of animals into that house that never come back out, except like the cat today. Every few days, an unmarked white van pulls into their driveway and stays for maybe twenty minutes. This cat is the second one we've found in the gutter; the other one was dead. It looked like this one, and we figured it had starved to death. We think they're stealing people's pets and selling them to laboratories. I read an article in a magazine about that, and it fits, what with that van that comes by."

"This is a serious charge," said Hardy. His mood had turned increasingly grim as they related the details. "We need to call the sheriff. Are you ready to tell him everything you just told me?"

"Of course. We want to put these people in jail if that's what they're doing."

Another client came in, so Hardy took the Masons to the back room and dialed Sheriff Downey. He gave the sheriff a brief rundown of what he'd been told and handed the phone over to Mr. Mason. Angela Mason stood by the cage with the cat, her fingers stroking its nose through the bars. Mr. Mason handed the phone back to Hardy.

"The sheriff wants us to come down and file a report. He says he can do a search if he can establish probable cause."

Hardy patted Mr. Mason on the shoulder. "You did real good, and I'll keep you posted on our patient here. If we had more people like you, the world would be a better place."

Hardy watched the Masons drive off to meet with Sheriff Downey, and then he checked the cat. It had opened its eyes and closed its mouth, a good trade-off. He pulled the baby blanket up around its chin, as he had done for Estelle earlier, and patted it lightly on the head. "Come on, baby, you can make it. We'll all help."

Later that day, Hardy called the sheriff, only to learn that at that very moment he was out on a bust at the Masons' neighbors. The white van had arrived, and the Masons, as instructed, had immediately called Mitch Downey. "From what I'm hearing over the radio," said a deputy, "it's just like your people suspected: a ring of pet thieves. Animal control has rescued all kinds of animals from the house. Man, those guys are going down heavy. And the lab that's buying them, it's in big trouble too, because the sheriff says they knew the dogs and cats were stolen. What a lousy racket."

Hardy named the cat Mr. Lucky. Although luck played a big part in the lives of most of the creatures he took home, this cat in particular, if he pulled through, deserved the moniker. He kept a close vigil on the animal, watching his temperature slowly creep back toward normal and his dehydrated cells re-hydrate with vitamin-filled liquid nourishment. A compromised immune system was inevitable, and he hoped pneumonia or some other opportunistic bacteria didn't invade and take advantage of the cat's weakened body.

Again, time was the healer—time and the doctor's dedication. When the day was over, Hardy debated whether he should bring Mr. Lucky home so he could watch him overnight but decided the ride would be too stressful. He would be better off lying quietly on his heating pad, gaining strength little by little. He switched off the light. "See you in the morning, Mr. Lucky." The cat raised his head at the sound of the voice.

When they pulled into his driveway, Hardy took a deep breath and yelled, "Look at that, Bella. It's our barn!" The knotty pine slats, fashioned into long panels and held together by a steel framework, were now fitted in place where they belonged. They formed the four sides of the structure. Bill, the burly man, and his helper sat atop the beams, attaching a corrugated tin roof. Hardy and Bella hurried to the site.

"Ahoy there," he yelled. "You men need any help from down here?"

"We're good," yelled Bill, waving his arms at the doctor. "We should have things wrapped up pretty soon. We'd better, 'cause I can't work in the dark."

Hardy waved, checked on the goat, and went into the house, while Bella remained with Flicker. When she whined at the door, trying to lead Hardy out to the field, he said, "No, your friend is not coming inside tonight, not after the mess he made last time. His new home will be ready soon, and you can stay out there if you like, although I'll miss you on my bed." She cocked her head and looked at him, as if she were deciding a great dilemma. "Come in and have your dinner. It's dinnertime." He opened a can of her wet food and added it to the dry, mixing in a little water to form a nice gravy, then he refilled the cats' bowls and scooped out the litter boxes. With the animals taken care of, he heated up his leftover chili and sat at the kitchen table, watching from the curtainless window as the roof was tacked to the barn.

As soon as he finished eating, he went out to watch the workers, and just before the sun set, Bill climbed down from his ladder for the last time and announced that the job was completed. He asked Hardy to do an inspection while he prepared the paperwork. The inside, a huge space, was light and airy, ventilated by narrow spaces where the roof met the sides. The dirt floor was scraped and leveled, ready for cement it he wanted it. Panels separated each wall into four box stalls, with a room at the end of each row. The roof itself peaked at a height of thirty feet, so it was tall enough to store plenty of hay.

"Looks excellent," said Hardy, as he began signing the stack of papers. "I'm amazed that you fellows can erect a structure like this in one day. It's not going to fall down on me, is it? On my little goat?" Hardy was kidding, but when Bill's face turned red and he stammered and stuttered, Hardy realized he had hurt the man's feelings. "Just pulling your leg, Bill. I'm absolutely confident in your wonderful barn, my wonderful new barn."

He watched as they drove the heavy truck down his drive to the county road, and then he hurried to free Flicker and introduce him to his new space. The little goat followed along behind Bella as she sniffed each stall.

"Pick any one you want, or you can have all of them for now. I'll have to order a load of hay." He moved the trough of alfalfa pellets and the water bucket into the building and scattered what bedding he had in the first stall. "We need a giraffe with all this head room. When Marion sees this, she'll probably arrange to find us one." The little goat settled down in the first stall, and Hardy looked at Bella. "What's it to be girl, Flicker or me?" She looked from one to the other, then lowered her head and followed him to the sliding barn door. "Atta girl. I hoped you'd see it that way."

# CHAPTER TWENTY-ONE

Hardy, sidetracked by the goings-on, had forgotten to phone Estelle, so he called when he returned to the house. "The barn's up, and the goat's inside, and it's quite beautiful. It makes a nice improvement to my little ranch, and I've always wanted one. Marion's going to be very jealous when she sees it."

He told her about Mr. Lucky, and she was anxious to help with him if she could. "And the sheriff already arrested those people? Thank God. What a terrible thing to be doing. I hope the animals they impounded will be reunited with their owners."

"I'm sure the paper will do a big article on it, and the shelter's holding the animals indefinitely, so I was told, waiting for them to be claimed."

"They won't put them to sleep, will they?" shuddered Estelle. "If they've been stolen," she gasped, frantically, "the owners need time to find them."

He tried to reassure her. "I'm sure they won't. There will be a ton of publicity about this, and the shelter would look terrible, not to mention being liable for lawsuits, if they did that."

She became belligerent. "Well, I'm going to call them in the morning and warn them not to put any of them to sleep. You can't trust anybody in a case like this. It's the poor animals who need the help. The police ought to be guarding them."

"Now, honey, you're overreacting. The shelter's not going to screw up."

"In the morning, I'm going down there and stand guard, Hardy. I'm being proactive, like Marion. You know there's never enough help on the side of the animals, and humans can do so much damage so quickly. That's what I'm going to do. That's where I'll be if you need me." She slammed down the phone, and Hardy sat staring at the receiver, wondering if he had really talked with Estelle or something Marion had cloned.

But what she'd said was true. There never was enough support for the animals, and humans held the ultimate hammer over their heads, so Estelle might be doing just the right thing. Good for her, she was coming along nicely. He went to bed, confident that Flicker was safe from predators in his fancy new barn and happy that Bella was where she belonged, lying across his feet. Estelle, apparently, could take care of everybody else.

Will banged the kitchen door when he came in and dropped the newspaper on the table. Hardy was already up and sitting there waiting for him, a mug of coffee in his hand.

"What do you think of my new barn?"

"It really is nice looking. They did it in one day?"

"Yup, Big Bill and his helper. Now I gotta go free my little captive, unless he's eaten a hole in the wall." When Hardy slid the door open, Flicker pranced out, looked around, and pranced back in, baaing for Bella to join him. "Go ahead, girl. I still have to get dressed."

Will was reading about the bust of the animal thieves on the front page. "Sheriff Downey Scores, Hero Again," he read aloud.

"There's a lot of nasty things going on around here, Will, and somebody's got to take credit for cleaning them up. Might as well be Mitch Downey." He hurried into his bedroom, pulled on his pants, grabbed a shirt, and returned to the kitchen. "I'm anxious to check on Mr. Lucky. Estelle's on patrol down at the animal shelter. She's afraid they're going to put all those rescued animals to sleep before they can get claimed. God bless her little heart." He buttoned his shirt and tucked it into his pants.

Will laughed. "I hope she didn't bring along a gun. I wouldn't put it past her."

Hardy stopped short. "Really? You think she's capable of handling a firearm? Estelle?"

"I do," Will said, emphatically. "She's become so passionate since you and Marion got her all riled up about anything having to do with animal welfare. Haven't you noticed the change in the woman? Maybe you're too close to see it."

"Well, that wouldn't be good," he said, making a clucking sound like a chicken laying an egg. "No, no, not at all. I'd better go down there." He hurriedly pulled on his boots. "Come on Bella, let's roll. I'll meet you at the clinic," he called to Will, "and please check on Mr. Lucky first thing."

The animal shelter was on the outskirts of town, set back off the main street and hidden in a grove of old oak trees, as if the town was ashamed of it. It was a plain building, gray stucco, depressing as hell both inside and out.

The staff turned over constantly, unable to deal with the emotional toll of the job, for they did kill animals at the shelter. Putting them "to sleep"—what a serene misnomer for a horrendous deed, thought Hardy. A tall chimney rose at the very back of the building. Hardy tried not to go there if he could avoid it, because it always left him feeling miserable. The county had tried to become no-kill, but they couldn't make it work. People didn't cooperate and spay and neuter like they were supposed to. As a consequence, there were too many unwanted pets. Hardy planned on spaying Bella as soon as she had her one litter and her pups were spoken for. He knew he was trying to rationalize his decision, for he felt guilty for bringing more dogs into the world when there were so many strays. He parked under an oak and got out, commanding Bella to remain in the truck. "You don't want to be running around loose at this place," he warned.

Inside the building, dozens of people milled about, presumably in hopes of retrieving a stolen pet. And there, in the middle of the room, standing on a plastic chair holding a poster, was Estelle. Her sign read, *DON'T LET THE BASTARDS PUT THEM DOWN*. It was done in red letters on white cardboard, with drops of paint dripping to look like blood. It was quite effective, he thought, and when he finally got her attention, she flapped it at him. He squeezed through the group and stood at her feet, calling up at her, "You don't have a gun, do you, sweetie?"

He should have called more softly, for when the woman standing next to him heard, "gun," she screamed, "She's got a gun!" Panic erupted. People fell over each other trying to escape the shelter and the crazy lady with the poster and the gun. The girl behind the Plexiglas counter dialed 9ll, and before he knew it, Sheriff Downey and his men arrived. One of them tackled Estelle and threw her to the ground as the room emptied of distraught, frustrated pet owners who only wanted to find their animals and take them home. Hardy had been pushed to the floor and trampled but had had the good sense to turn over onto his stomach, protecting his vital organs. While the sheriff's deputies slapped the cuffs on Estelle, patting her down in a search for the gun, he rolled over and watched. She hurled vehement slurs at the men, and he waved at her, trying to tell her to shut up and be quiet, but she wouldn't. Adrenaline surged through her body at warp speed, fueling her transformation into a wild, raging, angry woman. They dragged her off, threw her in the back of a black and white, and away they went, to join the pet thieves in the county jail.

Hardy sat on the cold cement floor, clutching his knees. He was the only one left in the room. Other than a few bruises, he didn't think he was injured. How did this happen? And had there been a gun? He looked about. There in the plastic magazine rack attached to the gray wall, wedged down at the bottom beneath an issue of *People* magazine, was a small pistol. He stood, hobbled painfully forward, and retrieved the gun, shoving it deep in his pocket. What would they have done if they'd found it on her? Did she have a permit to carry a gun? Was it even loaded? He scoffed. Of course it wasn't. She'd just brought it along for effect, he concluded, to scare people.

As he limped to his truck in the parking lot, he pulled the pistol from his pocket and laughed at its tiny size and the thought of Estelle brandishing a loaded firearm. He playfully aimed it at the ground and squeezed the trigger, sending an unexpected bullet tearing through the left rear tire of his truck. A terrified Bella yelped, flailing at the rolled up windows. Air wheezed out of the tire, and Hardy reacted, hurling the weapon into the bushes. A moment later, thinking better of his action, he fished it out, placed it carefully in the glove box, and called road service with his cell phone.

Poor Bella shook with fright, and he hugged her, stroking her, hoping to calm her. Who was this woman he had affiliated himself with? Did he even know her, or was her behavior all his doing?

As he sat waiting for road service, he assured the girl from the shelter that he had not heard a shot, maybe a backfire, but definately not a shot. He phoned the clinic to ask about Mr. Lucky's condition. The cat was improving. Then he told Will what had happened. How could he not have seen the change in Estelle? he asked himself. And now he'd have to bail her out. She really hadn't done anything wrong. The sheriff didn't know about the gun, so how could they hold her? Mitch Downey would let her go. Hell, he certainly owed Hardy a few favors.

# CHAPTER TWENTY-TWO

The county jail was around the corner from the clinic, so when his truck tire was changed, he drove directly there, feeling it his duty to free Estelle as soon as possible. The place was a madhouse, cops everywhere, which was to be expected, but the citizenry had also converged upon the building, angry at not being able to claim their pets because the sheriff had ordered the shelter closed until things could be sorted out.

Hardy found a friendly deputy who led him down a dark hall to the women's lockup. There, all by herself in the damp, clammy cell, sat Estelle, looking serene and satisfied, her battered poster propped beside her on the bench. She jumped to her feet and grabbed the bars when she saw him. "I knew you'd come to spring me," she beamed. "I did it, didn't I? I stopped them from killing those animals." He winced. She had no idea of the problems she'd caused, delaying things.

"The sheriff closed the shelter down, and nobody can take their pets home. You caused such a disruption, there are a million people in the other room clamoring for justice. You'll be lucky if they don't form a lynch mob and drag you outta here. Yeah, you really did it, Estelle." He spoke harshly, crossing his arms and nodding his head for emphasis.

The tiny, gray-haired woman shrank, collapsing on her bench, stunned by what he had said and the way he'd said it. She had not meant to hurt, she whined, she had meant to help. She began to weep, covering her face with her hands.

Softening, he admitted, "I know you thought you were doing the right thing." He lowered his voice to a whisper. "But why in hell did you bring a gun to that place?"

She sniffed and looked at him through her fingers. "It wasn't loaded. I just wanted to scare them."

"The hell it wasn't," he shouted, louder than he should have. "The slug put a hole in my tire, and I had to call road service before I could drive down here. Where'd you get a gun?" he growled, lowering his voice again.

"You mean to tell me it went off?" she gasped. "That old thing? It belonged to my mother. I had no idea it could really shoot."

"That's how accidents happen, Estelle, usually with little kids, not grown women." He folded his arms across his chest again and shook his head slowly, back and forth, hoping to shrink her down to size. She stared at her feet and remained silent. When he figured enough time had passed, he said, "Sit tight, I'm going to find Downey and see if we can't sneak you out the back door."

Now that he had the disturbing influence in custody, the sheriff had allowed the shelter to reopen. The disgruntled pet owners deserted his jail, hoping this time to succeed in their efforts. Hardy explained Estelle's misguided fervor and assured Downey there never had been any gun and that it was just a hysterical woman's reaction to his misstatement. Downey bought it. He didn't want to keep Estelle anyway; she looked like trouble. The little ones sometimes were, he said, so he let her out and told her to behave herself. She wanted to keep her poster, but he wouldn't let her take it, saying it had contributed to the riot. She started to say something about free speech, but Hardy dragged her off and put her in his truck with his other girl, the one who didn't cause any trouble and kept his feet warm. Bella licked her cheek, and she threw her arm around the dog. "I don't know what we'd do if we lost you, Bella. I just hope those poor people find their loved ones."

He had spent half the day chasing after Estelle, and now he brought her to the clinic so he could keep an eye on her. He wasn't sure she was back to normal. How she had strayed so far from normal in the first place, he wasn't sure, but he wanted her back the way she had been. When he looked in on Mr. Lucky, the cat raised his head and tried to meow, but just a squeak came out.

"He's looking stronger," said Will. "I think he's going to make it. The Masons phoned, and that's what I told them. They also inquired about the bill he's accruing, and I told them it's on us."

"Absolutely. Can't charge people for doing the right thing. No animal should be refused medical service because of money."

"Can I open the cage and pet him?" asked Estelle.

"If you just stroke his head softly. His body's so boney that any weight is apt to be uncomfortable." He slid a stool beside the cage, and she sat, talking to Mr. Lucky and petting his head.

Hardy made cheese sandwiches from the supply in their little refrigerator, then wrapped them in paper napkins and handed her one. "Better than the food at the jail, I'll bet."

"Let's forget that ever happened, can we please? I've never been in jail before." She cocked her head toward the cat. "He's purring, Hardy. That's a good sign."

"He's happy, and I think he likes to be around people. He seems to respond to our voices. He's going to be a nice pet, if he pulls through."

"But he will, won't he?" she asked, a frightened look in her eyes.

"Unless something unforeseen pops up."

Hardy had placed two orders for sedatives and darts of various sizes, and now he put in a third. That was probably all they would need, but he wanted an update from Marion. They had a meeting scheduled for later that week, and he was hoping she had relevant news. Will and Lois were leaving the next day for their Las Vegas trip, and Will briefed his father on the two animals under his care. "Estelle, maybe you'd like to come to work as my assistant until Will gets back, what do you say?" Martha had quit, and so Hardy, anticipating the need for a helper during Will's absence and wanting to keep an eye on Estelle, offered her a job, thereby killing two birds with one stone, a quip he despised.

"Really? I'd like that. Can I wear a white coat?"

"I don't see why not, but you can't pretend to be a doctor."

Hardy took her home after work, and then they remembered her car was at the shelter, so they had to drive back there to pick it up. It seemed like the day had been seventy-two hours long. He wanted to call it a night, and she said she had things to catch up on, so they agreed they'd see each other in the morning. "Stay out of trouble, take a hot bath," he called, as he drove away.

He was looking forward to an easy meal and an early bedtime, but when he pulled into his driveway, he was greeted by a welcoming committee of three horses and a mule. They gathered around his truck as he opened the door, and Bella jumped out, bouncing about, making instant friends.

"Where did you guys come from?" he asked, running his hand down the neck of the buckskin mare. She nuzzled him, looking for food, and then she threw her head up and down, and shook it sideways, all the while digging the dirt with her hoof. The other two horses, a bay and a pinto, held back. Then the big mule, who stood taller than any of them, came forward and whinnied, pushing the mare aside with his bulk.

"Okay, come on, then," said the doctor, "follow me. Bella, let's put these guys in the pasture with Flicker and the new barn."

He had ordered several bales of oat hay from Otis, his neighbor, and he found them stacked neatly inside the barn.

"Good timing, you boys and girls act hungry." He undid the ties on one bale and scattered the hay in three stalls. The goat ate hay alongside the horses, holding his own, but he returned every now and again to his alfalfa pellets, which he was reluctant to share. Hardy hung water buckets in each stall and returned to the house, hungry for his own dinner. It occurred to him that these nomads could be leftovers from the freedom raid he'd orchestrated a while back. It was certainly possible that they could have been wandering the valley. He'd check to see if there were any bulletins for missing horses in the morning. The mule was special, a magnificent specimen. He'd give it a try, but if he couldn't find owners, he'd keep them. Perhaps the herd he'd wanted had found him instead. He'd gotten his barn just in time. He thought of calling Bill to ask if his Built-Rite barn came with a supply of stock, but realized he'd probably just confuse the burly man.

# CHAPTER TWENTY-THREE

Hardy counted the days until Bella would give birth and figured she was due on or about December 25. He hadn't planned for there to be Christmas puppies; that was just how the days added up. In a few weeks, he could do an ultrasound and make sure she was pregnant, but of course Bella already knew. The rains were coming regularly now, and it grew colder each day. The outside cats wanted in and the inside cats wanted out; every year it happened that way, and he didn't try to understand it. The creek was swelling too; each rain made it higher and wider. Will and Lois were in Vegas, Estelle was assisting at the clinic, and their meeting with the Movement was scheduled for seven that evening. Mr. Lucky was now sitting up, off his heating pad, and eating like a champion. Hardy could find no one who was missing horses or a mule, so for the time being they were living in his pasture, enjoying the new barn. Flicker was happy to have company all day, but the horses, and especially the big mule, would have nothing to do with Bella's herding business. When the mule laid back his big ears and charged her, Bella turned tail and ran, jumping into a feeding trough to escape his long teeth. She did not try to herd him again.

Estelle did a good job helping at the clinic. She liked talking with the clients and tolerated the people who brought them in. Hardy believed she was back to normal, as normal as she ever had been. They neutered Hardy the cat, and she assisted, chucking his testicles into the garbage with an overhand shot worthy of Kobe Bryant. The operation took only a few minutes, males being so much less complicated than females, and he was already up and hobbling around an hour afterward. She left the clinic a little early that day, wanting to settle him down and make sure he was okay before Hardy picked her up for the meeting at Marion's.

They were both excited and hoping to learn more details about the upcoming mission, for Hardy had questions and Estelle was spoiling for a fight, something she could really sink her teeth into. The hacienda was lit up like Christmas, and a jovial crowd had congregated on the deck, bundled in jackets and heavy sweaters and drinking hot toddies. Marion greeted Hardy and Estelle, and after handing them each a steaming mug of the brew, she climbed onto a small redwood end table to address the group.

"So glad to see so many of you here tonight," she began. "Our covert operatives have learned a great deal about the situation I touched upon at our last meeting, code-named 'Banned Hunt,' and I believe we are now ready to proceed with direct action against the enemy. As with the geese, refuge for the animals is top priority. We know the organizers of the killing field have brought in tigers, lions, and several other species of big cat, so we've arranged their transfer to our cat person down south. The elephants— believe it, they've got two of them—are going to an elephant preserve in the Central Valley, and we've found someone in Washington State who will take the three bears— yes, three grizzly bears. So the problem kids are already placed, and now we need space for the antelopes, buffaloes, and range animals. Transportation will by large van and truck, and Dr. Johns will provide tranquillization when necessary—for the animals, folks, so don't get your hopes up." Polite giggles rippled throughout the crowd. "We can celebrate when the operation is complete. We know where they are, and we know how to get in. The doctor and I will take care of the guard, and most of the hard reconnaissance is done. Now we need to coordinate among ourselves and decide who's doing what. Let's adjourn into the house, where it's a bit warmer, and we'll break into groups and pass the signup board around."

Everyone knew the drill, and they found the people they were comfortable working with and formed groups, signing up for the things they were best equipped to handle. The meeting lasted for an hour and a half, and when people started to leave, Marion asked Hardy to wait. She wanted a one on one with him. He and Estelle lingered in the living room until the others had left, and Marion refilled their mugs and sat on the hearth in front of her flagstone fireplace, warming her back. "How's our supply of drugs?" she asked.

"I think we have enough for the cats and the others, but we certainly can't dart elephants. We'd never be able to move them. If they were zoo animals, maybe we won't need darts; maybe they'll just walk into the trucks. That would be the best way for everyone concerned. How many guards did you say were there at night?"

"They have a small office and a caretaker. Only one man's there at night, and hell, I was thinking we could stick him with a dart. Why not? Put him out and back the trucks up to the gates. And, like you said, if the animals are tame enough, they might cooperate and walk right in."

"Tell Marion about your new barn," said Estelle, poking him in the ribs.

Marion's eyes lit up. "You have a new barn?"

"It's a really big one," said Estelle, "and he's got a goat, three horses, and a huge mule to go with it."

"When did you acquire all the animals, Doctor?" Marion's interest was piqued.

"Very recently. They kind of came with the barn. You missing any stock?"

"No, but the mule sounds fascinating." She leaned forward, clasping her hands together and resting them on her knees. The fire crackled and snapped behind her, adding intensity to her demeanor. "They're such smart animals. I've always wanted one."

Hardy paled, uncomfortable with her confession. "I've become rather fond of Montrose myself."

"Montrose?" drawled Estelle, a look of surprise on her face. "Yes, it suits him, don't you think?"

"I do," she agreed, "it's quite regal."

"So, getting back to the barn, if we need to hide a few animals for a few days, you could handle it?" asked Marion.

"Is there a giraffe? I have a thirty-foot ceiling, so he'd fit if he stood right in the middle, but we'd have to keep him hidden. Folks would start asking questions if I turned him loose in the pasture."

"I don't think there's a giraffe, but I'm not sure. These people bought everything they could get their hands on."

"Seriously, I can take anything that eats hay. I've got some of that now, and we should think about notifying Sheriff Downey as soon as we have the animals out of there, so he can make sure these creeps don't try it again. Another coup for Downey. He's going to win sheriff of the year."

"Is there such a thing?" asked Marion.

"I have no idea," said Hardy, "but there ought to be."

Marion stood. "All right, then, the group has tentatively agreed on two weeks from tonight as the target date. We'll meet here first as usual. I'll let you know immediately if there's any change. And if you decide to get rid of Montrose, you let me know."

"That's not going to happen, Marion. Order yourself a Built-Rite barn, and maybe you'll get one too."

Relieved that the date was set, Hardy and Estelle discussed their duties on the way home. Again, Bella would be important, but they had to be careful how they used her. She certainly couldn't herd lions and tigers. Hardy figured the best way to trap those animals was to bait cages or, if that didn't work, the tranquilizer darts. Marion had borrowed six sturdy cages from the woman who was to receive the cats. The animals could always be tranquilized once they were caged, if Hardy used his long pole syringe or the blowgun. Tranquillization was often safer for wild animals who had to travel long distances, but it all depended on the individual. "We'll just have to wait and see how each animal reacts. We can be ready for any scenario."

"I like Marion's idea of darting the guard," said Estelle. "Can I do it?"

"Ha! You'd like that, wouldn't you, you little hell cat." He pinched her thigh and grinned at the thought of his tiny girlfriend blowing sedative darts at the big bad man. Why not? She'd brought a gun to the animal shelter, and she wasn't squeamish. "I'll tell you  what, if you practice and convince me you can hit the target, the job is yours."

"It is?" she squealed. "I'll practice, I promise, and I'll get really good at it, you'll see." She slid across the seat, snuggling close, and he felt himself becoming aroused by the subject matter and the way she grabbed hold of it.

# CHAPTER TWENTY-FOUR

Since Will was not there to drop the newspaper on his kitchen table, he let it sit in the road, as was his custom, and would pick it up when he came home at night. Of course, that meant he was a day behind when he got around to reading the headlines, but by then Estelle would have brought him up to date on anything important. He was bored with the paper, and he thought seriously of not renewing his subscription next time around. The only enjoyment he got out of it was reading about Sheriff Downey scoring a bust, and he usually knew about that ahead of time.

Estelle was practicing with the dart gun and the blowpipe every chance she got, and he had to admit, she was dead on. She'd shredded the target of the torso he'd pinned to the big oak in his front yard. Will and Lois would be back soon, and he had a job he wanted to take care of before they returned, mainly to avoid his son's intense scrutiny and endless questions. It was on his list, and he intended to ask Estelle to help, for she was what he needed, a stand-in.

That night when she'd finished blowing the target completely off the tree, he brought her inside, sat her down, poured her a scotch on the rocks, and explained what he had in mind. Bella also listened, wagging her tail as if she understood.

"This is something that has needed to be done for a long time, and now that you are so capable, I think the two of us can pull it off," he said, hoping flattery would engage her. "On Route 29, out by the old cemetery, a gang of misfits runs an illegal puppy mill. They've got a big shed behind the house where the keep the dogs, and every time animal control and the cops go out to bust them, they hide the cages somewhere. I think they've got a basement under the structure and someone tips them off, probably a cop or a shelter worker. They breed Westies, West Highland white terriers, which are fine little dogs, but these particular puppies, the ones I get to see, are sick and often die in a few months, leaving a trail of tears that leads right back to that house. The heartsick owners signed disclaimers, waivers, you name it, and usually they're too beaten down to go after the sellers anyway, and they've paid twelve to fifteen hundred dollars for all this misery." He refreshed her drink and poured himself another.

He leaned forward, his elbows on the table. "Okay, here's what I have in mind. They run an ad in the paper, it's always there, and you call and tell them you want a puppy. You play it real sad. Tell them your Westie just died and you want another one. So you make an appointment to go out there and look at the dogs, but you've got to get in that building behind the house and see what's there. I'd go with you, but they know who I am, local vet and all."

"How do I do that?"

"I don't know. I'm trying to figure it out."

She sipped her scotch and leaned back in her chair. "So, we're up against the mystery of the disappearing dogs," she mused. "What if I took Bella along, and she ran off and ended up in the building in the back, and I had to chase after her?" Bella's ears pricked to attention. "Yes, I said *you*, pretty girl."

"That might work. At least you'd get a look-see."

"But then what?"

"Then we steal the dogs. We sneak in there and take them."

"Why don't we just do that and skip the rest of it? You're sure they're there, right? Let's just sneak in at night and take them. I can dart them to sleep—the people, not the dogs."

Hardy was silent, thinking about what she'd said. Perhaps she was right. The direct approach was the way to go, a blitz.

"All right, we'll do it your way, Estelle," he declared, banging his glass on the table, "tonight, right now. You haven't had too much to drink have you?"

"Tonight?" she stammered. "So soon? Isn't this awfully abrupt? And no, I haven't had too much to drink," she added, indignantly.

"I want to do it *now*. I'm all fired up. You've got me all fired up, kiddo." He grabbed at her, but she dodged, setting her empty glass in the sink.

"You sure *you* haven't had too much to drink?"

"I'm sure," he grinned. "Okay, I'm going to hitch my trailer to the back of the truck, 'cause I know there'll be lots of cages. You bring the blowpipe, and we'll stop at the clinic and pick up some loaded darts. Anybody gets in our way, you put 'em down. I *like* it."

He really liked it. He hitched up the trailer and wondered why he hadn't just suggested it in the first place instead of using all his roundabout gimmicks. He'd thought about it too long and too often, that was the problem. These things worked best when you just did them. Thoughts weren't any good unless you put them into action.

"Let's roll!" he yelled, "C'mon, Bella, you can help."

She pounced into the cab, taking her place in the little back seat, her head resting on his shoulder. They stopped at the clinic for the darts and headed out to Route 29. Estelle gripped the blowpipe, her knuckles white, her eyes glowing in the darkness, and her adrenalin-filled blood pumping through her body with each beat of her pounding heart. He knew she was ready.

"Here we go," he said, as he passed the little cemetery on Route 29. He killed the lights and slowed to a crawl, parking the rig across the street and up from the driveway. Lights were on in the old, single-story wood house, but no light shone from the building in the back. They slipped through the shadows, sliding along the house to the rear yard, flashlights in their pockets. Estelle was ready with the loaded blowgun. There was no moon, so they stepped carefully, not wanting to make any noise. The building in back was long and low, and Hardy recognized it as an old chicken coop. The large door was held closed by a metal bar, and, to his surprise, there was no lock. The windows in the side of the coop were covered with canvas tacked tightly to the weathered gray boards. Hardy motioned Estelle to follow, and they snuck down one side, around the back, and up the other side, encountering no one. When they were once again in front, he lifted the bar, set it aside, and pushed the door open. It creaked and swung wide. Hardy's flashlight revealed a dismal sight.

A long row of small metal cages sat on wood pallets pushed end to end, and each cage was crammed with at least three full-grown dogs. They shone their lights down the rows, and some of the little dogs stood, looking into the beams, their ears pricked forward. Their naturally white coats were dirty brown, matted with their own feces; their small water bowls were green with algae. The stench in the shed was thick with urine and disease, and the pathetic little animals didn't whimper or make a sound, so broken were they in body and spirit.

Estelle advanced, her face twisted with rage. She raised the blowpipe, hoping for a target. "This is disgusting," she whispered, "let's get these dogs out of here."

"Look," said Hardy, stumbling over a loop of rope that protruded from the planks beneath his feet. He grabbed the loop and pulled, and a trap door sprung open, revealing a ladder down to another space. "Ha! This is where they hide them when the sheriff comes. Shine your light while I climb down and look around. I don't want to leave anyone behind." She did, and he found more pallets but no cages. Just then they heard a click and footsteps coming toward them from the house. They doused their lights and flattened themselves against the wall beside the open door. Estelle raised the blowpipe to her mouth and took a deep breath. "Come on, baby," whispered Hardy.

Once the figure stepped into the shed, Estelle let fly. The dart caught the tall, thin man in the back of the thigh. He yelped, wavered a moment, and then collapsed in a heap.

"Man, that stuff works fast," she said.

"Good aim, honey. I wonder if he's the only one home tonight. It'd make our job a whole lot easier."

"I suspect we'll know the answer to that question very soon. Let's throw him in that hole where they put the dogs." The dragged the limp body to the cellar trap door and slid him down the stairs, feet first, paying no attention to the way he landed. Hardy kicked the door closed. He'll be out for at least three hours. C'mon let's start loading." They found a flat dolly that held three cages at a time, and they loaded it, wheeling it in and out with abandon, angry and ready for a fight should anyone dare try to stop them, but no one came. They loaded thirty cages into Hardy's trailer. Each cage had three grown dogs, and some even had four or five, so they knew they had at least one hundred animals. "I feel like throwing a match to this place," said Estelle, as they rolled the last load to freedom.

"Sheriff Downey will take care of them. We'll tip him right now. Let's get out of here."

They'd left Bella in the car, thinking better of letting her loose, and she was excitedly diving back and forth between the seats. "Take it easy, girl," said Estelle. "You have your babies to consider. And all these poor dogs, how many babies do you think they've had to produce this year?"

"They keep them pregnant, birthing litter after litter. It's a rotten racket." He got the sheriff on the cell and told him what they'd done.

"You mean you actually found the hiding place? A trapdoor, huh?"

"Yeah, and there's a man down there. He'll be waking up in about three hours. We're going to take these dogs to the clinic, do what we can for them, and then to the animal shelter. I'll notify the Westie rescue group, and they should be a big help with rehabilitation. I hope you can put this human scum in jail and keep them there for awhile, Sheriff."

"This is what we needed, Hardy. My men never could find that spider hole. Thanks."

They spent all night working on the dogs at the clinic. Hardy examined each one and treated the sickest. They washed the dirtiest, but it was a job for many hands. He called the shelter director's emergency number, and she arranged to meet him at the shelter at six in the morning with a crew. Once again they loaded the cages, using the doctor's own supply so as not to crowd the dogs so badly, and then they delivered them to the sanctuary. Members of the Westie rescue society were excited at the prospect of so many new little faces; they arrived later that morning, eager to help, and Hardy volunteered free medical treatment if it was needed. A reporter from the newspaper who had a scanner tuned into the sheriff's dispatch caught Estelle and Hardy as they were leaving and pestered them for an interview. "Sheriff Downey finally nailed the bastards," said Hardy. "He's a fine man, and he ought to run for president. And you can quote me."

# CHAPTER TWENTY-FIVE

Hardy took Estelle to his house, where she picked up her car and went home to sleep. He threw out handfuls of hay to his newly acquired herd, left the barn doors open, fed the cats, changed clothes, and drove back to the clinic. People and animals depended on him, no matter if he'd been up all night. Bella stayed with Flicker, for she needed her rest.

As soon as he unlocked the door, Sheriff Downey phoned, wanting to bring the doctor up to speed on the arrests. "We pulled that fellow outta the cellar, and he was still woozy, but when he sobered up, he told us his buddies had gone to Oregon to pick up more dogs. *More* dogs, Hardy! So we staked out the place. And, sure enough, a few hours later, up comes their truck, full of more dogs. So we arrested the whole bunch. I got them sharing a cell, smallest one I have, all six bastards crammed together. Wish I could stuff 'em in the toilet, let 'em know how it feels, but then I'd get a reprimand, and I don't want to tarnish the image you got going for me. Anyway, thanks again. We really appreciate the tip."

He felt good about their accomplishment. It was a big victory, and Estelle had played a major part. He needed to let her know how proud he was of her, and so he decided to buy her a present of some sort. But in the meantime, he phoned the newspaper, identified himself, and asked to speak with the reporter who had been at the animal shelter that morning, for he had important additional information. When a male voice answered, Hardy said, "You should give special mention to the fact that Estelle Greenwood, my assistant, single-handedly brought down the guard, thus enabling the rescue of the dogs. She is a true hero, and you should be sure she gets the credit she's due."

"Thank you, Doctor, this will be a great addition to my story. How did she accomplish the feat, may I ask?"

Hardy hesitated, considering how much of their personal business he should reveal, and then said, "She did an expert job on the guard with the blowpipe."

"I see," said the reporter, sounding a bit confused. "Well, thanks, I'll put it in."

The remainder of his day at the clinic was uneventful, which was good, for truthfully, he'd had enough events to last him awhile. He dozed in his chair with his feet on the examination table until it was time to close up and go home. He stopped at the candy store and bought a big box of mixed chocolates, deciding Estelle would appreciate candy more than flowers. After they'd eaten dinner, she opened her present. "How thoughtful of you to buy me candy," she said, offering him a piece.

"It's a reward for being such a good helper last night. I think the newspaper's going to mention your name as well. Be sure to check in the morning." He smiled and winked.

"Really," she purred. "I'll certainly do that."

They sat together on her sofa, eating chocolates and talking about the upcoming operation and how he was going to let her handle the darting because she had proven herself. Then he kissed her and went home, for his weariness was catching up with him. And Will would be back in the morning, and that meant he'd have to talk to him all day.

Will liked to talk while he worked; Hardy preferred to remain quiet. They achieved a happy medium by avoiding each other as much as possible, one in the back room, the other out front. Hardy likened it to his sex with Estelle: he could indulge if he wished, but he didn't have to.

Bella, happy to see him, ran to meet him at the front door. He gave her a bowl of food, opened more cans for the cats, and put on his pajamas. The stock took to bedding themselves down in the barn at night, and all he had to do was close the barn door. Montrose stuck his big head over a stall divider and whinnied at him.

"Good night, big fella," called Hardy. He wondered if any of his new animals were saddle broken and would let him ride. He needed tack: a saddle, halters, bridles, blankets. This animal kingdom had come upon him so suddenly that he was not prepared to be a cowboy. Montrose would make an awesome mount. Marion would be jealous beyond belief. He made a mental note to visit the saddle shop, for what was the point of having riding stock if you didn't ride? Perhaps Estelle would like to learn too. She'd look good on the buckskin mare.

He climbed into his bed, and Bella assumed her place stretched across his feet. He wondered for the first time how she could sleep that way, for it didn't look very comfortable. If she was pregnant and her belly began to swell, she would probably have to choose a new sleeping place. The other side of the bed was still available, and it was hers if she wished. She could even have her own pillow.

He woke early but lay in bed staring at the ceiling, trying to remember a dream he'd just had, but it was no use. It faded, disappearing into some secret alcove in his brain. He heard the kitchen door bang and his son yell, "Anybody here?"

He sat up, slipped into his slippers, grabbed his robe, and pulled it on as he shuffled down the hall. "I'm coming, Will," he yelled. "Glad to have you home."

Will stood at the table looking tanned and rested. He dropped the newspaper and smiled. Bella licked his hand and wagged her tail, and he stepped to the door and let her outside. "You look great," said Hardy. "Have a good time?"

"We did." He nodded and pointed at the paper lying on the table. "Looks like you had your hands full too. Finally got your nose into the puppy mill racket, huh, Dad? Good for you. And Estelle, who knew! Quite a write-up of the whole affair. Sorry to have missed it. It sounds like it was fun."

"Fun?" asked Hardy, picking up the newspaper and reading the headline. "I don't think I'd call it fun. 'Sheriff Closes Down Puppy Mill,'" he read aloud. "You find something funny in that, Son?"

"Keep reading," he said, filling the coffeepot with water.

Half the front page was devoted to the rout, with photographs of the spider hole and the inside of the awful chicken coup. When he read the first column of the reporter's story, however, his face turned red and he began to cough and sputter. "Good Lord, when Estelle sees this, she'll kill me." He read aloud: "'Dr. Hardy Johns, the town's beloved veterinarian, credited his assistant, Estelle Greenwood, with the capture of the gang member guard, praising her proficiency at delivering blowjobs.' Oh," moaned Hardy, "this is terrible. I knew that kid didn't understand what I was telling him. I probably ought to leave town. I think I'll saddle my mule and ride off into the sunset."

"Mule?" asked Will.

"Montrose. He appeared with three horses the night you left. Kinda came along with the barn. I'm waiting for wise men bearing gifts."

Just then the phone rang. No one called this early except Estelle or the sheriff with an emergency. He moved slowly toward the jangling beast, as if it would strike out and bite him, inflicting a deadly poison. He was almost right.

"Yes," drawled Hardy, "but he got it wrong, he mixed up my words." Will could hear the screaming on the other end, and he stifled a laugh. "Of course I didn't say that. We don't even *do* that. Why would I say something we don't even do?" A long pause and more screaming. "If it makes you feel any better, I'm canceling my subscription. ... Yes, just as soon as their office is open. ... I don't know the kid, Estelle, and I don't know if he knows what it means. ... No, I'm *not* going to explain it to him. I'm sure everybody he works with will take care of that. ... Okay, see you later."

"I was going to cancel my subscription anyway," he muttered.

# CHAPTER TWENTY-SIX

The phone at the clinic rang all day long with eager male voices asking to speak to the woman named Estelle, who, after recovering from her initial shock, was threatening to come into town.

"This will blow over," Hardy said, when he called her at noon, instantly regretting his choice of words.

"Did you cancel your subscription?" she rasped, her voice strained from yelling at him.

"Yes, of course, as soon as they opened." He had called the paper, but everyone was so busy guffawing, they could hardly hear him. But when the girl realized who he was, the noise stopped cold, like a door slamming shut. "And I gave them what for, believe me. That young reporter is going to send you a letter of apology. He offered to print a retraction, but I said no, 'cause I was afraid he'd screw it up worse and mention those words together again in the same sentence. We just have to let it die, and it will."

He didn't dare tell her about the lewd calls they'd received all day or about the excessive number of vehicles that circled the block hour after hour, slowing as they passed the clinic, hoping for a glimpse of the talented woman. "Take a few more days off," he coaxed, "let everyone forget about you. Low, low, low profile, that's the ticket."

"But I like to help at the clinic. Don't you need me down there?" she whined, "I'm bored with just sitting home with the cats."

"Of course I need you, but Will is back, and it's not terribly busy." He lied, for they had been swamped with patients, nothing serious, just minor annoyances, but her presence would create chaos. All at once he had an idea.

"If you must go out, Estelle, would you like to run an errand for me? Do some shopping?"

"Shopping?" She sighed, sounding disinterested. "For what?"

"Tack. Bridles, saddles, blankets, and all the things we need to be horse people. Go to that nice saddle shop downtown, and I'll meet you there later and write a check, and then we can go horseback or mule back riding together. Can you ride?" he asked, hoping to redirect her thoughts and pique her interest.

"I can ride," she said, defensively. "I had a horse when I was a kid, and I was a good rider." He heard her self-confidence returning.

"Excellent. So, you want to do it? Shop?"

"I suppose I could," she sighed, "if that's what you want."

"Great! Call me when you're finished, and I'll meet you there."

"Is she all right?" Will asked, having overheard the conversation.

"She's just down in the dumps 'cause she's stuck in the house. She'll perk up when I spend some money on her."

"Well, if you're not too preoccupied, I'd like you to help me with the golden's spay."

"Gladys? Is she here today? She had a lovely litter. I understand all the pups have found homes, too. I want to do an ultrasound on Bella. It's almost time, but I'm sure she conceived. You want to bet me on it? Hundred dollars?"

"No, because *I'm* sure she conceived. I have that sixth sense, you know."

"How about number of embryos? "

"No, I don't want to bet on Bella's babies."

Hardy prepared an injection for Gladys. "I hope you were more fun in Vegas, 'cause you're sure not much fun around here."

The two men were silent, working with the big golden retriever, shaving and swabbing her belly, then making the incision and removing her reproductive organs. When they were finished, Will wheeled the sedated dog to a cage and placed her on a thick pad of blankets, taking care to lay her tongue out the side of her mouth.

The phone rang. Hardy picked up the receiver, listened to the drunk on the other end, and said, "She quit, not enough action. Try the clinic over in Parkston. I think she took a job there."

"Lois and I are engaged," Will shouted from the backroom. "She wants a Christmas wedding."

Hardy braced himself against the examination table. "Can you come in here and tell me about it?"

"Not much to tell," said Will, joining him in the big room. "I asked, and she said yes."

Hardy grabbed his son and hugged him. "Good work, my boy. Actually, I was afraid you'd never get around to asking, and that if you did, she'd say no. Wrong on all counts, thank goodness."

"You say she wants a Christmas wedding? What does that mean? You get married on Christmas Day? That would be a little hectic, wouldn't it, what with Bella having her puppies?"

"No, not on Christmas Day. A few days before, probably. We wouldn't want to compete with Bella giving birth. We'd lose for sure, and we do want you to come to our wedding, Doctor."

"Make it the twenty-second. That's a good day," suggested Hardy, studying the calendar on the wall. You might suggest it to Lois, but I don't want to interfere. Of course, Bella was first. She got pregnant before you got engaged. That ought to count for something, right? And there's nothing we can do about the gestation period; nature has these things pretty well locked up."

Will patted his father on the back. "I'll talk to her about the date, and I'm sure it will work out. Lois is a reasonable person."

"And an animal lover," added Hardy.

"Right."

"Whatever happened to that little dog of hers? She doesn't bring it around anymore."

"That's a funny story," said Will. "She borrowed that dog to get to me. It belongs to a friend. See how I affect women? The things they'll do to gain my attention?"

"Huh, not surprising. After all, you are Hardy John's son."

Estelle called him at four thirty. She was at the saddle shop, ready to spend his money. Could he come now? He congratulated his son again and left for the day, eager to see what she'd chosen and hoping her mood had improved.

Tacky's, the Western store, was a few minutes from the clinic, and he arrived in short order. She greeted him wearing a fringy leather jacket, a wide-brimmed Stetson, and cowboy boots that rose to her knees. "Howdy, pardner," she drawled, a big grin on her face. "Come on in and set a spell."

They were the only customers in the store, and the salesgirl, a shapely young blond with a huge mouth full of white teeth, smiled and remained quiet, letting Estelle close the deal. Hardy was overjoyed that she seemed happy again and back to her old self. Shopping was the magic cure. "Look at you," he gushed. "You look like the real deal, honey. You need some jeans is all, and maybe one of those kerchiefs around your neck, you know, the kind the bandits pull up over their noses. What have you got for us in the way of tack?"

She grabbed his hand and led him to the back of the large store. "I had so much fun today picking out all this stuff, with Ellie's help, of course. She's the salesperson, and I feel much better now. You're so smart." She put her hands on his cheeks and kissed him, her big blue eyes appearing meltingly soft despite the harsh fluorescent lighting overhead.

"Ellie put all my choices back here so nobody else could buy them." She gestured to an area that he took to be at least twenty by twenty, stacked with an assortment of items. "Of course, you can add things if you want."

He browsed the aisles Ellie had thoughtfully provided, pulling Estelle along behind and stopping now and then to ask, "What does this do? Do you really think we need one of these? Where's my saddle? I want to sit in it and make sure it fits." He had not seen his, only hers, a silver-plated dazzler that cost a small fortune, and he wasn't sure the depths of his remorse ran that deep. It was the reporter's fault, after all.

"Ellie said you had to be here to try on your saddle, so they're over there." He found the row of tooled leather saddles sitting on custom-made racks, some with silver, some without, and he picked a rather plain looking one and sat in it. It felt comfortable and had plenty of butt room, and it did have a nice silver horse head on the horn.

"I like this one. Let's add it to our pile."

"It's so plain," protested Estelle. "Are you sure you don't want something fancier to match mine?"

*Mine?* The word struck home, and he knew he was stuck. "I'm a man, Estelle, and I think a man's saddle *should* be plain. Let the lady sparkle. Know what I mean?" He winked.

"So we're good to go then?" asked Ellie, hovering in the background. "Shall I start ringing up your purchases, Doctor?"

"If you think we have everything we need to be horse, mule, and goat people, please do. Do we have enough saddle blankets?"

"Only two."

"Better throw in two more. My son and his fiancée will be riding with us now and then. If they want their own saddles, they'll have to come try them on."

"Certainly. Do you want to pick out the blankets?"

"You do it, please. I'll limber up my check-writing hand."

Estelle finally processed what he had said. "Fiancée?"

"Yeah, Will told me they're engaged. She wants a Christmas wedding. How's that for soon? I told him the twenty-second, so it wouldn't interfere with Bella's date."

"That's a surprise. They haven't really known each other very long. About as long as you and I, isn't that right?"

"I think it is, Estelle." He watched as Ellie rang up their purchases, stuffing what she could into bags. When she'd checked off the last item, she rang the total: $4,685.95, half of which went for the silver-encrusted peace offering.

"Do you want to wear your hat, jacket, and boots, Estelle?" asked Ellie.

"Oh yes, please, and, Hardy, we forgot your hat! You've got to have a Stetson."

"Of course I do." He found a nice, textured straw hat with that a wide brim Estelle favored and paid cash, having already written his check.

It took several trips to load the bags into the truck. He set the saddles on top of the blankets, like Ellie told him, so as not to damage their trees, a term he had not heard before.

"What a nice day this turned out to be after all," said Estelle, cuddling close. "Thank you for the lovely saddle and the other things. You're my hero, and you know what I discovered today? Not everybody reads that old newspaper. Ellie didn't even know who I was."

"She does now."

# CHAPTER TWENTY-SEVEN

Estelle followed him to his house and helped him unload. They decided to designate the front of the barn as the tack room, and they set the saddles on their racks on one side and hung the bridles, halters, and ropes on the other. Hardy had convinced Ellie to throw in the saddle stands, figuring he'd spent enough to justify her gift of a few well-constructed sawhorses.

The animals were curious, especially Flicker. Since he didn't want the goat eating the leather goods, he reminded Estelle to always keep the door to the tack room closed when Flicker was loose. Will stopped by after work, wanting a closer look at the horses and the mule. He was very impressed with his father's new equipment.

"You have a nice setup going here, Dad. Montrose is quite some mule."

"Marion wants him. She says she's always wanted a mule, and she keeps hinting that I ought to let her have him, but I want him myself." He turned toward the mule's stall and yelled, "I love Montrose," and the mule stuck his head over the side of the stall. Hardy stroked his forehead and planted a kiss on the soft muzzle. Montrose stretched out his neck, raised his head, and curled his upper lip, showing off his long mule teeth. "Yes, you're beautiful, and you're mine," sang the doctor. "Marion can go find her own mule."

Estelle had been fixing dinner in the kitchen, and now she joined them, congratulating Will on his engagement. "I think it's just great," she said, "and you and Lois make a perfect couple. You have so many things in common, what with your mutual animal connection. Can you have dinner with us? I made spaghetti."

"Thanks, Estelle, but my fiancée is waiting for me. You know how that is," he grinned.

"Not really," she said, shaking her head.

Hardy felt a distinctly chilly draft as she fluffed her apron and went back into the house.

"Why'd you have to say that?" he whispered. "Did you see the way she reacted? Like she was the only woman in the whole world who doesn't have a fiancé?"

"Well, nothing I can do about that," said Will. "That's your problem." Quickly changing the subject, he said, "Listen, can Lois and I go riding this weekend? She asked me to ask you. She loves to ride, and apparently she's quite good at it."

"Our clinic is open on the weekends. We work those days, remember?"

"Come on," Will wheedled, "I can take off a little early on Sunday."

The doctor capitulated. "Use our saddles, then. You'll look real pretty in Estelle's silver casket. I got one rule though: hands off Montrose. He's mine. And remember, those horses haven't been ridden since they came to me. I don't know anything about them. For all we know, they may not even be saddle broke. If Lois is such a hot shot, she can find that out. See you tomorrow."

Estelle served her meatless spaghetti cheerfully enough; the tension he'd felt seemed to have dissipated. Their day had ended on such a high note, he didn't want anything to spoil it. That night she stayed over, and they made love in his bed. Everything seemed back to where it had always been, and he was relieved. He slept like a happy man, but she lay awake, staring at the moonlight on the ceiling, wondering whether he'd ever ask her and whether she'd be able to say she was somebody's fiancée.

"No paper today," said Will, as he made the morning coffee.

"Nope, cancelled it like I promised. It's just the bearer of bad news, and who needs that?" He sat, waiting for the coffee to brew. "So, you and Lois are riding Sunday?"

"Right. She's all excited. I hope those horses are broke."

"Find out soon enough."

"I see Estelle's car. Everything okay?"

Hardy smiled, thinking about their lovemaking. "Things are great. I guess I was a little paranoid yesterday, worried about nothing. Sorry."

"Women," declared Will. "It's true what they say. Can't live with them, can't live without them. Coffee?"

"Yeah."

He poured two mugs and sat with his father. "Seems funny not having a newspaper to look at with your coffee."

"Well, there's no way I can have one of those things back in this house as long as Estelle's around. I got an idea. Why don't you have the paper delivered to your house? Then you can drink coffee and read over there."

"Who's going to wake you up if I don't come by?"

"Ha! I wake myself up. Don't misunderstand, I love seeing you like this so early in the morning, but it's not like we don't spend all day together."

"You bringing Estelle in today?"

"It's up to her. She can come in if she wants. Our shopping spree revived her. You know how much that saddle of hers cost me? Twenty-eight hundred big ones, so sit with pride, my boy, you're riding high on the hog. But you better take the big bay, 'cause that sucker's heavy."

"Maybe you and Estelle can ride in the Labor Day parade next year, now that you have all the accoutrements. She should be able to handle the press again by then."

"The press? What press?" demanded Estelle, slipping into the room, her bare feet silent on the cold linoleum.

"We were just talking about riding in the parade next year, you and Dad. It might be fun, and you could get all cowboyed up."

She poured herself a mug of coffee and pulled Hardy's terry cloth robe tight around her tiny frame. "We'll see. That's a long time off." She sat with them, sipping from her mug, and Bella dragged in and plopped down under the table between their feet.

"She's acting sluggish. I think it's time to do that ultrasound. You want to come in and help with it, Estelle? See the *babies*?" cooed the doctor.

"No need to patronize me, Hardy Johns. You know I do." She hurried back down the hall, and Will set his mug in the sink and stretched, spreading his arms and puffing out his chest. "Shopping and babies—gets them every time," said Hardy. "See you at work."

Bella roamed the clinic, padding along the row of cages, checking new patients, smelling each spot on the floor for a possible surprise. When she had performed her recon, she went to her mat, pawed it to a pleasing shape, and collapsed, her head resting on her foreleg. She watched as Estelle and Hardy and Will, the humans she loved most in the world, prepared to look inside her womb. Hardy disinfected the steel able again, having done it once already, and then he rolled a small table with the ultrasound machine alongside and turned the machine on. He handed Estelle a tube of gel and called Will to come help lift. The two men set Bella gently on the table. Since she trusted them, she lay quietly, letting Hardy stroke her belly and clip her long gray hair.

Estelle applied the clear gel, which acted as a conduction agent, and Hardy pressed the ultrasound probe against Bella's soft skin, rolling it gently in circles, looking sideways at the screen on the black box. Immediately he saw what he was looking for. "There," he whispered, "right there. Can you see them? One, two, three!"

Will looked over his shoulder, taking up the count. "Four, five, six, seven. I count seven, Dad."

Estelle squinted, peering into the screen, seeing only splotches and one big mass.

"Can you point them out, please? I can't see any babies."

Will stepped to the box and pointed, "See, there's one, and there's another, here's a third."

"Oh yes, uh huh, I see, uh huh." She wanted to act professional and not totally stupid, but in truth she couldn't tell what he was pointing at. But if he and Hardy saw seven puppies, they must be there.

When they were finished, the men set Bella back on her mat and praised her for being such a good dog and fine mother-to-be. "Great, just great!" enthused Hardy, "and everyone wants one. I'll bet Marion would want a Bella baby. Remind me to call and ask her, Estelle."

Hardy suggested she let either him or Will answer the phone, since he didn't want her encountering drooling nutcases like the men who had called yesterday. But cars no longer cruised the building, so he felt it was safe to let her walk to the corner store for groceries at noon, as they were out of cheese and mayonnaise for their sandwiches.

When she got back, they made lunch and sat at the exam table, eating and discussing Bella's due date and Will's wedding. "Lois had picked that Saturday, the twenty-second, anyway, Dad, so it's all good. We're not sure where to have the ceremony. That's what she's working on now. Personally, I don't care where we do it as long as it gets done."

"Why don't we have it at my place, and you can say your vows on horseback. Old Harold Oates will do the service. You can wear cowboy clothes, and we'll invite your friends and have a big party. Suggest that to Lois and see what she says."

Hardy had meant it as a joke, but Will thought the idea was great. "That might really be fun. It would certainly be different. I'll bet Lois would like it. She likes things that are left of center."

"What do you think, Estelle?" asked Will. "What's the woman's point of view?" Estelle was not happy talking about another woman's wedding. She tried to be happy, but she wasn't, yet she did her best to conceal her discomfort. "I think you'd better make sure those horses will let you on their backs before you include them in your wedding party." She shrugged. "Otherwise, it sounds fun," she said, mustering a weak smile.

# CHAPTER TWENTY-EIGHT

Operation Banned Hunt was fast upon them, and Marion phoned Hardy to check on his supplies. "We're on for this week. We'll meet as planned," she told him, keeping her words intentionally vague in the remote chance someone had tapped their phone lines. You could never be too careful nowadays, what with the current administration's lax attitude toward personal privacy. They all had to watch what they said and did, especially when they targeted legal operations, for then they had the law to consider. Illegal operations, such as the current target, had no resource to fall back upon and no laws to back them up, so the perpetrators usually disappeared, thankful not to have been arrested.

"Congratulations on the puppy mill, Hardy," said Marion. "I especially enjoyed the write-up in the newspaper praising Estelle's heretofore unknown talent. The poor thing, she must have been mortified."

"She was, believe me. It took a twenty-eight-hundred-dollar silver-plated saddle to pull her out of her misery, but she's fully recovered now."

"How's Montrose, my beautiful mule, doing?"

"*My* Montrose is excellent, thank you. He's a wonderful ride, by the way, smooth and powerful, everything you'd want in a mule." He told her this to get her goat, for he hadn't yet tried to throw a saddle on Montrose and had been content just to admire the handsome beast. "I did want to tell you that my Bella is pregnant. We counted seven puppies, and we expect them on Christmas Day. I could let you have one of *those* if you're interested. The dad is another Border collie, a handsome stud, so they should be fine animals."

"Baby Bellas! I want one for sure, a female if possible. That will be a wonderful Christmas present, Hardy. Thanks for the news."

"You're on the books, then, and we'll see you soon, at your place."

"Over and out."

He and Estelle arranged their supplies, carefully packing the items they would use. The preloaded darts went in one section of his waterproof container, and the chemicals he could load himself and the empty darts went into another. It was important that both of them knew exactly where everything was in the event they got separated. They had the infamous blowpipe and the dart gun, and Estelle could use whichever fit the need. They zipped the case and set it on a shelf in the clinic, ready to load into the truck the following night. The strategic implementation of Operation Banned Hunt was underway.

Will knew nothing about the planned raid, and that's the way Hardy wanted it. That he'd brought Estelle into the Movement was stressful enough, for he did worry constantly that she might let something slip and jeopardize the group. It was simply that these missions meant so much to him, and he wasn't sure she grasped the depth of his commitment. He wasn't sure anyone could.

That evening, he and Estelle had a quiet dinner at her house. Hardy the cat ate with them off his own special plate. He sat primly on a high stool, craning his neck over the edge of the table to select morsels of shredded tuna fish. It was her routine to share her evening meal with the cat, and Hardy the doctor saw nothing strange in the behavior. He thought it lovely to have such a polite dinner companion available and waiting each evening.

"Marion wants one of Bella's puppies," he said. "She really wants Montrose, but of course that's out of the question. Let's saddle up the mule and the buckskin mare and see how it goes. I want to beat Will and Lois to the punch on this riding thing. Are you game?"

"Tonight? It's dark."

"We can find out if they'll take the saddles and ride around the front yard. Come on, be a sport."

"I think I've been a pretty good sport, so far, don't you?"

"Yes, you certainly have, so why stop now? Come on. Don't you want to use your saddle before someone else does?" He talked her into it, but they drove separate vehicles, because she wanted to get a good night's sleep.

The animals were at rest, their heads drooping and their eyes closed. The horses stood lopsided, hips locked into place. Montrose, who occupied one stall, snapped to attention when Hardy switched on the overhead light. He had risen to group leader immediately, the others respectfully deferring to his size and demeanor, and now he stood self-appointed sentry, turning his big head and watching as they stepped into the tack room and emerged with two bridles. "I'll try Montrose first, and then we'll do the mare." Estelle stood back out of the way, not knowing what to expect.

Hardy approached slowly, speaking softly, and when he stood at the mule's head, he stroked the animal's face with one hand and lifted the bridle with the other. He grasped Montrose's chin and pinched, forcing his mouth open, and slipped the bit over the big, lower teeth, raising the bridle, pulling the mule's long ears through the straps at the top. Montrose adjusted the metal in his mouth, moving the center roller with his tongue, and looked at Hardy as if to say, "Yeah, so what else you got?"

He led the mule to the tack room and wrapped the reins once around his wooden hitching post. Then he chose a saddle blanket and placed it high against the rounded withers. Montrose waited quietly as Hardy fetched his saddle, grabbed the horn, and heaved it onto the mule's broad back. The animal switched his weight from one foot to the other, stretched his head into the air, and stuck out his upper lip, showing off his big teeth again.

"You are a beauty, son," said Hardy, "and you're a good boy so far. Let's see how you like it when I tighten the cinch." He reached under the mule's stomach, grabbed the thick sisal band, and brought it forward, wrapping the saddle's latigo strap through the brass ring on the cinch. "Easy now." Hardy slowly pulled the strap, wrapping it through the brass cinch ring, pulling the cinch tighter and tighter around Montrose's belly. He completed his wrap, dropped the stirrup, and adjusted the fender forward. Montrose craned his neck around and whinnied, bobbing his head up and down as if approving of the man's handiwork.

"Okay, okay," said Hardy, "let's go." He led the mule to the barn door and handed the reins to Estelle, who stood watching in awe at the ease of the operation.

"He didn't bat an eyelash," she said. "I hope my mare is as cooperative."

Hardy retrieved the buckskin mare, repeating the process. It was obvious that she'd been ridden, but she didn't like the weight of the silver saddle. She laid flat her ears when he cinched it up, and kicked with her back legs as he led her to the door. "I think we should get you another saddle for everyday use, honey. This is just too heavy for her. She doesn't like it, and I don't know how you're going to lift it and throw it up there. It's pretty, but it's not practical."

"I love this horse more than any saddle, so if it's too heavy for her, I'll get a lighter one. She reminds me of Dusty, the horse I had when I was a kid."

"Let's ride 'em around the front yard and see how it goes."

He swung his leg into the stirrup and mounted the mule. Montrose danced sideways, bucked a little, kicking with his rear legs, and pranced about the circle. Estelle followed, her mare angry and barely tolerating the insult. She walked flatfooted and droopy, tossing her head in defiance.

"At least we know they're saddle broke," he called.

"Yeah, but Dusty's not a happy camper."

"You calling her Dusty?"

"Why not? She needs a name."

"Good enough."

They continued their circle ride, Hardy testing the extent of Montrose's skills. "Back," he yelled, pulling the reins gently, and Montrose stepped backward rapidly, one foot behind the other, his hooves ringing like a jackhammer on the hard ground. He spun in circles to the left, then to the right. He turned when Hardy shifted his weight in the saddle and sprang forward when the doctor tightened his knees. Overall, it was an excellent trial run. "For a mule, he's very well trained. Someone did a good job, and I can't believe nobody's claimed him. He must have come from another county."

"My little girl will do better when I get a lighter saddle. Now I feel stupid spending all that money. Do you think they'd take this expensive one back?"

He called over his shoulder, "Keep it, and we'll get another. Will or Lois can use it, and it is kind of pretty. It'll look good in the parade."

"If you're sure."

"I am."

They put the animals back in the barn. When Hardy slipped the silver saddle off the little buckskin mare, she was visibly relieved. They gave all the stock a handful of oats, locked them in for the night, and then Estelle went home to her own bed, wanting to be well rested for her upcoming darting duties.

# CHAPTER TWENTY-NINE

When Will stopped by the next morning, Hardy told him about their successful ride with the mare and the mule, but he warned his son to be cautious with the other two, as they hadn't tried them out yet. Will wasn't overly concerned, reminding his father, "Lois is a great horsewoman, so we shouldn't have any trouble."

Hardy had bigger fish to fry, for this was it, OBH day, and when Estelle met him at the clinic later that afternoon, they checked and rechecked their bag and loaded it in the truck. He left a little early, giving Will no further explanation other than, "I have to," and met Estelle at his house. They fed the animals, downed a tall scotch, and went on to Marion's. Bella occupied her usual place in the back seat. The atmosphere was tense, and they spoke little as he guided the truck over the bumpy country roads.

"I wish I'd had another drink," he said, at last, breaking the tension.

"Me too. Do you think Marion would give us one?"

"Probably, if we ask."

"Let's ask."

"Okay, you do it."

"No, you do it, you know her better than I do, and she wants Montrose and a Bella puppy, so how can she refuse you a scotch?"

"You're right; she practically *owes* me a scotch."

He parked his truck in a space between two very tall vans, wondering if, indeed, there was a giraffe in the herd. All the vehicles were trucks or vans capable of transporting many animals. As they pushed through the group milling about on the deck, they spotted Marion, who beckoned them inside. She dragged Hardy and Estelle into her kitchen and closed the door. "Here," she said, "one for the road." She poured three half-full glasses from a bottle of Johnny Walker Black and raised her glass in a toast, "To our continued success." They downed the liquor in several quick gulps. When Estelle placed her glass on the sink, she said, "How did you know?"

Marion smiled, her wrinkled face glowing from the warmth of the whiskey. "It's tradition, and it's always scotch for Hardy and me, and now you, Estelle. It's for good luck."

Hardy winked at her.

"So you always drink before a mission?"

"Yup. Just us, not the rest of them. Too many people. Besides, I know Hardy can handle his liquor, and the last thing we need is a bunch of drunks chasing after Thomson's gazelles and tigers. Okay, let's go brief everyone and get going. I think it's dark enough." Marion led the way out to the deck and called the group to order.

"All right, people, I'm riding with Dr. Johns and Estelle. We will lead you to our destination. It's on a dirt road, and there are no signs, so follow carefully. When we arrive, park behind the vehicle in front of you. After the guard has been demobilized, one of us will come get you, and then you can bring up your trucks and get to work. You have your maps showing which animals are kept where, and those of you working with the big cats will need Hardy, so stay close to him and make sure your flashlights are working. There's no moon tonight, which is helpful for the mission but not good if your batteries die. Okay, you're all well versed in your tasks, so good luck and let's roll!"

The air was cold. A curtain of black sky hung overhead as they wound around the paved country roads, a convoy of vans and trucks on a desperate mission to save the innocent. Hardy followed Marion's directions, and after thirty-five minutes they reached the turnoff, a narrow dirt path that looked like a private driveway. As instructed, all the vehicles turned off their headlights. He took the turn slowly because his vision was obscured by overhanging branches and the ever-present darkness. As his truck rocked in the well-worn ruts, he shuddered at the thought of how many vehicles might have gone before. Estelle glanced over her shoulder, trying to see how close the others were. Bella was excited, so Marion rode with her arm around the dog, holding tight as they hit the bumps. "It's just up ahead. I was out here once with our recon man, Tim. He pretended to be a customer and was scared to death he'd have to shoot something. He got out of it by throwing up in the guard shack. Told them he had the flu."

"He threw up?" asked Estelle.

"Yeah, nerves. All over the guard, too," laughed Marion. "Okay," she said, pressing her nose against the window, "pull over. This is the entrance. The guard shack is through that gate to the left."

Hardy parked the truck and they waited, giving the others time to catch up, and then they stepped into the darkness, Estelle carried the weapons, Marion talked softly to Bella, and Hardy brought the all-important bag of tricks.

"This way," whispered Marion, and they followed behind, creeping to a metal gate that she quickly unlocked with a key. Hardy had learned long ago not to ask how she accomplished what she did. Beyond the gate lay a path surrounded by scrubby brush, and in the distance was a small cabin. Light glowing from a window illuminated the figure of a man.

Estelle carried her blowpipe in one hand and the dart gun in the other. Both were loaded. Which one she used would depend on how the guard reacted. When they reached the side of the building and were squatting in the dark, she handed Hardy the gun and proceeded around the corner with the blowpipe, moving toward the door. Bella wanted to follow, but Hardy blocked her with a hand command.

Banging her fists on the door, Estelle began her act, yelling, "Help, I need a doctor. I've been in an accident," but the guard didn't answer. Suddenly the house became dark. She banged and pleaded, but no Good Samaritan came forth, so she rejoined Hardy and Marion at the side of the house. "Does he think we don't know he's in there? Turning off the lights makes him not home?"

"Plan B," said Hardy, handing Estelle his night-vision goggles and exchanging the blowpipe for the dart gun. "I'll break the glass and you shoot. If he's going to play it like this, we don't want to take any chances. Let him have it."

The window was half way down the side of the house, and they slid sideways, Marion ducking beneath the opening, flattening herself against the wall. Estelle figured she was just tall enough to lean over the edge and get off a good shot, using the sill to steady her aim.

"Ready?" asked Hardy.

"Ready," she said, drawing the gun up to eye level.

Hardy smashed a well-padded elbow into the single pane of glass. As it shattered, Estelle leaped into position. The goggles lit up the heat-releasing prey like a fluorescent popsicle. She fired once, a beautiful shot, hitting the target in his right shoulder. The dart easily pierced his thin tee shirt. They watched as he staggered around the room, bumping into the furniture and finally falling to his knees and then flat on his back.

"All right!" yelled Hardy. "Good work, Estelle. We'll leave him right there, and I'll alert the others."

The two women warriors waited in front of the shack, shivering with expectation, hearts pounding in their chests, and then slowly and magnificently the surrounding terrain began to glow, awash in light as the rescue vehicles rumbled forward, rolling over the chain link fence like tanks. They lined up to form a long row of headlights and searchlights that illuminated the vast area.

One by one the gates of the enclosures were opened, and the crews positioned their vehicles in the fields and began rounding up their animals. They used secured bales of hay as bumpers inside the trucks, and as soon as one vehicle was loaded, it rolled out of the way to make room for the next. Bella rounded up the antelopes, zebras, and buffaloes, barking and nipping at their feet until they obeyed and climbed their ramps to safety.

Hardy and the crew who were working with the big cats located them in several small cages behind the guard shack. The tigers, alarmed by the lights and the noise, were agitated and stalking restlessly. Hardy decided darting was the only safe way to move them, so Estelle went to work with the blowpipe. Once they were sedated, the men transferred the felines to their trucks and put them in the borrowed cages. Sadly, they were too late to save one of the lions. It was missing from the pride, and that left one cage empty on the long drive to Southern California and a new life.

Bella was taken aback by the size of the elephants, for she had never seen such animals. Thankfully, they were gentle creatures. Having been circus captives, they were used to people jabbing and prodding them, so this particular duo did not rebel but instead lumbered slowly up their ramp, capitulating to humans who were once again deciding their destiny.

Marion's worst fears were realized when Hardy discovered the gorillas. It was a tragic sight: two gorillas huddled together in a small enclosure, their arms around each other, shivering in fright. "How in the hell did these jokers get their hands on gorillas, for crissakes?" he yelled, shaken by the scene in front of him. The depth of man's cruelty hit him in the gut. "There but for a few hundred thousand years go all of us, and look at them!"

Marion had not mentioned gorillas to Hardy. She had not even been certain they were really here, and she knew it would anger him terribly if it turned out to be true. She had arranged for a new home, just in case, and now she put her arms around him and looked into his eyes. "We have a good home for them, Hardy. Their suffering will soon be over. Come on, now, let's get the job done." She nodded at Estelle, who stepped forward with the blowpipe and looked at the doctor.

"Is it all right?" she asked. "Do you want to do it?"

He shook his head and took her arm, leading her to a place nearest the cowering creatures. "Aim true and get it over with," he said stoically. She rested the pipe on the cage bar, took careful aim, and expelled the first dart. The gorilla winced and grabbed his mate, burrowing his head into her chest. As the chemicals took effect, Estelle shot again, hitting the second gorilla, who stared into Estelle's eyes for a long moment before her legs buckled and the two of them collapsed, locked in an embrace.

"Get them into the truck," yelled Hardy, "and be gentle. My God, be gentle!" He laid his arm across Estelle's shoulder, walking her away, hoping to find a place that was not lit up by their lights. He found a fallen log, and they sat, staring into the darkness.

"I'll never forget the look in her eyes," she said.

"You must never forget it," he said. "Never forgetting will make you better. It's all we have."

When all the gates had fallen and the fences lay buried in the dirt, Marion stood atop a tall truck in the glare of a spotlight and addressed the crews. "Mission accomplished!" she yelled. "Now drive with caution and deliver your precious cargos. We'll meet at the hacienda in one week for a celebration and debriefing. Congratulations on a fantastic job." A roar of victory swelled from the crowd, and she watched in pride as they climbed into their vehicles and slowly drove their loads out of the killing fields.

"No giraffe?" asked Hardy, a little disappointed.

"No giraffe, but I'll find one for you if you'll trade me Montrose."

"Get outta town," Hardy scoffed. "C'mon, let's us do that before Little Bo Peep wakes up and finds out he's lost a whole lot more than his sheep."

# CHAPTER THIRTY

There would be no announcement in the newspaper about this rout, for the killing field was an illegal operation at a secret location. Marion also wanted to keep a low profile for her organization. Rumors that such a place existed had circulated through the animal underground, but no one outside of the Movement was certain, and now there was no proof.

Although their victory was total, Hardy felt unfulfilled. He promised himself if he ever discovered the organizers, he'd kill them. For the gorillas. During the day following the mission, he became increasingly obsessed with thoughts of revenge. He finally called Marion and told her of his feelings.

"We don't know who the big honchos are," she told him, "just the lackeys who ran the day-to-day operation." Marion was worried by his confession and tried to console him. "The mission was a great success. The animals are safe. Why not let it go, Hardy, and be satisfied with the result?"

"You know they're going to do it again somewhere else, Marion. I can't forget those gorillas."

"Look, I'll ask around and try to dig up some information for you, okay? Relax, go for a ride on my mule." When he didn't counter with some cute remark, she became alarmed. "Listen, take it easy, big guy. I'll find out who's responsible. I promise."

He hung up and tried to focus on other things. If Marion promised, then it was just a matter of time. Estelle had slept late. She usually did sleep late after a completed assignment, and when she finally arrived at the clinic, she brought a picnic basket lunch for the three of them and Bella. She smiled and set her basket in the back. While Will was working on a client up front, she kissed Hardy's cheek and watched as he unloaded his bag of tricks, returning unused supplies to their places on the shelves.

"You okay?" she asked. "You look stressed."

"I'm bothered by whoever set up that operation in the first place. I want to get them and put them away before they can do it again somewhere else."

"I see," said Estelle, sensing the deep undercurrent of Hardy's despair. "How can we find out who they are?"

"Marion said she'd work on it, and that's pretty good, having her working on it. So I'll just wait to hear from her."

"Well, I'll help, whatever you do."

The bell tinkled and Will joined them. "Lunch? I'm starving. Whatta ya got in there?" They disinfected the exam table, spread out paper towels, and Estelle unloaded tomato and onion sandwiches, homemade macaroni salad, cheese quiche, cookies, milk, and dog biscuits.

"Quite a spread," said Will. "I wish Lois could cook as good as you. She doesn't have time, she says, and I feel guilty asking her. But guess what, she likes the idea of getting married on horseback! The only thing is, it's going to be cold this time of year if we do it outside."

"Well, we sure as hell can't do it *inside*," grunted the doctor. "The animals won't fit, and it'd be messy. Lois may not like to cook, but I'm not that into cleaning. I never thought she'd take me seriously," he grumbled.

"But she did, so now what?"

"I don't know," he said, annoyed and wanting to change the subject. "See if the horses will let you ride 'em first. Estelle, today's a good day to go pick out another saddle. How about it?"

"Good idea. I don't have anything planned for this afternoon." She laid a biscuit in Bella's mouth, and the dog carried it to her mat, set it down, and rolled onto her back, exposing her tummy.

"She's becoming noticeably pregnant," said Estelle.

"Yup," said Hardy, his mouth full of tomato and onions. "It won't be long now."

"You want to come with me to the saddle shop?"

"No, you go. Just don't go overboard this time, okay? Keep it simple. Tell Ellie to put the charges on my new account."

"Gotcha." She packed up the remains of the lunch, and Hardy carried the basket to her car.

"Will doesn't have an inkling about last night, does he?" she asked.

"Nope." And we can't talk about it in front of him, remember."

"Gotcha."

He watched her climb into her car and kissed her on the cheek. "Have fun shopping, honey. Come over later?"

"Of course. I'll bring my new saddle."

Hardy recapped the silver saddle situation to Will. "So use it on the big bay. I call him Jim, by the way, Big Jim, and the pinto is Lucky. So there's Montrose, Dusty, Lucky, Big Jim, and Flicker the goat." He hung his thumbs in his breast pockets and stuck out his chest: "My little herd."

Ellie was surprised to see Estelle back in the store so soon, but she quickly understood the problem with the heavy saddle. "I was wondering how you'd be able to handle it. I figured you'd have a man around for that."

"I do, but my mare, Dusty, says it's too heavy, so I have to get another one."

"That would be very humane of you," said Ellie, leading Estelle to the long row of saddles. "You know the drill," she grinned, her white teeth gleaming green under the fluorescent lights. "Call me if you need any help."

Estelle strolled the aisle of saddles, feeling the smooth leather seats beneath her hand, twisting the saddle strings in her fingers. She stopped at a rather plain one that was similar to Hardy's and had the same beautifully carved silver horse head on the top of the horn. She sat in it, and it fit; not too big, not too tight. It was just right. When she returned to the counter, Ellie was in the back room talking on the phone. Estelle couldn't help overhear, for she was talking loudly, as if the person on the other end was hard of hearing. At first she didn't pay attention, but suddenly a word grabbed her, "… gorillas, you'll never find another pair like that. How could this have happened?" Ellie's voice rose to a shrill crescendo, but it fell flat as soon as she realized Estelle was standing at the counter. "I have to go, I have a customer. I'll call you later."

Estelle felt the blood draining from her head, and Ellie noticed. "Are you feeling okay, Estelle? You look awfully pale. Do you need to sit?"

"I'm just overly tired. I was up late last night."

Ellie stared blankly. "So, you found one you like?"

"Yes, I'll show you. Dr. Johns said to put it on his account."

"Just like the one he bought for himself! How nice, you two will match. I'll write it up." Ellie finished the paperwork and loaded the saddle in Estelle's car. "Come again soon," she called, as Estelle slammed the car door.

"Thanks, I probably will."

Estelle, in a daze, drove her car on autopilot back to the clinic. Hardy was surprised to see her so soon and even more surprised when she grabbed his sleeve and pulled him outside where they could talk.

"Did you get another saddle?"

"I got a lot more than a saddle," she said, her voice quaking with emotion.

"Again? I told you to take it easy this time," he whined.

"No, no, not that. Listen to me! I was waiting at the counter, and Ellie was in the back talking to someone about gorillas. She said, 'you'll never find another pair like that,' and I practically fainted. There's only one place that's missing a pair of gorillas, Hardy. She's mixed up in the canned hunt game somehow."

Hardy listened, his mouth hanging open. "That pretty little thing?" He shook his head. "Are you sure that's what she said? You may have misunderstood."

His words made her furious. That he didn't credit her with enough brains to overhear the conversation of a 'pretty little thing' and get it right was insulting, especially a conversation as important as this one. "I don't care how pretty she is, that's what she said, and she's *not* little." Estelle stomped to her car, climbed back inside, slammed the door, and screeched away from the clinic, leaving him on the curb, his mouth still agape.

When her car turned the corner, Hardy stepped inside, went to the phone in the back room, and called Marion to tell her what Estelle had overheard.

"Trust no one," said Marion. "You know that better than I, Hardy. I'll check into it. It's a solid lead, at least, and more than I have going. Estelle's got a good head on her shoulders."

# CHAPTER THIRTY-ONE

Estelle swallowed her pride and pulled into Hardy's driveway. He saw her coming from the kitchen window and hurried to meet her, handing her his scotch on the rocks and apologizing for his behavior earlier in the day. "I was just taken aback by the mental picture it conjured. But I phoned Marion right after you left, and she snapped me back to my senses. *Trust no one*, that's our mantra, and there's no reason that young girl couldn't be involved. You did a wonderful job of overhearing, honey. Please forgive me, okay?" He kissed her cheek and put his arms around her waist, drawing her close.

Estelle was appeased, for he did seem properly chagrined. But she decided to exploit his remorse a bit longer, so she finished his scotch and handed him the empty glass. "May I have another? I think I've earned it."

He led her into the kitchen, refilled her glass, and fixed another for himself. She sat at the table watching as he stirred a pot on the stove. "I'm making beans and rice," he offered. "I didn't think you'd be by. Please don't ever stay mad at me, Estelle. I can't stand it."

She joined him at the stove, took the wooden spoon from his hand, and began stirring. "You sit. I'll stir for awhile."

He took a seat, carefully composing the words in his head. He wanted them to come out just right after his afternoon gaff. He cleared his throat. "So, in line with the big clue you uncovered today, I have an idea, and I want your opinion."

"That's flattering," she quipped, trying not to sound too pleased with herself. "Go ahead, run it by me."

"Okay, then, here it is." He sat on the edge of his chair and posed the premise eagerly. "What if you went in there, the tack shop, and casually mentioned that you wished you knew of a place your son could go to shoot a tiger, or a lion, or some other exotic animal. You tell her your son is nuts about hunting, and he wants a trophy for his wall." He considered his folded hands and continued, "I don't think you should bring me into the picture. I'm afraid I'd scare her away, given who I am and my reputation. If you can gain her confidence, maybe she'll take the bait, and we can find out who's running the show. Whatta ya think?"

"My son?"

"Your pretend son. You can call him whatever you want."

"Thank you. Does Marion know about this plan of yours?"

"No, because I just thought it up. Thing is, I don't see what harm we could do, even if nothing comes of it. All Ellie has to do is play dumb."

"That's true," she said, nodding her head and furrowing her brow. "If she doesn't want to clue me in, she won't. No harm, no foul. Good idea. I'll go back tomorrow and give it a shot. Now, I think your beans and rice are done, see?" She raised the spoon with a gummy glob attached. "It's sticking to the bottom."

"Do you want to eat with me?" he asked, timidly. "It's all I've got, that and some bread."

Unable to maintain her haughty shell a moment longer, she melted. "That's all I need, beans and bread and thou. I know it sounds corny, Hardy, but it's the truth."

They ate the meager meal and drank a bottle of wine. The food tasted better than anything he had ever eaten, he said, and she agreed. And although he suspected it was because they were together in spirit and body, he didn't tell her that. He was not ready yet, and she, a plainspoken girl, had already said it all.

The next day, Sunday, Estelle went home to change clothes and practice what to say to Ellie at the saddle shop. Hardy, meanwhile, went to his clinic and waited impatiently for her to stop by to rehearse in front of him, because he wanted to screen for any flaws in the delivery.

Will was dressed like a cowboy under his white doctor's smock. This was the day of his horseback riding date with Lois.

"Good for you, Son. You're going to look pretty, even if you don't stay in that saddle for long."

Will ignored the comment and said he was leaving at two.

"Have Lois call me from the hospital. I can come visit when I lock up here." Hardy chuckled, disappearing around the corner as the bell tinkled and Estelle walked in.

"He's in the back," said Will, "and he's full of it today."

"Today?" she sneered. "So what else is new. Hey," she noticed his boots, "today's the day you go riding, huh?"

"Yeah, and he's been giving me a bad time about my equestrian skills, or lack thereof."

"Don't pay any attention to what he says. Those horses are probably as tame as Dusty, the buckskin. You'll do fine, I'm sure." She patted him on the back and joined the doctor.

She wagged her finger in his face. "Don't be teasing Will. This is important to him. Shame on you, Hardy."

"Just kidding around. So, let's practice." He leaned against the wall and assumed a judgmental pose. "What are you going to say to the girl?"

"Okay." Estelle paced the length of the room, gathering herself, and then she stopped in front of Hardy and began talking. "Here's the story. My son, Daniel, that's what I'd have called him if I'd had a son, is coming for a visit, and he likes to hunt. He wants me to pay for a trip to Africa so he can kill big game, but I hem and haw and beat around the bush, and whine about how I wish they had those hunt places here like they have in Texas, blah, blah, blah. At this time, I'd be hoping she would say, 'oh we *do* have those places here,' and help me out."

"What if she asks why you don't just send Daniel to Texas?"

Estelle frowned, totally engrossed in the game. "Well, I haven't got the money to do that, see, I'm broke. You're the one spending all the money on saddles, and I'm too embarrassed to ask you for a loan."

"You know I'd loan you money, honey," he said, putting his arms around her shoulders. "Not to send Daniel on a killing spree, but anything else."

Estelle rolled her eyes at him. "We're getting off point, here, Hardy. Let's focus. So that's it, and besides, she or her friends aren't going to make any money if Daniel goes somewhere else to kill his lion."

"How are they going to make money if you're broke? There's a big hole there, Estelle."

"Yeah, you're right." She thought a moment, paced and turned to Hardy. "All right," she declared. "I've decided, for the right price, I *will* come to you. It's for my boy's sake, after all, and my boy means *everything* to me. Lord, forgive me for raising a kid who loves to shoot animals."

"Okay, okay, that's good. Just get her talking about who and where. That's all we need. She seems to like to talk."

Estelle left the clinic, determined to succeed in her deception and convinced she could wheedle information out of the young girl. Hardy was chafing at the bit, hoping she was as good as she thought she was.

The familiar smell of the leather and saddle soap was pleasant. It lent a unique atmosphere to the shop that Estelle was becoming fond of. She'd also discovered the smell in their tack room, just not on such a grand scale. Ellie was alone in the store again. It seemed there were never many customers, but the goods were expensive, so all they needed were the right customers, like Hardy Johns. She looked up, surprised to see Estelle again.

"Back again so soon? Another saddle? How many horses do you have out at that place?"

"No, no," giggled Estelle. "I only need a few little things. Thought I'd browse. I really love the atmosphere in here. I think it's the smell, all the leather."

"You feel free to browse to your heart's content," said Ellie, turning her gaze back to her *People* magazine.

Estelle cruised the aisles and inspected the merchandise, and then she chose several inexpensive items, laid them on the counter, and commenced her performance, opening with a huge sigh. "I just don't know what to do for him," she said shaking her head.

Ellie looked up from the magazine. "What's the matter, hon? Do for who?"

"My son, Daniel. He wants me to send him to Africa on safari, and I just don't have that kind of money. He wants to shoot big game, a lion or a tiger or something like that." She shook her head. "What's a mother to do? At least he's not asking me to buy him drugs. I suppose I ought to be thankful."

Ellie listened, a hint of a smile on her face, a knowing look in her eye. "How old is this boy of yours, Estelle?"

"Daniel's thirty-five," she responded, stealing her daughter's age.

"My," said Ellie, resting her elbows on the counter and her chin in her hands, "and he wants to shoot big game? How'd he get that bug?"

Estelle rolled her eyes again (she was becoming very proficient in the facial gesture) and crossed herself. "His father, rest his soul, was a big game hunter, and I guess he passed it on through his genes. I wish we had those hunt places here like they have in Texas. That would make things easy. I might be able to afford one of those."

Ellie's blue eyes narrowed, and she chewed on her lower lip, her thoughts almost visible. "Estelle, you've been a really good customer, and I might be able to help you out with this dilemma. Sometimes we can help our good customers with their special needs." She winked and nodded. "Can you wait right here while I make a phone call?"

"Why, of course."

"I'll be right back." Ellie grabbed her magazine and flitted around the corner. Estelle couldn't hear what was being said this time, but when the salesgirl returned, she had a big grin on her face.

"You're in luck, Estelle," she gushed, "and I'm so happy for you and Daniel! You see, my uncles, Hirim and Burt, have a little side operation in addition to their butcher shop over in Zelma. They receive all kinds of products for their special customers."

Her face lit up as she continued. "Hirim said he might be able to arrange for Daniel to shoot his very own lion! He's expecting to receive one in a day or two." Having delivered this information, Ellie paused, her face a mixture of caution and excitement as she awaited Estelle's reaction.

Estelle knew she was on the hook, and she responded with what she hoped was the proper amount of awe and graciousness. "How in the world does someone just receive a lion? That sounds too good to be true."

Now totally engaged and convinced Estelle was sincere, Ellie became engrossed in her sales pitch, explaining in detail how the covert activity functioned. "See, people raise exotic pets, and when they get too big and hard to handle and they can't keep them anymore, they bring them to Uncle Hirim and Uncle Burt. Somebody's got to kill the animals, right?" Ellie shrugged nonchalantly. "Can't just turn them loose. After all, this isn't Africa. So, it might as well be your son does the killing, and isn't that wonderful news?" Ellie placed her hand over her heart, radiating benevolence.

Estelle gushed, "It is! Wonderful! How can I ever thank you?"

"Nonsense, girl, your happiness is all the thanks I need." Ellie scribbled on a note pad, tore off the sheet, and handed it to Estelle. "All right, now, here's the address of the shop, and the phone number, so call, and one of the boys will tell you when to come by and how much it will cost—you know, all that. And I'm so happy this worked out."

"Daniel will be thrilled! He's a good-looking boy, Ellie. Perhaps I'll bring him in with me next time." Estelle winked and grinned, as though naughty thoughts were filling her head.

"That would be nice. I'd love to meet him," cooed the salesgirl.

Estelle left the shop, light headed and giddy, for she had almost believed the story herself. That Daniel, what a schmuck he turned out to be, just like his father.

# CHAPTER THIRTY-TWO

Estelle sat in the clinic relating her story, and Hardy was blown away by her prowess and courage under fire. "How you managed to get all this out of her I can't imagine. She must be really stupid."

"I beg your pardon, how about *me* being really smart, outwitting her, being a good actress? Although, I have to say, she is pretty ditzy. She fell for my act, and she trusts me, stupid girl. *Trust no one*, that's the mantra."

"All right," declared Hardy, his adrenaline level rapidly rising, "you have to call and arrange the details, then you and I will meet these butchers and fry their bacon. I'll let Marion know what we've discovered." He cleared his throat and corrected himself. "What *you've* discovered."

As they tidied up and got ready to leave, the phone rang and Estelle answered. Her face drained of color as she listened. "Hang on he's right here."

Lois was calling from the hospital. "Will got thrown and his arm's broken. They're sending him to radiology for a full body scan to check for internal injuries. It was the big bay, Jim. I should have ridden him, but Will insisted. The horse didn't like the silver saddle for some reason. Whoops, gotta go, they're taking him up. I'll call with any news." She slammed down the receiver.

"Wouldn't you know it," moaned Hardy. "It's probably all my fault, but I was just kidding around with him. Come on, we need to go to the hospital."

Rosemont Hospital was on the outskirts of town. It was just a mediocre clinic for minor injuries like broken bones and stitches. But serious cases were sent on to the Critical Care Center in Waterston. Heart attacks and the like were delivered by helicopter, a thirteen-minute trip, and every time a life flight whirred overhead, the citizens on the ground speculated about which of their neighbors was in trouble.

Hardy and Estelle hurried up the stairs, bypassing admitting, for they knew where radiology was. Lois paced the small waiting room. "How's he doing? Any update?" asked Hardy, hugging the worried girl. She wore jeans, now dirty from kneeling in the dirt, a western shirt, and cowboy boots.

"He's still in there." She pointed to a big door with a sign that said, "Radiology: No Admittance." "He was doing so well. We were riding along the creek, and when we turned away and headed up to the house, Jim took off, bucked a few times, twisting and turning like he wanted to get rid of whatever was on his back, and Will went flying, landing on his side. I think he hit a rock. I helped him up to the house, and we called 911. You know the rest."

"Where's the horse?"

"He hightailed it directly to the barn and started rubbing up against the stall, trying to kill that saddle. I felt sorry for him and took it off. He's a happy camper now, munchin' grass in the pasture."

Just then a nurse, Nora Belcher, according to her name tag, rolled a gurney through the double doors. She smiled. "He's fine, no further injuries, just the arm."

Will looked up at them, his eyes glassy and unable to focus, and warbled, "Hi, Dad, hi, Estelle. How's it going?"

"They gave him a shot of painkiller, and he's higher than a kite," whispered Lois.

Nurse Belcher pushed the gurney down the hall, and they followed to room 213, where she rolled Will onto a bed and tucked the sheets up around his chin. His injured arm was secured to his body with a tight sling. "The doctor will be in shortly to prepare a cast," said the nurse. "You can wait with him if you wish."

As they sat beside the bed, Lois talked softly into Will's ear, and Hardy fidgeted, uncomfortable with his guilt. "We might as well go on back to work," he told Estelle. "There's nothing we can do here, and he's out of it."

Lois agreed. "You go on along, and I'll call you if there's any change. It's going to be a long wait, I'm afraid."

"Yeah, we can come back when he's awake. I'm feeling real guilty about the way I teased him this morning. I even told him to call me from the hospital. It's almost like I caused this to happen," said Hardy.

"Nonsense. It's coincidence, nothing more," reassured Lois.

It was late when they opened the clinic doors again. There was no one waiting in the parking lot with an injured animal, so Hardy used the solitude to call Marion.

"We know who the organizers are, so there's no need for you to look any further." He told her the details of Estelle's one-act play that morning, and she was both shocked and bewildered.

"They run a butcher shop and sell this meat? The meat from the murdered exotic animals?"

"That's what it sounds like. We'll know more after we meet with them. Daniel has come down with the flu, so I'm going in his place. We'll need a home for the lion."

The line was quiet, unusual for Marion, and finally she said, "Good luck."

"I expected more from you. No warnings or admonitions?"

"Not this time, Hardy. Just be careful, cover your tracks, and nail the bastards."

That night they ate an early dinner together at his house, and when they were finished, Estelle called the number Ellie had written down. Hardy listened over her shoulder as the man on the other end, talking loudly, apologized for his deafness. They made the appointment for the next day, after he closed the shop. The animal would have been delivered by then, he said, and they'd have the facilities to themselves. Estelle told him that was perfect and that she and Daniel looked forward to the adventure. Hardy called Marion again to give her the time and place. She told him to call when the job was completed, and she would send her van to transport the lion. It was as Hardy preferred, all ducks neatly in a row.

They returned to the hospital at seven to find Will still groggy and his arm in a cast that ran from wrist to shoulder. Lois explained that the doctor said there were several compound fractures, so the whole arm had to be completely immobilized for at least eight weeks.

"Will this affect your wedding plans?" asked Estelle.

"We'll probably postpone. There's no reason we have to get married at Christmas time, and we want to go scuba diving in Aruba for our honeymoon. Will can't do that in this cast."

"For sure," said Estelle.

"So maybe we'll let Bella be the Christmas star. We won't detract from her big event."

"Yeah," said Hardy. "That would be nice. We can all concentrate on Bella's babies."

# CHAPTER THIRTY-THREE

It was the middle of November, Thanksgiving was sneaking up, and the weather was cold and clear. Will had come out of his drug-induced stupor, but the doctor wanted him to remain in the hospital one more day, and Lois concurred. She was in no hurry to take up nursing duties, for he would require intensive help until he got used to the cast, as he'd broken his right arm and he was right handed.

Hardy and Estelle opened the clinic the next morning, hoping it would not be a busy day. They were closing early, no matter what, to keep their appointment with the butcher in Zelma at five that evening. The atmosphere was electric, as always before a confrontation, and the time dragged by. A few patients dribbled in, and Estelle trotted off for sandwiches at the corner store.

This action was different. Hardy had no plan, and he wouldn't know what he was going to do until he was face to face with the enemy. He hoped they would both be there, a twofer. Estelle asked him how he was going to handle it, and he couldn't tell her.

"The only thing I know for sure is that the lion is going home to Marion."

She left it there.

They closed the shop at four thirty, loaded his bag of tricks in the truck, dropped Bella off at his place, and set out for Zelma, a few miles down the road. As he drove, a sublime peace overwhelmed him, and the realization that he was about to put and end to the deaf man's hearing problem bathed him with an inner warmth.

They found the shop easily. It sat in a field at the far end of town, lonely and isolated, a perfect spot for the butchers to ply their trade. A neon sign of a happy, frolicking pig hung over the door. They drove through an open gate and parked in the rear, as Hirim had instructed, and then stood by the truck, waiting for someone to greet them. The dirt field adjoining the shop was enclosed with a solid chain-link and wood fence. It was twelve feet tall, making it private enough to run animals and high enough so they couldn't escape. The top was strung with three lines of double razor wire slanted inward, which would be impossible to climb without inflicting serious injury. Spotlights were mounted to the uprights at fifty-foot intervals. It looked like a prison yard or a concentration camp. Hardy estimated the land area to be no more than an acre, so apparently they didn't want to make the hunt difficult. Brown stains clung to wide indentations in the dirt, and arrow shafts littered the dry grass that clumped here and there. No noisy gun? A real nightmare of goings-on in Zelma, 'The Town With Heart'.

The back door opened, and a big man stepped out. He wore overalls, a dirty white tee shirt, and a blood-stained apron open from the waist down. He was bald, probably in his sixties close to Hardy's age. His work boots were spattered with blood, old brown blood and new red blood. He grinned at them, his teeth the color of coffee and cigarette tar. He cupped a hand around his right ear and yelled, "I'm Hirim. You Estelle?" He nodded at Hardy. "This can't be young Daniel."

Hardy stepped up and grabbed Hirim's elbow, shouting in his ear. "Daniel's come down sick. I'm here to take his place. Can't let a good thing go to waste, no sir!"

Hirim considered the statement and nodded. "That's right," he grunted. "Good enough, we've still got a deal."

"Absolutely," shouted the doctor.

Estelle stood back, letting Hardy make the contact.

"Come on inside then, and let's get to it," said the butcher. The cement-block warehouse was cold and dark, illuminated only by one fluorescent fixture suspended from the lofty ceiling. A smaller door at the end of the big space opened, and another man emerged, a duplicate of the first, maybe a few years younger, more hair, less smile. He came forward and introduced himself. "How do, I'm Burt. You Daniel?"

"Daniel's come sick," said Hirim, explaining the substitution to his brother. "I don't see it matters whose money we take, right?"

Burt nodded. "Reckon not."

"Exactly how much money is this going to cost?" asked Estelle. "We never did get around to discussing price."

Hirim spoke first, preempting his brother. "This particular critter's a beaut. He's gonna run ya five hundred. If that's too steep, we got other folks want him, so it don't matter no way."

"No, that's fine," assured Hardy. "Where is the critter? I'd like to see what I'm getting for my money."

The brothers chortled. Phlegm rattled in their lungs and worked its way upward till they had to spit in unison or choke. Having spat, they wiped their dirty hands on their aprons. "Reckon we should give you a tour," said Burt. "You might end up reg'lar customers."

Burt opened the door to the room he'd been working in, releasing a rush of foul odors—blood, bleach, and wet sawdust—causing Estelle to gag. He motioned the guests to have a look. "This here's our butcher shop, where we sell over the counter to customers. It's closed now, after five, but we do a good business all day long. See, we provide specialty meats, things you can't purchase at most shops. We call it customizing." He winked at this brother and they chortled again. Estelle felt sick to her stomach.

"Come along," he said, leading them back into the warehouse. They followed him to a hallway with several doors. He opened the first, stepped aside, and grinned. "There you go. How's that look? He worth a bullet or two?" At the end of the long, narrow, windowless room, sat a medium-size male lion in a large, heavy steel cage. He looked at them curiously, his head cocked to one side, as if he were about to ask, "When will I be let out, please?" Hirim stepped forward, grabbed a metal pole off the cement floor, and jabbed it through the bars, poking at the animal. The confused beast moved away, cowering at the back of the enclosure. The man snorted with each thrust, an evil glint in his eye.

"Stop! That's enough! Leave some for me," yelled Hardy, grabbing the end of the pole.

Hirim dropped it on the ground and spat at the lion. "You'll get yours," he growled, taunting the terrified creature.

"Come on, let's get on with it," said Burt. "We'll get back to him soon enough."

They left the lion, and Burt opened the second door, a heavy double-insulated metal affair. "This here's our freezer," he said proudly. "This is where we store our special cuts for our special clientele."

Estelle gasped. Hardy maintained his composure, but she knew he was having a hard time controlling himself. Hanging on the meathooks were duplicates of the animals they had rescued. They still wore their skins: antelopes, buffaloes, zebras, bears, one lion, but thankfully no gorillas. Had there been gorillas, Estelle knew Hardy would have lost it. "We prepare them when the customer's ready, specialty cuts. We have a connection in Africa shippin' us bush meat. That's a hot item. Big markup on that stuff. Only thing is, they're running out of animals, so the prices have gone sky high. It's good and it's bad, but whatta ya gonna to do?" He shrugged and pushed the freezer door closed.

"So, that's our little operation. We can get you anything you want. You ought to get on our preferred client list," said Hirim, expelling another wad of phlegm.

"Yeah, we'll have to do that," said Hardy, struggling to hold it together.

"Okay, then. Now, how do you want to kill your lion, bow and arrow or rifle? You name it, we got it."

"Where do I do it?" asked the doctor.

"You do it right there, in the room. Won't make no noise. It's all insulated. Whole building's insulated. Can't hear nothing from outside."

"Not much sport in that," said Hardy, feigning disappointment. "I thought I'd get a chance to run him around outside. Looks like there's been a lot of blood let in that field of yours."

"Yeah, right, but not the cats. We let folks do the antelope and other stuff out there, but the cats are too dangerous. You got to shoot them in the cage. We had an operation where we let 'em loose, but someone stole all our stock. Happened just a few nights ago. Too bad you missed it," said Burt, shaking his head. "Yeah, lost a lot of nice meat to them guys. If I ever catch who did it, I'm gonna skin him alive, you got that right. He'll be hanging next to that grizzly, for sure. Maybe we can butcher his ass and pass it off for chicken breast." He stomped his foot and gurgled at the thought. Hirim slapped his brother on the back.

"Give me the rifle," growled Hardy, his eyes narrow slits, his breathing shallow and rapid. "That's what I want."

"One rifle coming up," said Hirim, unlocking a cabinet on the wall. "You got the money?"

Hardy handed him a wad of bills, and the butcher counted it. When he had satisfied himself, he handed over the gun.

Estelle slid backward, wanting to stay far from the action. The brothers led the way back toward the lion's den, and Burt stopped and asked, "You want us to butcher it? Or you taking it with you?"

"The lion's coming with me," declared Hardy, his voice so deep and sinister it scared Estelle.

Hirim moved to open the first door, and Hardy said, "Wrong door, it's the next one down."

"No, this is the lion's room," said Hirim, grinning. "Easy mistake."

He moved toward the door again, and Hardy raised the rifle to his shoulder and pointed it at the brothers. "I said next door down. Open it."

"But," Hirim looked at Burt and stammered, "but … that's the freezer."

"Right, open the freezer," commanded Hardy, his voice an echo, rumbling deep and urgent, a volcano ready to explode.

Hirim pulled the heavy door open, and Estelle stepped close to Hardy. He motioned with the gun, pointing it at the men. "Inside," he said. They looked at each other, their mouths hanging open, not understanding. "Inside," he said again, motioning with the gun. Burt started toward Hardy, but Hardy leveled the gun at his face.

"Look, mister, we ain't goin' in there," whined Burt, stopping short. "What's the matter with you? You come here to kill a lion or what?"

"Or what," said Hardy, his eyes aglow. "Now, you going in that freezer or am I going to have to shoot you up and drag your sorry asses in myself? If I do it, you're going on the hooks; if you do it, you can sit on the bench, it's your call."

Hirim lunged, and Hardy fired, hitting him in the shoulder. The shot slammed him backwards into the freezer and the arms of the grizzly. The man bellowed as he tried to regain his balance, but the swinging bear knocked him to the ground. Hardy thought it poetic that a block of frozen bear sought revenge.

Burt shivered and wrapped his arms around his body. "You're the ones, aren't you?" he stammered. "You stole our stock."

Hardy slammed the butt of the gun against the man's head, gouging out a deep chunk of flesh and propelling him into his brother. "You're damn right I'm the one, you rotten son of a bitch. And there's a lot more like me."

"And I'm the one," yelled Estelle, stepping out from behind Hardy. "You're both dead meat, and the lion's going free. We ought to let him eat you, but he looks too timid, and you'd probably give him food poisoning."

Burt grabbed the grizzly's hand and pulled himself to his feet. Hirim moaned, his blood congealing in pools on the cold cement.

Hardy smoldered as he stood blocking the door. He spoke slowly and deliberately, taking delight in each word. "I want you to know and think about what I'm going to do next. I'm going to close this door, and you're going to freeze to death. And I want you to think about that until your brains are numb and you can't think any longer. When they find your bodies, everyone will know what you've done, but you'll be dead, so you won't care. Now, time for those last thoughts."

Hardy began to push the door closed and Burt threw himself against it, but he wasn't strong enough to counter Hardy's rage. The door slammed shut, and Hardy laid the lever across the bars, locking it tight. The brothers had been right about one thing: the insulation was excellent, for they couldn't hear the men scream.

Estelle put her arms around him, hugging him, and he whispered in her ear, "I wish I could kill them again and again, Estelle. It's not enough."

"You were great, honey. It's all we can do."

"Not all. We need to find their client list. We can do a lot of damage with it.""Call Marion first. Let's get that poor lion out of this awful place."

Marion's van arrived quickly and Hardy sedated the lion for easy transfer. They wiped away their fingerprints using alcohol from his bag of tricks, donned thin surgical gloves, and searched the butcher shop drawers, finding lists, records, and all the paperwork they needed to bring a chilling indictment against the brothers' operation.

"How long does it take for a person to freeze in a room like that?" asked Estelle, as they drove away.

"Not long enough," he sighed.

# CHAPTER THIRTY-FOUR

When they arrived back at home base, it was eight thirty. Hardy called Marion to check on the lion's arrival. She said he was still a bit woozy but safe, and she had arranged for him to join the other felines down south, for they were one lion short anyway.

"And the brothers?" she asked.

"On ice," he said.

"You wiped everything clean?"

"We did."

"There was no other way," she said.

"They were human garbage. Now we need to handle the people on their list. We need to scare the hell out of them, expose them, ruin them," said Hardy.

"The members will take care of that. When will the subjects no longer be viable?" she asked.

"It's over now, too quick. By tomorrow they'll be popsicles."

"Good work. Let's stay way back and watch the show."

Bella sniffed their clothing, her hair bristling at the odors of blood and gunpowder, things that frightened her. Hardy and Estelle threw the clothes they'd worn in the washing machine and showered. Once dressed in bathrobes and warm socks, they made hot chocolate, and Hardy built a fire in the fireplace. They snuggled together, staring at the flickering flames, unable to expunge the filth they'd uncovered at the butcher shop from their minds. "Never forget," he said comforting her, "just put it in the proper place."

The following morning, Lois picked up Will from the hospital and then stopped by the clinic on the way to her house. He was on pain medication and a bit loopy, totally useless as a helper but fun to talk with. Hardy put him through the ringer, asking him questions.

"I tole you, Dad, is not right. My arm isss broke hard. I can hep you soon whem I fixed."

"Come on, honey," Lois coaxed. "We'd better go on home and get you to bed. You remember what the doctor told you about rest."

"Sees you, Dad, I loves you, Dad."

"Me too, Son."

Estelle stifled a giggle and folded towels, robbing Hardy of his favorite pastime. They had heard nothing yet, but Hardy knew someone must have found the men by now. There was nothing to do but wait. At noon, the phone rang, and Estelle answered. It was the sheriff, and he asked for Hardy. Estelle handed off the receiver as if it were a hot potato, and Hardy accepted, answering glibly, "Howdy, Sheriff. What's up?"

"We've got a real lulu over in Zelma, a double homicide, and I wondered if you ever had any run-ins with the deceased, as they seem to have been quite the animal collectors."

"Really? What have you got?"

"Coupla butchers found hanging out in their walk-in. Walked in, but couldn't walk out because someone barred the door. Looks like one of them has a gunshot wound in the shoulder, but it's full of ice. Anyway, these guys have a whole freezer full of exotic animals, some of them endangered species—zebras, antelopes, even grizzly bears—made me sick to my stomach. What the hell is this all about? Is there any truth about canned hunt clubs around here? What's the underground say? Tell me what you know, Hardy. I feel like I been caught with my pants down here."

Hardy wanted to tell Downey everything but knew he couldn't. Mitch was a decent person. He recognized there were often conflicts between what was morally right and what was legal, but he was sworn to uphold the law. Shooting people and locking them in freezers might be morally right, but it wasn't legal, and Hardy wasn't going to jail.

"Who found the guys?"

"Some kid making a delivery. Opened the freezer and there they were, staring at him with their frozen eyeballs. He's really freaked."

"I'll bet."

"So, you ever heard of them before? What they got in there isn't above board."

"I'll tell you what I know, Sheriff, because those guys were all the way bad. They ran a hunt club. Supplied their clients with all sorts of rare and endangered animals. Estelle overheard Ellie, the girl who has the saddle shop in town, talking on the phone about exotic animals, and we believe she's mixed up in it. The hunt club was recently shut down, but it sounds like what you found in the freezer, along with the killers, is the kill. Some pictures on the front page of the paper might shake up the right people, know what I'm saying?"

"You got any idea who would have killed them? Not that it sounds like a great loss."

"No, I don't, Mitch, but you know whose side I'm on, so it's all good in my book."

"I respect you, Hardy, and I want to warn you, keep way clear of this. This is nasty business."

"Not any more."

Sheriff Downey said nothing further and hung up the phone. If he had suspicions, he kept them to himself. Hardy Johns was the best man in the county, to his way of thinking.

Estelle had heard the conversation and she sat waiting for Hardy to share his thoughts.

"I shouldn't have taken you with me. It was too big."

"Nonsense, I can hold up my end."

"I know that, honey, it's the exposure that worries me. There'll be pictures in the paper tomorrow, and there's going to be an investigation. It's a high profile murder, a double one at that."

She waved her hand, dismissively. "We did the world a favor, getting rid of those vile specimens. They should be engraving our names on trophies, for heaven's sake."

"Sheriff said to stay wide of things, so that's exactly what we do. You heard what I told him. We say nothing more, we know nothing more."

"Ready for lunch?" she said.

"Yeah, let's make tomato and onion sandwiches. Those were great."

Hardy tended to the afternoon clients, and Estelle helped with the assistant duties, holding cats' legs so they couldn't scratch while he administered shots, weighing dogs on the big scale, cleaning cages, and doing laundry. She was becoming an indispensable part of the operation, especially with Will in sickbay. That night when they locked up, he offered to take her out to dinner, and she said that would be lovely, so they went directly to the Mexican restaurant, a fun treat. Bella slept on the backseat, having had her dinner at the clinic, but she devoured a half-eaten chimichanga they brought out with them, for her appetite had become insatiable with the pregnancy. They left Estelle's car at the clinic and drove to his house, their mood mellow and fatalistic, two against the world—three, including Bella.

# CHAPTER THIRTY-FIVE

He had no morning paper, so he topped off his crime spree by borrowing his neighbor's, fully intending to return it when he was finished reading about his other, more serious crime. Estelle sat drinking coffee as he laid the newspaper on the table in front of her. When she saw the article, she choked on a big gulp of the hot brew and had to spit it back up into her napkin.

"Good God," she exclaimed, "they didn't spare much, did they?"

The front page was a collage of photographs of the frozen animals hanging on their hooks, the butcher shop itself, the blood-stained yard, and close-ups of the razor wire fence and the grizzly's head. The headline read, "Monsters in Our Midst."

"A very good choice of words, I think," said Hardy. "Quite apropos."

They read the long article together, turning to page A9 for the complete details.

"An investigation is ongoing, it says." She looked at him for a response. He shrugged. "So? It's none of our concern. Let them investigate. Come on, let's go out for breakfast. I feel like celebrating some more." They went to Beulah's, *the* spot for good breakfasts in town, and while they waited for their order, Hardy offered to buy food for a Thanksgiving dinner if she would cook. She agreed, warning him that Lois and Will would probably expect to eat turkey, and they most certainly would want to be invited, if just to get out of their house.

"To each his own," he said, a benevolent position reserved for his family.

Lois had taken the week off to nurse Will, and, bored to extinction, she called the clinic periodically to chat with Estelle. "Of course we'll come," she said.

"How's the patient doing?" asked Estelle, for the umpteenth time.

"He's getting better, a little less pain as the days go by, but this is tougher than I'd ever imagined, because it's his right arm. I have to spoon-feed him. He tried to eat with his left hand and made such a mess, it was easier for me to help him. He's sleeping right now."

Exasperated by Lois's frequent calls and drained of any meaningful conversation, Estelle politely excused herself, saying Hardy needed help with a cat.

"Is there anyone else you'd like to include for Thanksgiving dinner?" she asked him.

"Let me think awhile on that," he said.

At three in the afternoon, Sheriff Downey phoned and asked if he could pay a visit. Hardy told him to come on by. Estelle was worried, and although she tried to hide it from him, she didn't do a very good job. "What do you think he wants?" she asked, folding a thick terry-cloth towel and placing it on the shelf.

"Honey, I have no idea. We'll just have to let him talk and find out. Don't volunteer anything. In fact, don't say a word except hello."

"Should I make a pot of coffee?"

"That would be nice, hospitable. The sheriff likes hospitable folks."

Downey arrived at three sharp, and as luck would have it, the clinic was empty of patients. They sat at the examination table, and Estelle brought two mugs of coffee. The sheriff was appreciative, for it had been terribly long day, he said, what with the investigation still going on at the butcher's place.

"Still at it, huh?" said Hardy, sipping his coffee.

"Yeah, it's pretty much routine. A lot of evidence to inventory and collect. We should be finished today."

"What do you do with the animal carcasses, Mitch?"

"For now, nothing. We got no better place to store them, so we're leaving them hanging there as evidence."

"Evidence against who? Who are you charging with the murder of those animals?"

"Not murder, Hardy. It's more a misdemeanor crime, and I know you think different, but murder's a charge reserved for people killing people, not people killing animals. I'm not sure how the DA's going to charge anybody we can shake outta the woodwork."

"Homicide? All those rare and endangered species? There must be a felony in there somewhere. Come on, Mitch. There's got to be more justice available for the innocent than that. The pictures the paper ran were great. They showed people what's going on right in the middle of their town."

Mitch Downey fiddled with his mug, pushed it around and moved it back, drank from it and set it back on the table. He looked at Hardy, smiled, his face cracking in a maze of creases and he said, "There's a room in that place, the warehouse, with a big cage. Ugly looking thing, and I'd hate to think what went down in there, 'cause forensics found blood residue everywhere, animal blood all over the bars. They're looking for fingerprints now, on whatever they can find, anything a person might have handled, a weapon, I don't know, just anything." He finished his coffee and stood. "Well, thanks for seeing me, Hardy. I just wanted to let you know how it's going."

When he left, Estelle was approaching hysteria. She darted around the room, pulling shades open and then closed, banging cabinet doors with her fist, then she unfolded the towels and folded them again. Finally she said, "What was all that talk about? What was he saying? I don't get the point of his visit. I don't get it at all."

Hardy had listened carefully, trying to understand the meaning behind the sheriff's words. Now he became thoughtful. "I think he was trying to warn us, Estelle. I took the rifle. It's been disposed of. What else did we use? Is there something we might have touched and not wiped properly? Can you think of anything?"

She could not, and she retraced their movements, recounting everything as it had happened. "What did you touch, Hardy? All I can think of is the gun and the freezer door. We wore gloves when we went through the paperwork."

"He talked a lot about the cage with the lion. Why was he making such a big thing about that room? Blood all over the cage, the bars, *the bar!*" Hardy's face turned pale. "That bar, that pole Hirim was jabbing at the lion—did we wipe it down?"

"The pole? I don't remember a pole," she gasped. "I don't remember seeing a pole, Hardy."

His memories played rapidly now. "I grabbed the end and told him to stop. He dropped it on the ground. I didn't wipe it off. I didn't see it again. It must have rolled under the cage. It'll have my prints all over the end."

Estelle pressed her hands to her mouth and whimpered. Tears filled her eyes and began to roll down her cheeks. "What can we do?" she asked, her voice quivering.

"Nothing," he said solemnly. "There's nothing we can do if they have the pole except wait until they run the prints and match them with mine. They'll find mine easily enough because of my profession, and I have to think the sheriff would look at me first. Mitch is no dummy. He probably already suspects I had something to do with the murders."

"Maybe if we invite him to Thanksgiving dinner, Hardy. Would that help?" she sniffed.

Hardy had to laugh. "Beat a murder rap with a Thanksgiving dinner invite? Sure, why not, invite Mitch, maybe we can squeeze in a dinner before I go to jail. He's not married, so he'll probably come, unless he's got some reservation about dining with suspects."

The mood at the clinic was somber and strained. Hardy went about his usual business, tending to patients, and Estelle assisted. At night they went home, fed the animals, ate dinner, went to bed, and waited for a knock on the door or a phone call from the sheriff, advising him he was under arrest. Will was off his pain meds, of his own volition, and Lois was planning to return to work as soon as the holiday was over.

Sheriff Downey accepted Estelle's invitation to share the Thanksgiving meal, so when the day arrived, she and Lois cooked and set the table, while she and Hardy wondered in secret if he would be leaving in handcuffs after dessert.

Not knowing what the sheriff knew put a damper on things, but they tried to act as if nothing were amiss. Hardy built a nice fire in the fireplace. The smell of turkey and pie filled the house, and drinks a plenty mellowed everyone's mood. Willa's old piano sat against a wall in the living room, an upright, and Estelle decided she would entertain. Although she hadn't played in years, she had been a good pianist at one time, she said. She sat thumbing through the sheet music until she found something she recognized and began to play. Hearing music in the house again brought tears to Hardy's eyes—that and the scotch, and the belief that he was going to jail when dinner was over. It all came back to her, and she played and they sang those songs they knew. It was a heartwarming gathering.

The sheriff proposed a toast: "To fine folks and good food, and many more happy years for us all," and then he carved the turkey, at Hardy's behest.

Estelle's ears tingled, and Hardy smiled, hope swelling his heart for the first time in a week. Lois steered Will's left hand toward his mouth, and he practiced with his right, now that he could hold a fork with it, so he managed to pack in enough food to become pleasantly full. Being a good vegetarian, Hardy ate around the turkey and filled himself instead with vegetables and cornbread dressing. After the pie, coffee, and a snifter of brandy, Sheriff Downey thanked everyone for including him in the lovely holiday and asked Hardy to walk him to his truck. Hardy sighed, looked wistfully at Estelle, and said, "Can Bella come along?"

"Of course, she can," answered the sheriff, puzzled by Hardy's need to ask such a question about his own dog at his own house.

They stood by the sheriff's truck, and the lawman said, "I got something for you. You do what you want with it." He reached into the bed, pulled up the iron pole, and handed it to Hardy. "I'd a tied a bow around it, but I was running late for dinner."

Hardy took the gift in his hands, the cold steel flooding his brain with memories. Never forget.

"Thanks, Mitch, you're the best man I know."

"That's what I tell everybody about you," said the sheriff.

# Chapter Thirty-Six

Hardy told Marion of his brush with fate and the sheriff's benevolent gesture.

"So you see, he's on our side, Marion, as much as he can be without losing his job. I still think he ought to run for president."

"Where's the pole now?"

"I dropped it in your pond."

"Like hell you did," she yelled.

"I used it in the barn, to hold up a post."

"The members are scaring hunt club people out of their skins, major pun intended, threatening them with exposure. These deviates paid a lot of money for the privilege of killing their animals. Maybe we should turn over the names to the sheriff, anonymously of course, and let him deal with them. Whatta you think?"

"Give Mitch his Christmas present early. Help him tie the man to the carcass, because there's a lot steeper penalty for an endangered animal, and he's still holding them in the freezer."

"Good. That'll free up our people for other things."

Now that the rains had begun in earnest, the creek at the rear of Hardy's property widened and rose, filling in the niches carved over the years, allowing him to predict with some accuracy the probable severity of the season. This year, if he was reading the rocks correctly, the rains were ahead of themselves, for the higher niches were already awash with the clear, cold, fast-running water. He enjoyed the noise it made, but Estelle likened it to a freight train, and it wore on her nerves, beautiful yet violent. She now spent most of her nights with Hardy, so she closed the windows when they went to bed, shutting out the distant roar. The animals waited out the stormy days under the cover of their barn, venturing to the pasture when the rain stopped to run and kick and graze on what little green grass remained. Will was also back to work. He couldn't do much, but he could drive his car and manage to give a shot with his right hand.

At four on this early December afternoon, all was quiet at the clinic, so Hardy and Estelle left an hour early to go riding. She hadn't yet tried out the new, lighter-weight saddle, and there was a nice break in the weather. Bella was excited as they saddled up Montrose and Dusty, knowing she was in for a romp. The crisp air invigorated her, helping to counteract the listlessness she felt from her pregnancy. Estelle easily set the new saddle onto Dusty's back, and the mare didn't flinch or kick out in displeasure as she had with the heavier one. The other animals were enjoying the pasture as Hardy and Estelle mounted their rides and headed out of the barn. Bella trotted alongside Montrose, keeping pace with the mule's long strides. They decided to follow the perimeter of the fences, turning at the creek and riding along its banks to the opposite fence and back up around the house to the barn, a big rectangle.

They walked, content with the leisurely gait, not wanting to push Bella into anything too strenuous, for they knew she would follow blindly, whatever they did. The long grasses in the meadow hit her at shoulder height, and she delighted in tearing off mouthfuls as she ploughed along beside them. Hardy smiled, a look of contentment on his face as he rocked back and forth in tune with Montrose, his hands resting on the horn, the reins flapping loose, the wind lifting his gray hair in soft gusts.

"What could be better than this?" he asked.

"It's perfect," she agreed.

They reached the end of his fence at the creek and then headed up a rocky ridge to a well-worn deer trail that followed along the water's edge. The noise of the water rushing over the rocky creek bottom was loud, and Bella crept forward, climbing down to a small niche where she could drink. The mule shied sideways, uncomfortable with the sound, but Dusty stepped forward, tossing her head, craning her neck, pushing toward the water. Estelle loosened the reins so she could drink. The horse bent her knees, sinking her muzzle deep and letting the cold water rush around her nostrils.

They continued to follow the trail along the bank, and as they cleared a small rise and started down, they heard a terrible bleating over the sound of the rushing water. Bella and Dusty stopped abruptly, their ears pricked forward, and the mule danced nervously, snorting and clicking the bit in his mouth, working up a foam  that spilled down his chin.

Estelle saw him first. She jumped off her horse and ran toward the water. "I'm coming!" she screamed. Flicker was marooned in the creek, his foot jammed beneath a rock. He was fighting to keep his head above the surface as the pull of the torrent dragged him under. Montrose carried Hardy away, frightened by the bleating sound, and Hardy had to rein him back as Estelle plunged into the icy cold water, struggling to move against the current. Bella followed blindly, plunging in from upstream, and the water slammed her against Estelle, almost knocking the woman over, but she managed to remain upright and hold onto the dog. But she was unable to move forward.

Hardy jumped from the mule, loosened his rope, tied one end around Montrose's neck and the other around his waist, and fell into the water, straining against the current to reach them. He pushed forward, yelling for her to hang on. Estelle clung to the dog, fighting to stand. When Hardy reached them, he grabbed Bella around her swollen middle, freeing Estelle to grab his rope.

"Back," he yelled at the mule, "back, Montrose." The mule gathered himself, craning his neck, and backed away, tightening the slack between himself and his people. Estelle pulled herself along, hand over hand, and Hardy followed behind, one arm around Bella, the other on the rope. When they reached the bank, Hardy handed Bella off to Estelle, who gripped her tightly.

"Don't let her follow me," he yelled, plunging back into the creek, this time after the goat. The mule held fast, keeping the rope taught. And as Hardy needed more slack, Montrose stepped forward. Hardy reached the stranded Flicker and pushed his weight against the animal's body, struggling to hold him upright as he felt beneath the surface. When he shoved the boulder aside with his foot, the goat bellowed. Hardy held fast as the current fought to snatch him away. He slung the slack around the goat's middle and then, pushing his head above water, yelled for Montrose to back away. Estelle yelled too, gripping Bella, who fought to join Hardy and Flicker. Montrose backed up like a champion, pulling the man and the goat out of the torrent.

Bella finally twisted free of Estelle and bounded to the two friends, licking them and rubbing against them. Gulping great, deep breaths, Hardy collapsed on the bank with the goat in his arms, and Montrose snorted, lifted his head high, and curled his upper lip, showing off his big teeth.

When Hardy's breath returned, he checked the goat's leg. It was bruised and skinned but not broken. The little animal, wobbly, scared, and cold, was not willing to move, so Hardy remained with Bella and Flicker while Estelle led Montrose back to the barn and returned with the truck. They loaded the goat and Bella in the flat bed, and Hardy sat with them as Estelle drove slowly over the field to the barn.

"He's cold," said Hardy, as he watched the shivering goat and tossed hay to the other animals. "I'm worried about his temperature."

"Let's bring him inside and light a fire in the fireplace. The house will warm him up."

"You know what happened the last time I had him in the house."

"But this time he's not up to high jinx, Hardy. He almost died."

Knowing she was right, he relented and carried the goat into the house. Estelle made a thick pad of towels and blankets in front of the fireplace. Hardy changed into dry clothes and built a fire, and the little goat sat in the warmth, eyes closed and head nodding. Bella ate her dinner alongside her friend, and Hardy and Estelle heated up a can of stew, his pantry stand-by.

The animals lay side by side, and Hardy and Estelle sat together on the sofa, drinking coffee and watching the two friends who had bonded immediately from the beginning.

"He would have died today if we hadn't left an hour early and gone for our ride," said Estelle, staring into the fire.

"We all could have died today, Estelle—Bella, you, me. You did a brave thing, jumping into the water like that. I was dumbstruck, and you were already in action." He put his arm around her and pulled her close. The fire danced, illuminating their faces, and she melted into him, serene and content, wanting only that this moment would last forever.

"I need you in my life, Estelle, always. Will you become my wife?"

Tears welled in her eyes, and she nodded. "Yes, Hardy Johns, I will."

# CHAPTER THIRTY-SEVEN

"If ever two people belonged together, it's you and Hardy," Lois proclaimed when Estelle, finally having something newsworthy, called her the next morning. "My God, how scary that sounds. The creek, I mean, not the getting married. You might have been washed away."

"I didn't even stop to think. I just went into the water," said Estelle, wondering herself why she had done what she had. "It's strange how our minds are programmed."

Hardy wanted to check Bella with another ultra sound, just to make sure things were all right after the "big swim," as he now called their narrow escape. The babies looked viable and everything was as it should be, so once again he relaxed, comfortable with the health of his little family. Flicker had slept by the fire all night, making only one mess when Hardy didn't open the door fast enough in the morning. And he was hungry, which was always a good sign. Hardy had fed him alfalfa pellets and a ration of oats, letting him eat as much as he wanted, and then released him back to the open pasture.

He reminisced at the clinic, telling Will, "You know, Montrose was the real hero, pulling us out like he did, backing when we yelled at him. He's some mule, all right. Wait until I tell Marion how he saved our lives."

"You're just teasing her," said Will, as he stuck a tongue depressor up inside his cast, trying to scratch an itch. "You know she covets him."

"Of course, that's why I do it."

Will was not surprised by the revelation of his father's marriage plans. He said he'd seen it coming.

"That so," said Hardy. "Why didn't you tell me, then? We could get married together, all of us. How about that?"

Will took it with a grain of salt. "I'll mention the idea to Lois."

That night they turned in a little early. Estelle tossed in the bed beside him, rising at three to use the bathroom. She couldn't fall back to sleep, her mind replaying the harrowing events of the big swim, and at four thirty she had to use the bathroom again. She fell asleep sometime after that, awaking in a cold sweat at seven with an image in her head, a dream she remembered from somewhere, but now it was vivid—and terrifying. She yelled to Hardy, and he sat up, half-awake himself.

"What's the matter? What is it?" he asked.

She grabbed the sleeve of his pajama top. "It's a dog, and they've buried him, but he's not dead, and he comes up out of the ground, out of his grave. Hardy! The dirt moves and rises in big clumps, and he comes up and shakes himself off, and it's terrible. I can see his eyes, and he's so sad. He shakes the dirt off his body. He's a big brown and white dog with sagging jowls, and he looks at me with big brown eyes, and he wants to know why they buried him. And we keep saying, is he dead? No, he's alive. And we look at the hole where they buried him, and it's empty, and he staggers around, drool running down his chin, but he's not dead, and they've buried him! Oh, God, what does it mean?" She covered her face with her hands and began to cry as he held her in his arms.

"Nobody knows what dreams mean, honey. They can be unnerving, but usually we forget them."

"But I remember this one now. I've had it before." Her body shook, and he held her tighter.

"It's just a dream, Estelle. It will pass." He dabbed her cheek with the blanket and climbed out of bed. "I'll start the coffee."

She calmed herself and put on her bathrobe, but the dream didn't pass. It remained in her consciousness, a terrifying specter.

They arrived at the clinic ahead of Will, greeting several patients who were waiting in the parking lot. Estelle went directly to the back room and began to arrange the laundry, moving the folded towels from one shelf to another, separating blankets from sheets, washing things that weren't dirty. No matter what she did, the dream wouldn't go away. The big brown and white dog followed her around the room, his eyes pleading, wanting to know why. She heard the clients talking in the other room and thanking the doctor, then Will came in and hung his jacket in the corner. She helped him pull the lab coat on over his cast. "Takes me longer to dress with this thing," he said, apologizing for being late.

"Yes, of course," she said, absentmindedly.

At noon, she went to the corner store for lunch things, and they made sandwiches and sat at the examination table, eating and talking about

Bella and what they should name the pups. She heard them but couldn't concentrate—she was distracted by the sad dog's eyes.

After lunch, she returned to the back room, fussing with the cages, wiping the stainless steel, and wiping it again, anything to keep her mind busy and drive the dream further away. But now she saw the dog reflected in the window glass, and she covered her eyes and stood facing the wall, afraid to look. She heard the bell in the other room and voices as people entered. Will and Hardy were talking, and she heard the click of a dog's nails on the examination table. They were old people, a man and a woman. Their voices cracked as they talked. They wanted the dog put down. He was sick, they said, and they couldn't take care of him any longer. Hardy protested, telling them the dog was old, not sick, and old age was no reason to end a life. Will remained silent. Being old themselves, Estelle thought they would understand what Hardy was telling them, but they didn't. They insisted the dog be "put out of his misery," although the doctor told them he wasn't in any misery. Hardy never killed healthy animals to accommodate bored or lazy owners, but he knew there was a vet close by who would do it without thinking twice, so he always tried to change people's minds.

As if someone had pushed her from behind, Estelle stumbled through the doorway into the room. When she saw the dog on the table, she gasped, for it was the dog from her dream. His shaggy brown and white coat was caked with dirt, and his big, sad, droopy brown eyes stared at her, just as they had all day. The old couple stepped aside as she walked directly to the table and wrapped her arms around the dog's neck, drool running down her arm. The dog reacted, licking her face and butting his head against her shoulder, as if they were old friends.

"It's him," she whispered to Hardy, "it's the dog from my dream. He doesn't want to die."

The old couple stepped back, startled by the sudden display of affection between the two. And the woman said, "You want him, honey, you can have him. He seems to like you a lot. Don't seem so miserable."

"Yes, we want him," said Estelle, her arms around the dog's neck. "Is it okay, Hardy?"

"It's okay," he declared with finality. "What's the dog's name?"

"Buford," said the old man. "Named him after my uncle Buford Tilsdale, a miserable man, turned out. Reckon you'll give him a good home then?"

"We certainly will," said Hardy, escorting the old folks to his door.

Hardy set the big dog on the ground. "He's a St. Bernard, Estelle, and he's in dire need of a bath. You want to clean him up so we can take him in the house?"

"I will. How old do you think he is?"

"Seven or eight. Still got some good years. This is the dog from your dream?"

"Yes, don't you see? It was a premonition. We were meant to save Buford's life, and we did!" She grabbed Hardy and hugged him. "Oh, I love you so much."

"I find this very spooky, my dear. I don't know what else to say. You described him to a tee."

Will listened, taking in the facts, adding that he believed in such paranormal phenomena. "Someone wanted you to have this dog, Estelle, to save his life." He hugged her. "It's a miracle."

She bathed Buford and blow dried his long silky hair, and he swiped his big tongue over her cheek. She clipped his nails, cleaned his ears, wiped his droopy eyes, and gave him a brand new collar, his old one being worn and grungy. When it was time to go home, he looked like a new dog, and he smelled of strawberry shampoo.

"I hope Bella will tolerate Buford," said Hardy. "She's a little cranky lately, what with her condition."

"How could she not fall in love with this guy, Hardy? Look how he cleaned up. This better mean I won't have that terrible dream again. I've done what I was supposed to do."

"You should find out soon enough, according to my son." He shook his head. "Will never talked about this kind of thing with me. Takes a woman to bring out the sensitive side of a man."

They brought Buford in the house on a leash, not knowing what to expect from Bella. She had remained at home. Her time was drawing near, and the nesting instinct had kicked in, so they had provided her a bedroom to herself with a large cardboard box that once held a refrigerator. She loved it, snuggling against the back in the towels Estelle had arranged. Now the sweet-smelling Buford arrived, wagging his big tail, drooling his long strands of silver drool, and sniffing eagerly at Bella's box. She snarled at him, warning him away.

"That's what I was afraid of," said Hardy. "We'll just let them alone, and he'll get the hang of things. Bella's territorial and probably jealous. Her hormones are all goofed up, but I don't think she'll kill him."

"Kill him! Bella?"

"Don't underestimate the female of the species, Estelle. I have, in times past, and it's a big mistake."

# CHAPTER THIRTY-EIGHT

Buford quickly realized that Bella didn't want him anywhere near her box. He was such a loving, sweet animal, Bella's rejection made Estelle feel guilty, so she lavished attention on him, for she knew she was responsible for the big dog's life, and she definitely did not want the dream to return.

"After the pups are born, she'll mellow out," said Hardy, "then she'll be happy to have the company, you watch."

They had chosen to celebrate Christmas at Hardy's. Estelle found a live tree in a lot downtown, which Hardy bought and lugged into a corner of the living room. He and Estelle strung it with tiny lights and hung gold ornaments on the branches. They shopped for presents, wrapped them, and set them beneath the tree. It felt like Christmas was supposed to feel. They had all decided on ham for the Christmas dinner, all except Hardy, that is, who stuck to his principles, so Estelle planned to make cheese lasagna for him. Now, as the days counted down, Bella stayed in the box for longer periods of time. They didn't bring her to the clinic, for climbing in and out of the truck was a chore. Hardy revised his date for the birth, changing it to the twenty-second, and that was a relief, as nobody wanted to deliver puppies on Christmas Day. He had kept Mr. Hollis informed of the progression of Bella's pregnancy. The man called often to check up and to reiterate that he did indeed want the pick of the litter for Buster's services, as agreed.

Lois took a week off, and Will's cast was due to be removed the week after the holiday, so plans for their wedding and honeymoon were back on the burner, simmering. Hardy and Estelle didn't talk much about getting married. Just knowing they had made the commitment seemed enough for the time being. As she did every year, Lois made pinoche, a brown sugar candy, very sweet and creamy. She wrapped each piece in red cellophane and presented Estelle and Hardy with a platter full. It was her mother's recipe and a family favorite, she said. The weather was cold and blustery, so Hardy brewed hot toddies every night, and they sat together on the sofa and counted their blessings. Hardy could feel himself becoming soft.

He and Estelle went to Marion's Christmas party and shared their plan to wed with the members of the Movement. Having people he cared about to celebrate with was meaningful, and the group toasted the couple and wished them well. He appreciated the members, because they shared a common goal, but on a good day, he could barely tolerate most of his clients anymore. His patience was growing short as his years grew long, and he began to think he should turn over the clinic to Will before he said the wrong thing to someone, got himself sued, and ruined the business for his son.

When he sat by the fire, with Estelle beside him, a hot toddy warming his innards, the dogs at his feet, and the cats scattered around, he was more than content. But several names remained on his list, and he wanted to wipe the slate clean before he hung things up.

He was dead-on with his date. On the morning of the twenty-second, Bella curled in the back of her box and went into labor. Hardy and Estelle stayed home, Estelle sitting in the box with her, offering encouragement. It was over quickly. The seven babies slid out one after the other, and Bella licked each of them clean, tearing off the membrane, and eating the afterbirth. The little ones nosed about like blind moles seeking her teats, and she sprawled on her side, nudging them into place with her snout. Hardy prepared a post-delivery ritual, a sloppy meal of milk and bread and shredded chicken, and she lapped it up on her way back from a hasty trip to the yard.

Buford stuck his big head into the open doorway, but Bella growled and bared her teeth, warning him to stay away. Estelle made him a sloppy bowl too, and watched as he lapped it up, his big, pink tongue slurping the soggy bread all over the kitchen floor. She moved the bowl and he cleaned it up, eagerly devouring every scrap.

"Who are you, Buford?" she asked, earnestly, kneeling and taking his huge head between her hands. She was convinced the dog and the dream were more than paranormal coincidence. Her suspicion was that he might be her dead husband, Bernie, reincarnated. Hardy thought she was heading toward the deep end and told her so, not wanting to tarnish the St. Bernard's appeal by giving him a human identity, even if that human was dead.

"If you want to keep Buford in the bedroom with us at night, you'd better curtail that line of thought, Estelle. I have enough hang-ups without having Bernie watching us. Let's go on the assumption that Buford's just a dog."

Will and Lois came by to deliver presents on Christmas Eve. It was icy cold outside, so Hardy had a big fire going in the fireplace. They visited, drinking toddies and ogling the puppies. Bella seemed to enjoy the attention her youngsters were attracting. She didn't stay long out of the box. She only made short trips to the yard to do her duty, and they fed her in the bedroom to minimize her stress. Estelle had prepared a blanket along one wall, but for now, cozy was best. Lois sat in the mouth of the box, running her fingers over the sleek puppy fur, talking baby talk, and drinking her toddy. Will watched from the doorway, a glow on his face. Thoughts of their future ran through his head. They had decided to drive back to Las Vegas for New Year's Eve and get married.

"Yeah," he told Hardy and Estelle, "the cornier the better. We like that kind of kitsch. We might even Elvis it up a bit, and you're invited, if you want to come. I know it's a long drive, so don't feel you have to. We'll understand if you don't. One of us should probably be around the clinic, for emergencies anyway."

Hardy was not fond of long drives, and neither was Estelle, so he said they'd think about it. Will already knew what their decision would be, and it really didn't matter. He just wanted to get married. He was tired of talking about it, tired of waiting. He was in a hurry to have the cast removed too, and he wanted to skin dive nude in Aruba. The new year was full of promise.

They left late and said they'd be over in the morning to open presents.

"That was nice," said Estelle, as she poked the fire. "I don't want to drive to Las Vegas, but it's up to you."

"Nah, Will's okay with it, and someone should be on call. I usually always have an emergency on New Year's Eve. It's tradition."

"Really?" she said, wondering if he was pulling her leg.

"Yup."

They went to bed, with Buford snoring and drooling on the rug on her side and the cats curling up wherever they found a spot between and around the human forms. When Estelle woke at three, she stepped over the dog and tiptoed to the hall bathroom. On her way back to bed, she looked in on Bella, who was lying on her back with her pups cuddled against her. She slipped silently across the hall to the bedroom, stepped over the snoring Buford, and crawled back into bed, rearranging the cats who had kept her place warm. As she snuggled beside Hardy, she marveled at the family she had acquired.

# CHAPTER THIRTY-NINE

The Christmas sun was a dull orb in the east, rising slowly over the icy hills. Hardy was awakened by the jangle of the phone and hurried to the kitchen, not wanting to bother Estelle with it, for she slept soundly. He lifted the receiver and looked at the clock on the wall. It was six thirty. The sheriff was calling, probably not to wish him Merry Christmas. He sat and listened, his bare feet cold on the linoleum floor, his pajamas hanging open. "Hardy." Mitch Downey's voice was raised and urgent. "We got an emergency out on Highway 53 and the 29 turnoff. A horse trailer's overturned, and it's down the bank. Good God, man. It's full of horses, and they're goin' crazy! You gotta come, now. Bring your darts!"

Hardy slammed down the receiver and dialed Will, waking him, yelling at him to meet him at the scene. Then he ran to the bedroom and threw on the shirt and Levis he'd worn the day before. He woke Estelle, briefed her on the situation, and told her to take care of their animals and to stay put. He'd be home when it was over. He carried emergency supplies in his truck, and now he hoped he had enough of the things the horses would need. The accident was ten minutes away. He cursed when his cold truck didn't turn over immediately, but it caught the second time, and he roared out of the yard, throwing up a hail of gravel.

To his surprise, Will's truck was already sitting on the shoulder, door open, when he arrived at the scene. As he parked behind it, he saw his son scrambling back up the bank. Hardy grabbed his bag of tricks from the back seat and jumped out of the cab.

"This is really bad, Dad. We've got to sedate them quickly before they kick each other to death. There's six horses, and they're flailing around, and

I think a couple of them have broken legs." He grabbed the injection stick from Hardy's hand and started back down the hill. Hardy followed behind, dragging his bag to the overturned rig and the screaming animals.

It was a ghoulish nightmare of shrieking horseflesh. Sheriff Downey and one of his men tried desperately to calm the crazed, struggling, beasts, who foamed at the mouths, their coats lathered with sweat. The trailer had overturned after it broke away from the driver's truck and had skidded down the icy slope on its side, throwing the horses on top of each other. Now, as they fought to right themselves in panic and fear, they were inflicting perilous damage on one another. The back door had sprung open on impact. The sheriff was at the door, working with a young filly. Her head lay in his lap, but her rear legs and body were trapped beneath one of the panel dividers that was supposed to keep the horses separated. He was using a towel to clear the blood running from her nose so she could breathe. He saw Hardy and Will and yelled, "Thank God, you're here! Can you help me?" The filly's restricted movement was working to her benefit, and although her eyes were wild with fright, the doctors didn't think she had been mortally injured. Hardy loaded the syringe, and Will immediately plunged the liquid into her shoulder as Mitch held onto her head. In a minute, her eyes drooped, her struggling stopped, and her breathing became calm and steady.

"Good deal," said Mitch. "Now, the others are harder to reach, but if we can slide her out of the way, it might be easier."

As they struggled to lift the panel from the dead weight, Hardy asked, "Where's the driver of this thing? How'd he manage this nightmare?"

"He's on his way to my lock up," spat Mitch. "The goddamned asshole was drunk, that's how. Been drinking all night, and decides to take the horses for a ride. At least he didn't try to run away, and a passerby called 911. Son of a bitch, wait till I get him in my sights again. I had my deputy run him in before I did serious damage. It was coming to that."

They called the remaining deputy over, and the four men gently slid the filly out onto the dirt, rotating her body so that she rested with her head higher than her feet on the steep slope. They reloaded the tranquilizing syringe, and Will climbed in the trailer and was able to stick another horse in the rear, instantly calming him. Now they went about un-stacking them, sedating the thrashing bodies one by one. The slope of the trailer helped the men slide the horses to the ground. The final victim, a big palomino gelding that had been slammed against the steel, was fatally injured. Now he fought for breath as he strangled on blood from his internal ruptures, and jagged spikes of bone protruded from the skin on his forelegs. Hardy had no choice but to put him down, for he was suffering terribly.

The veterinarians examined each horse, feeling their legs, listening to their heart and chest sounds, and looking into their glassy eyes. Mitch sat on the hillside, his head,  trapped between his knees, his fingers laced together, holding on.

"Merry Christmas, you guys," he yelled, raising himself and dusting off his rear. "We need to transport these animals to a holding pen. Are they going to be fit to travel, Doc?"

"Looks like they're going to be sore and hurting for a while, but I don't see any life-threatening problems. Can I borrow that cell phone of yours?"

Downey handed it off to Hardy who called Marion. "Merry Christmas, sweetie. Sheriff Downey and Will and me got some presents for you." He proceeded with the details of the accident, and she volunteered her pasture and said she'd have drivers and trailers there within the hour. "Will they be under that long?"

"Oh yeah, more likely two more hours, but let's not take chances. Have the folks come as soon as they can, what with the holiday and all. And honey, you're a stand-up gal. I knew we could count on you, and thank goodness, 'cause we got horses lying all over the hillside out here."

The horses started coming to by the time the trailers arrived and parked along the flat shoulder. As soon as the shaky animals were able to stand, the men led them up the hill and loaded them; they were still too drowsy to be further traumatized. They called the disposal unit to come pick up the palomino, leaving his body in the trailer, and Downey had the tow company haul the drunk driver's truck to the impound yard. The accident provided Christmas overtime for a lot of the locals.

"I hope my drunk's a rich dude, 'cause he's going to pay for this," said Mitch.

When it was just the three of them left standing along the highway, Hardy said, "Mitch, why don't you come on out to my place for dinner and what's left of Christmas? We all need a drink or two."

"That sounds good, man. I think I'll take you up on the invite."

It was three in the afternoon when they arrived home. Lois and Estelle were cooking, and the fire was flickering in the fireplace. Montrose and the horses hung their heads over the fence and watched as the two trucks drove into the front yard.

Estelle saw them coming and met the men at the door. She recognized the pain in Hardy's eyes but said nothing, knowing her words would not help. They made toddies for the girls, and the men drank their whiskey neat, one after the other, until they felt up to talking.

"I had to put a horse down, Estelle, a big palomino. I had no choice. He was almost dead anyway, and he was suffering." He told her this in the kitchen when they were alone, and she wrapped her arms around him and pulled him tight against her.

"Maybe this is it now, and there won't be a New Year's emergency," she offered. "You've gotten it over with, and it sounds like you men did wonders. Only one death? That's amazing, given the circumstances, honey." Just then Bella came looking for him. She stood on her hind legs and leaned into him, her front legs on his chest.

"She misses going with you and being your sidekick. She's mellowing out a bit now. She let Buford baby sit while she went for a run with Flicker."

"Did you give the animals their presents?"

"No, I was waiting for you to come home."

"Well, let's do it then," he declared, pulling her into the living room where the rest of them sat. "My girl and I have some gifts for our friends, the animals, and we're going out to the barn now to divvy them up. You all can come watch if you want."

Mitch, Lois, and Will followed, drinks in hand, and watched as Hardy and Estelle carried a basket of wrapped presents to the barn. The curious horses, the mule, and the goat assembled shortly, nudging the humans, seeking their treats  Hardy and Estelle handed out horse candy, molasses oat balls, carrots and apples, and big cubes of sugar.

Montrose whinnied, stuck his head in the air, and curled his upper lip. "Merry Christmas to you too, son," said Hardy.

# CHAPTER FORTY

The good news was that Mitch and his team had been able to use the names Marion sent anonymously. They had matched the tagged carcasses and clients with "purchase orders" from Hirim and Burt, and the district attorney was bringing charges. The saddle shop was under new management while Ellie scrambled, trying to hide her involvement, but Mitch was confident she'd be indicted as an accomplice in the illegal hunt club enterprise.

Now, as the week between the holidays limped along, Will and Lois prepared for their trip and Hardy and Estelle manned the clinic. The sheriff came down hard on the drunk driver. "They weren't his horses, Hardy," said Mitch, as the men ate lunch together at a downtown restaurant. "He was transporting them for an Oregon breeder. He's out on bail, but he can't leave the county, or I throw his ass back in the slammer. Your friend Marion arranged for someone to complete the delivery."

"What're you charging him with?"

"I'm not sure what all the DA's throwing at him; everything he can, drunk driving, reckless driving."

"How about felony drunk driving, he killed that horse."

The sheriff picked up his coffee cup and cradled it in his hands. "We'd like to, but killing a horse isn't a felony. You and I have had this discussion before, seems to me." Mitch stared into his coffee and shook his head, knowing Hardy wasn't satisfied with the answer.

"Well, it damn well ought to be a felony," grumbled Hardy, throwing a wad of bills on the counter.

When Hardy returned to the clinic, he found Estelle by the dryer, serenely folding a batch of newly laundered towels, warm to the touch and smelling sweet from the detergent. She lovingly smoothed and caressed them, holding them to her cheeks, running her hands down the folds, doubling them over, and stacking them neatly in a pile on the counter. She jumped when he rested his hands on her shoulders, for he had come in quietly through the back door.

"Shall we go with Will and Lois and get married too?" he asked, suddenly wanting her to belong to him. He pulled her close, nuzzling her hair. When she turned and looked up into his eyes, she saw the overwhelming sadness he tried to hide from her but could not. She stroked his hair with her hand and pulled his head down so that she could kiss his lips, for she wanted to be part of him more than anything right then. They kissed passionately, probing each other's mouths with their tongues. He pulled away long enough to lock the clinic doors and then hurried back. He lifted her gently onto her stacked towels and spread them around into a soft nest, and they made love, and no one came to disturb them. When they were done, ensconced between the still warm terry cloth, they giggled as if it had been their first time, and then they held each other tightly, sharing the unspoken knowledge that they weren't young anymore.

"I don't want to be married in Las Vegas," she said, buttoning her sweater. "Let's get married right here." She grabbed his arm. "Let's do it at the house with all the animals. That's what I want!"

"And Montrose can be my best mule, is that your idea?"

"Absolutely."

He leaned against the counter and pulled on his boots. "I like it."

Their marriage venue decided, Estelle and Hardy relaxed, taking their time with the rest of it, for they had no reason to rush, and her household already mingled happily with his, she having moved her cats in some weeks earlier, much to Buford's delight. They had discovered that the big St. Bernard was crazy over felines. He loved playing with them, sleeping with them, and eating their food, even their poop, when he could get hold of it. Hardy had to move the food and the litter boxes into the pantry and install a gate with a hole big enough for the cats but too small for the dog.

The day before New Year's Eve, Will and Lois stopped at the house to say good-bye on their way to Vegas. "Hurray, the next time you see us, we'll be Mr. and Mrs. William Johns."

"Drive carefully," said Hardy, "and don't stay gone too long. It's a brand new year at the clinic."

"Have a good time," said Estelle.

On New Year's Eve they sat in front of the fire drinking wine, eating snacks, and watching the celebrations on television. Bella eagerly ventured out of her room to join the party, steal cheese, and roam the house, and

Buford prowled behind her, trailed by a conga line of cats. Since it was their first New Year's together, they stayed up until midnight and watched the ball drop in New York. They kissed, and then they went to bed. Hardy pulled the covers over his head and said, "Probably won't be up again this late until next New Year's."

"Lois and Will are married now," she said, cuddling against him.

"Yup. We can be too, whenever you're ready."

"I know, honey, no hurry." She lay her head against his shoulder and fell asleep.

New Year's Day was cold and dreary, with gray clouds heavy overhead. Hardy bundled up and fed his stock. He released them to the field, but they didn't seem eager to venture out, preferring instead the relative warmth of their barn. Flicker nosed about the tossed hay, picking out the oats, and Montrose laid back his ears, challenging the smaller animal.

"Behave," warned Hardy. "Share."

"Just a bunch of selfish kids," he said, as Estelle handed him a mug of coffee.

The phone rang. It was eight in the morning, and Hardy fidgeted, not wanting to answer it. He was supposed to get a pass this year, because of the Christmas emergency. Estelle had promised. "You answer," he told her.

She picked up the receiver, talked a moment, and handed it off to Hardy, a look of foreboding on her face. "It's for you. It's Mitch."

He slapped his fist on the table and cursed, "Every year, no matter what."

Mitch Downey had a strange tale, not an emergency really, just something he thought Hardy might want to know about. "There's an operation been going on out at Bottomless Lake this past week. Old Man Rumsey disappeared some time back, and his son's been lookin' for him. They found a rubber raft floating out there, and the boy figured his father might have gone and got himself drowned. He hired some locals to fish around, and they pulled up a metal cage, and it's got a half eaten body inside, and this Rumsey kid thinks it's his dad."

Hardy listened, and Estelle puttered in the kitchen, catching a word here and there. That anyone could have found his cage and pulled it up was hard to believe, yet here was Mitch, telling him it was so.

"Hardy? Are you there?"

"Yeah, I'm here. I just can't believe your story. How would he get into a cage and end up at the bottom of that lake?"

Mitch Downey cleared his throat and harrumphed a few times. "Looks like somebody must have put him there, Hardy. He probably wouldn't have jumped in and drowned himself."

"Huh, sounds logical." Hardy squirmed in his chair and rolled his mug around between his palms. "So, how can I help you here, Mitch?"

"Don't know that you can, Hardy. Just keeping you up to date on local color, being it's New Year's, and you usually have something going on."

"I appreciate your thoughtfulness, Sheriff, and don't think I wouldn't have wanted to stuff that slime into a cage and shove him down deep, but it wasn't me."

"Why, I never said it was, now, did I? But I'd like to thank whoever's responsible if you hear anything. Happy New Year, Hardy, and give my best to Estelle."

Hardy hung up the phone and grinned. They worked well together, he and the sheriff, and the nature of their work was ongoing, list or no list. It never really ended. He found the thought of Gordy's son pulling up a mess of Gordy Rumsey from Bottomless Lake and seeing what he really looked like inside very satisfying.

# CHAPTER FORTY-ONE

The newspaper ran an article on the man in the cage in the lake, but they didn't include pictures, and Hardy was disappointed. He read the headline to Estelle. "Sheriff Puzzled, No Suspects Floating Around."

"This must be the same reporter who handled the infamous blowpipe incident," speculated Hardy, dropping his neighbor's paper on his table.

Estelle shuddered at the thought of the man being trapped and sunk.

"He wasn't a nice man, honey. He did terrible things to animals. Maybe *they* put him in the cage, turnabout's fair play."

"Well, good riddance to him, then," she snorted.

Will and Lois phoned from Aruba, where they had flown directly after their wedding ceremony. The weather was dreamy, the snorkeling delicious, she said, and they were having a ball. "Well, no need to hurry back," said Estelle, "we're managing just fine."

Hardy harrumphed. "Where do you want to go on our honeymoon, honey? We could take a few weeks and go play on some beach. Of course, Will would have to look after our animals, and I don't think he's up to it."

"Probably not, it's a lot of work, especially if you don't know the routine. And the puppies, we certainly couldn't go anywhere until they're given away."

"Might as well face it, Estelle, we're never going to escape this place."

"That's fine with me. I'm not anxious to 'escape,' as you put it. I never was one for sitting on a beach, and there's nowhere else I'd rather be than right here anyway."

"That's fortunate, 'cause we're pretty bogged down."

They left for clinic duty, stopping by the feed store to order supplies from Otis, Hardy's neighbor. Otis was an ordained minister, and Hardy had him in mind to perform the wedding whenever he and Estelle got around to it. Otis was happy to drop off the sacks of grain and bales of hay on his way home at night. He liked the mule, hinting he wouldn't mind having an animal like that if Hardy ever wanted to sell.

"How can you sell something that isn't really yours?" Hardy pondered. "I'm afraid every day that somebody's going to claim him. We don't know where he came from, and he surely belonged somewhere." The logic snuffed Otis's hopes, but Hardy had no intention of parting with the mule, even if the president of the United States called to say Montrose had escaped from the Rose Garden.

"I fear, my dear, that we are out of cheese. Do you want to take a walk to the corner store?" It was lunchtime, and the little fridge was almost empty, so Estelle agreed.

She had just set out when a dismal looking man entered the clinic dragging a sorry-looking German shepherd by a rope. Hardy recoiled, recognizing the filthy human as one of the remaining targets on his list. "I want you to buy this here animal," he growled, squinting up at Hardy, a twisted grin on his lips. "I know you got a soft spot and cain't say no, and I need the money. You don't take him, I'm going to shoot him in the head, boil him up, and pick his bones. I got a right, you know, he's mine."

Hardy stared at the old man, sizing him up. Long, greasy hair hung in clumps over his hunched shoulders, the sharp points of his upper teeth rested on his lower lip, his eyes were mere slits in a wrinkled, dirt-caked face. Tattered, decaying clothes hung on his body.

"Why have you picked me?"

Willard Mead, cackled. "'Cause what I said, you cain't say no."

Hardy took his measure, coolly declaring, "You're right, Willard, I can't let you shoot your dog in the head and boil him. How much do you need?"

Willard jerked the rope, pulling the shivering, emaciated animal off his feet.

"He's a decent critter," he snarled. " I need twenty dollars. Reckon that'll do me just fine." He grinned, looked up at the doctor, and stuck out his hand, waiting for a payoff.

Hardy took the rope from the old man and lifted the dog to his examination table. The frightened animal peed as his feet hit the cold steel, and Hardy sopped it up with one of Estelle's clean towels.

Willard watched carefully as the doctor ran his hands over the dirty coat of hair and protruding bones. The dog shivered at the human touch. Hardy marveled that the man had come to him, saving him a trip. "The dog needs food. How long since he's had a decent meal?"

"I don't have no food for dogs," Willard screeched. "Hell, I hardly got food for me. Why you think I need your money?"

"What did you do with your other animals? The cow, the horses?"

Willard cackled wickedly. "Shot 'em and et what I could. This here mangy cur's all I got left, and he ain't got much meat on him. I figure he's worth more to you than he is to me."

"You ate your horses?" rumbled Hardy, his voice high pitched and disconnected from the rest of him.

"I did! he spat. "Et them first off. They was good, too." He smacked his lips and patted his belly, taking pleasure in the Doctor's pain. Then suddenly he blurted, "Why you asking all the questions? Let's do the deal."

Hardy set the dog on the floor as Estelle returned, tinkling the bell over the door. When she saw Willard, she gasped and dropped her bag, spilling out the cheese, bread, and other edibles. Willard eyed them hungrily. Hardy lowered his head and stared up at her, a strange light in his eyes. "This is Willard, and he's here to sell us his dog." She gathered up the groceries and hurried to the back room, frightened by the evil-looking stranger and the sound of Hardy's voice.

Willard Mead stole stock from his neighbors and ate everything that crossed his path. There was speculation about a brother who hadn't been seen for quite a while. Willard filed his teeth to sharp points making it easier to tear the flesh from his victims; eating seemed to be his life's work, his agenda. People in the town avoided Willard, crossing the street to pass, for not only did his body reek vile odors, they were terrified of him. Hardy had a specific rendezvous in mind for Willard, and since the man had sought him out, the time was at hand.

"Let me get your money from the back," Hardy said, leading the dog to a cage that Estelle had prepared. She searched his eyes, desperate for a clue, but he just smiled at her and nodded, and said, "Lower the blinds, please, dear."

She hurried to the big room and lowered the blinds, glanced at the hunched-over man, and hurried back to Hardy. He tossed Willard's greasy rope on the counter and whispered, "Lock the doors, quickly."

He took a moment to fill a large syringe with sedative and then removed his money from his pocket, counting out twenty dollars. Returning to the big room, he said, "Here you are, Willard." He stood a ways back, requiring the man to extend his arm to take the bills. Willard reached, exposing his wretched wrist, and Hardy slammed in the needle, depressed the plunger, and quickly stepped aside, watching as Willard stared at the protruding syringe, unable to comprehend the deed, and then collapsed like a burlap sack to the floor. Foul, brown drool rolled out of his mouth, and Hardy dropped the wet pee towel over his head.

Estelle stood in the doorway, her hands pressed against her mouth, her eyes wide. She took a deep breath and said, "What are we going to do with him?"

"Not we, dear, me. And don't worry, I have a plan in place. First I have to move him into the truck. Can you bring it around to the back door?"

She parked the truck beside the door, and Hardy dragged the sleeping hulk to the passenger side, pulling him up onto the floor of the backseat.

"He'll be fine there for a while. Now, can you handle the clinic if I take a little drive? Tell anybody I'll be back I an hour. I'm out on an emergency."

"Where are you taking him?"

He held her tightly and said, "It's better if you don't know, Estelle, for your protection. Can you trust me with that explanation?"

"I can, Hardy, because I love you, but please be careful."

He grabbed Willard's dirty rope from the counter and climbed into the truck. "This won't take long. He's not going far. Pull the blinds and unlock the doors. We're back in business."

On the drive out to the country, he thanked his lucky stars for the drugs. Without them, he'd need to use his guns, for most men fought like wild animals when they were cornered. But no matter, he had the drugs. Point Hardy, score Hardy.

He crossed the creek at Meyer's bridge, made the left turn, drove on a few miles, and pulled off the dirt road in back of the hog farm. It was a vast operation, and the spot he'd chosen was remote and hardly ever traveled by anyone except the animals, big long- tusked hogs who enjoyed wading hock-deep in the lovely mud. He dragged his drugged cargo out of the truck, found the greasy rope, and tied one end around Willard's ankles and the other end around his neck. He pulled the sleeping bundle to the fence, cut the top three wires, and rolled him over into the muck. Willard made a flat, sucking sound when he hit bottom, notifying several nearby residents of his arrival. Willard had landed on his back, his head cradled in a thick pillow of mud. His eyes would open soon, so he'd be able to watch the goings-on. That was only fair, thought Hardy. He should have tucked a napkin under the old man's chin.

Hardy got in his truck, rolled down the window, and yelled at the hogs, "Dinner's ready, boys and girls."

Estelle was pacing the floor when he returned, and a client sat waiting, a golden retriever at his feet.

"Be right with you, Mr. Norton," called Hardy as he took her arm and led her to the back. "Everything's fine, not to worry. It's taken care of. Now, please start the German shepherd off slowly. Just a few spoonfuls of food at first, then maybe you could try to give him a bath. If he looks like he's going to bite you, we have muzzles. I'll help as soon as I'm free." He kissed her forehead, and she smiled, relieved .

# CHAPTER FORTY-TWO

Several days went by with no breaking story of poisoned hogs, and Hardy fought the urge to return to the scene of the crime and do a drive-by. The German shepherd was gaining weight, and Estelle had bathed him, but he suffered from terrible emotional and physical abuse, cowering when humans approached, hiding his head between his legs. Hardy had seen the behavior often; sometimes the victims came around, and sometime they didn't. A positive readjustment depended on a breakthrough, and this required the establishment of trust through love. Everything came about through love; it was the only thing that worked. So Estelle lavished attention on Rheinhard, the name she gave the dog, and took him for walks, read him stories, and asked Hardy if, when he was well, he could he come live with Bella and Buford and the cats.

"We'll see how his temperament evens out," said the doctor. "Give it a little time, and keep working with him. If he doesn't come around, we can call the German shepherd rescue people."

Will and Lois returned, suntanned, rested, and very much in love. Will's first day back at the clinic was mind numbing, for he talked nonstop, sharing all their snorkeling experiences, hotel waiter experiences, and rent-a-car experiences. The only experiences he didn't share were the actual honeymoon experiences, prompting his father to ask, "Was the sex any good?"

To which Will blushed and said, "Dad!"

On the fifth day after his visit to the hog farm, the story hit the front page, "Body Dumped at Hog Farm." Hardy again borrowed the neighbor's paper.

"Damn, why didn't they put pictures in with the story," he complained.

"I don't imagine people would want to see pictures like that," said Estelle. She tapped the table with a big wooden spoon, commanding his attention. "Did that man deserve that kind of death? Just tell me the truth, and I'll believe whatever you say, Hardy."

Hardy dropped the paper and searched her face, mining her expression for a clue to her inner feelings. "If anyone deserved a nasty death, it was Willard. You see what he did to poor Rheinhard. And the dog was lucky; the horses didn't fare so well. Talk is, he probably ate his own brother. Nobody's seen Waylan for months. Why are you doubting me now?"

"I'm not. It's just that I feel left out not knowing the details, and I want to be part of your whole life. It would be better if you let me share these things. You don't have to shield me, Hardy. We can be a team."

He was silent, dissecting her train of thought as she carried on, pleading her case to be included. When she had finished talking, he said, "Okay, Estelle, from now on, you're a full partner, but that means your exposure is equal to mine, and if I get caught, you probably will too. No more secrets, and a lot of it's not pretty, so don't go getting squeamish on me."

She smiled, took his head in her hands, and kissed him. "You won't be sorry, honey. I'll be a good partner for you. I thought the hog farm venue was terrific. You're very creative."

"I try to give like for like, and it seemed appropriate under the circumstances. Sometimes situations don't correlate, but this was perfect. Hogs eat anything, and so did Willard."

Mitch Downey called, and Hardy answered. "I suppose you've seen the headline," sang the sheriff.

"Yeah, what a thing. Hope I don't have to make a ranch call for any sick hogs. I imagine that Willard was no gastrointestinal delight."

Mitch was silent for a moment. "The county's getting cleaned up of its bad seeds, Hardy. I'm grateful, believe me, but if you had anything to do with this, I hope you covered your tracks, 'cause I'm getting heat from the top. We're getting too clean for our own good, if you know what I mean. The big guys think we've got a vigilante out here, and I can't really tell them otherwise. For God's sake, man, be careful."

He hung up and sat drinking his coffee and watching Estelle as she moved about his kitchen. And he knew it was the thing to do.

"Honey, now's the time," he said. "I want us to get married, and I think we should do it tomorrow. How about it?"

She stopped fussing and sat in his lap, running her fingers through his hair. "Why the sudden rush?"

"Because I love you more than life itself, and a wife can't testify against her husband, and visa versa. It's the smart thing, if you're going to be my partner, to protect each other."

She grinned ear to ear. "You're absolutely right. It is the smart thing. All right, then, tomorrow. I'll call Otis."

When they got to the clinic, they told Will, and he phoned Lois at her work, and she said she'd ask for another day off.

"We'll have to close the clinic for the afternoon," said Hardy. "I suppose it'll be okay. People can always reach me on the cell in an emergency."

Otis said he'd make time, and they set the ceremony for two in the afternoon. At least the weather was good—clear and cold.

"Oh goodness, what do I have to do?" said Estelle, panicking suddenly. "I know, I'll order some food. We should ask Mitch to come, and Mr. Hollis, and the Movement. Oh dear, this is going to be bigger than I expected. I'd better go home and get ready."

"Take the truck. Will can drop me off. And call Marion. She can let the others know; she's got them all on her e-mail."

Before she left, Estelle opened Rheinhard's cage door and hugged him. The big dog licked her face and offered his paw, a first and a definite breakthrough. "Come see," she yelled at the men.

They watched as the dog interacted, licking her cheek, and Hardy was overjoyed, for this was the sought-after magical connection that made their work worthwhile. "Wait until after tomorrow, and we'll bring him home," he said. "There'll be too much commotion at the wedding, and we need to give him our full attention."

"What a wedding gift from Rheinhard. His trust, can't beat that," she said, tears filling her eyes.

That night Will brought Hardy home, and they celebrated the upcoming nuptials with a bottle of champagne.

"Mitch is coming, and Marion's bringing the group. We're going to end up with a crowd, like it or not, honey. Do we have enough food?" asked Hardy.

"I think so. I ordered from the deli, and it's being delivered in the morning. I told them not too early, or everything edible will be covered with cat hair. Bella's excited, she knows something's up. You better go say hello and give her some loving."

The puppies were crawling all over now, and they had to keep the bedroom door closed. Bella sat in the middle of the rug, all seven babies fighting for her teats. She looked wide-eyed at her friend. "I want you with me tomorrow, babe," he told her, and her ears pricked forward and she smiled. He sat beside her, stroking her back, and she licked his face and pawed his hand. "You'll always be my first girl, honey." He kissed her wet nose and stayed with her until Estelle called him for dinner.

They sat by the fire after dinner and decided they would say their vows on horseback and mule back, and Bella and Buford would be there, and whoever else wanted to participate. She would wear her nice riding pants, a fancy shirt, and her new boots, and he would have to get by in a nice pair of slacks, for he had no riding pants. He did have a Stetson, however, but he wasn't convinced he should wear it. Neither one of them was able to sleep that night, keenly aware that the next day was a big one.

Mitch called while Hardy was making coffee and joked, "Funny how nobody ends up in the lake while you're busy getting married."

Hardy didn't think it was cute, and he warned his friend not to kid about some things. "This is serious business, Sheriff, getting married, and we shouldn't tempt the fates and disturb the critical balance, if you know what I'm talking about."

"I believe I do, and I'll say no more, as you're obviously sensitive to certain matters."

"Enough of this talking in tongues. What time you coming over? You're my best man, you know."

"I'll be there for lunch, around eleven. That okay?"

"See you."

"The deli delivered the food too early, and now where are we going to stash it so the cats don't find it?" asked Estelle.

"It's cold enough. I'll put it in the tack room," said Hardy.

"Be sure and close the door so the goat can't get in."

"I will."

The guests arrived early, but Otis was late. No one knew where he was, and they couldn't get married without him, so Hardy and Mitch took the truck and went looking. Sure enough, they found him a couple miles down the road hoofing it. He'd run out of gas.

They had plenty of beer and liquor, and Estelle had planned on putting out the food after the vows, but now that everyone was drinking, she worried they might get too drunk, so she asked Hardy to fetch it from the tack room.

Don't you know, Flicker had found the door unlocked and had picked and chosen his favorites among the delicacies. But, being animal lovers one and all, the guests didn't care. They just ate around the goat hair.

When the time was at hand, Estelle mounted Dusty, Hardy climbed aboard Montrose, and they pranced forth into the pasture, the other horses and Flicker following curiously, the cats hanging over the top rail of the fence, and Bella and Buford waiting patiently at the gate. The guests moved into the pasture, Montrose and Dusty bumped shoulder to shoulder, and Otis sat, sipping from a beer nestled beside him in a clump of tall grass. Lois stood beside Dusty, a bouquet of flowers in her hand, and Estelle clasped a lovely bunch of Shasta daisies and chrysanthemums. Otis rose, burying his beer can back in the grass, and stepped forward, standing at the animals' noses, and began to speak the words. It looked and sounded as if he were marrying the horse and the mule.

When he asked for the ring, Mitch handed Hardy a gold band, and Estelle, not to be outdone, took one from Lois. They leaned sideways, slid the rings on each other's fingers, and kissed, whereupon Bella jumped up between the horse and the mule, one paw on Estelle's leg, the other on Hardy's, and howled a long, mournful howl. Everyone laughed. "It's not like that," said Hardy. "I still love you, my girl."

# The End

Printed in the United States
208322BV00001B/201/P